ATOMWEIGHT

PRAISE FOR *ATOMWEIGHT*

Atomweight is a complex coming of age story that through sharp storytelling reveals the power and pain of existing in a queer body; a body that witnesses two very different yet dominant cultures push against one another. This is where the terrifying world of fighting is faced head on. The end result is a bold and gripping tale of identity, love and a poignant exploration of self.

CHELENE KNIGHT, author of *Junie*

. . . a powerful impactful novel that follows a duel narrative within one character. A narrative similar to the one many queer folks of colour navigate in their daily lives. Heightened by stressful fight scenes, and smoothed by strong lyrical prose: this novel takes the queer experience by its horns, and tames it for the readers on the page. It's a bright and wonderful debut by Emi Sasagawa."

DANNY RAMADAN, author of *The Foghorn Echoes*

"Everybody has a plan until they get punched in the mouth," Mike Tyson once said. In Emi Sasagawa's bold and searing *Atomweight*, we meet a young woman who makes her plans with her fists, sparring as a way to push away her doubts about her family, sexuality and relationships. Sasagawa writes like a fighter: nimble and devastating.

KEVIN CHONG, authot of *The Double Life of Benson Yu*

Atomweight

A Novel

EMI SASAGAWA

TIDEWATER
PRESS

Published by Tidewater Press
New Westminster, BC, Canada
tidewaterpress.ca

978-1-990160-16-5 (print)
978-1-990160-17-2 (e-book)

LIBRARY AND ARCHIVES CANADA CATALOGUING IN PUBLICATION
Title: Atomweight : a novel / Emi Sasagawa.
Names: Sasagawa, Emi, author.
Identifiers: Canadiana (print) 20230225004 | Canadiana (ebook) 20230225047 | ISBN 9781990160165 (softcover) | ISBN 9781990160172 (EPUB)
Classification: LCC PS8637.A75365 A86 2023 | DDC C813/.6—dc23

We gratefully acknowledge the support of the Canada Council for the Arts and the BC Arts Council

Printed in Canada

To Yumi

Grapes must be crushed to make wine.
Diamonds form under pressure.
Olives are pressed to release oil.
Seeds grow in darkness.

Whenever you feel crushed, under pressure, pressed or in darkness you're in a powerful place of transformation and transmutation.

LALAH DELIA

PROLOGUE

I took another sip of the too-sweet cocktail in front of me. "Surprise me," I had said to the middle-aged bartender when he asked me what I wanted to drink. I was sitting alone at a pub near Holborn Station, popular with the university crowd. I'd walked by it many times, but never been inside.

That Thursday, I'd counted on a full house; instead, the pub was nearly empty. Just a couple of businessmen having a heated discussion about the 2008 financial crisis and how the Bank of England intended to pump £75 million into the economy, and a group of five men who looked to be a few years older than me, early twenties maybe. In the six months I'd been attending the London School of Economics, I'd learned to recognize the overblown egos of a certain class of British schoolboy. With nothing to prove and little to lose, a few drinks were the only excuse they needed for bigotry or misogyny.

Somebody had picked up a girl at a party last night. "She was wild, if you know what I mean." Another one was waiting for the right time to text back after a first date—two days would suffice, one of his friends advised. A third one was bragging about a threesome he once had with two German tourists. "Thirsty tourists, I tell you."

Their remarks annoyed me, but this was just standard misguided masculinity. Nothing made my blood boil or my hands twitch. I itched for a confrontation, but they didn't excite me. No spark. I took another sip of my cocktail and wondered why more women weren't gay.

The front door swung open and slammed against a chair, admitting a frigid wind and a young South Asian man who took a seat at the bar and ordered a pint. I pulled my hair back from my face so I could see him better.

He was the definition of average: short—only a couple of inches taller than me—with straight, black hair perfectly parted to one side, wearing the caramel boots, acid-washed jeans and navy-blue bomber jacket typical of first-generation Asians on the rise. He and I were the same hue of brown, but where the hairs on my hands were thin and light, his were thick and black.

There was something about his features that reminded me of Ayesha. The nose, the eyebrows. He looked like Asad. Or was this just me, thinking all South Asian men looked the same? I inhaled deeply, stretching my arms above my head, then turned to the bar and took the last sip of my drink.

"Do you want another one of those?" The younger bartender, Teddy according to his nametag, came over.

"It's all right. Just a shot of vodka."

"You here often?" the Asad-lookalike asked. "I feel like I've seen you before." His right foot tapped on the footrest to the rhythm of the rain.

"I doubt it," I replied curtly, folding the napkin in front of me into a triangle. I looked at his biceps. Not much bigger than mine.

"Technically, I'm not supposed to drink." He moved a seat nearer. His eyelashes were so long they curled up, just like Ayesha's. I could smell the rain on him, mixed in with cigarettes. I missed how she smelled of cigarettes. He took a large gulp of his beer and then turned to me. "Muslims are not supposed to drink."

"Then why do you?" I asked, spurring him on, sizing him up. My jaw tightened in anticipation.

"I guess I don't like being told what to do." He laughed and downed the rest of his beer, keeping eye contact with me, inviting complicity in his religious transgression. "Another one," he called to Teddy.

I couldn't decide whether he was trying to impress me or if he was just a regular asshole. Maybe this was a straight courting ritual, one I was not familiar with. His attention felt forced, repulsive, and I welcomed the familiar heat rising to my head, a blend of anger and elation. He was pushing the right buttons.

I smiled as Teddy wiped the counter with a dirty cloth and placed a shot of vodka in front of me. He stretched over the bar, on the tip of his toes and leaned in. "Is he bothering you? I can ask him to move."

"It's fine, thank you," I said, tight-lipped. I'm sure Teddy's intentions were good, but I hadn't asked for help.

"Is he the boyfriend?" Asad-lookalike asked.

"No." My nostrils flared as I turned to face him. "Penises don't interest me."

The man's eyes widened. "That's a bold statement." He laughed louder than necessary, feigning ease.

I stared at him. "I guess I don't like being told who to like."

"Touché." He turned to face me as Teddy exchanged the empty beer glass for a full one.

I nodded slowly. The man and I locked eyes. He opened his mouth, but then looked away. We were close. I could feel it. Now was not the time to be coy. "It looks like you have more to say about this." I pressed my lips together and inhaled. "Please, do enlighten me on your unsolicited opinion." Idiocy only needs the smallest opportunity to make an appearance.

He sneered. "You should be careful who you go around saying

that to." He took a sip of his beer. "If you were my sister, I'd set you straight." He shifted his body in his seat and turned away from me.

Rage rose from the pit of my stomach, up my chest, all the way to my head. My legs shook under the counter. I moved my neck from side to side. Even then, in the thick of unrepressed anger, I wondered if I was enough—big enough, strong enough. At five foot four and just over a hundred pounds, I was an atomweight, lighter than straw. Maybe that's why he couldn't have known what would happen next.

"I dare you to," I said as I grabbed onto the counter with my left hand and pulled myself off my seat. I imagined a ball of energy rising from the centre of my chest to my fingertips.

He looked at me, bewildered, confused. Before he could reply, I pushed him off his chair. He fell backwards onto his butt.

"Are you crazy?" He dusted his hands off on his trousers and stood up.

"You have no idea." I looked him in the eye. "Set me straight."

"Crazy bitch," he said under his breath.

Images flashed in my head. The smell of grass mixed with rain. The London skyline from Hyde Park. Ayesha's face when she walked in on Sana and me. I closed my hand into a tight fist and lunged forward, my right knuckles meeting the man's left cheek. He slammed into a couple of chairs by the bar, the noise startling the other customers.

"Fight, fight, fight!" The table of men began chanting. The businessmen gathered up their belongings and headed toward the exit.

The man put his hands on his knees and looked up at me, the imprint of my knuckles reddening his cheek. I walked toward him. "Get up and set me straight, asshole," I whispered into his ear. I knew I only had a couple of minutes before someone would try to break it up. They would look at my opponent and assume I was the victim. Fuck being the victim. This was me in control of my own fucking life. I walked to the centre of the pub, where some space had been cleared, likely for dancing.

My opponent stood up, took off his jacket and charged toward me, right shoulder first. I jumped out of the way, but not fast enough to dodge his elbow. I felt a radiating pain between my top two left ribs, and for a moment thought I might pass out. The man lost his balance on impact and toppled over a table in the corner. I bent over, my right arm cradling my left side. The Asad-lookalike got up and came charging at me again, baring his teeth. This time I kicked his shin with the back of my heel, the impact sending shooting pain up my calf.

He screamed in pain, fell to the ground and rolled into a fetal position, holding onto his left leg. "What is wrong with you?"

Behind us, applause from the twenty-somethings, clapping between points as if they were watching tennis. I couldn't help but laugh at the Englishness of it all. Behind the bar, Teddy, looking younger than ever, paced back and forth, seeming to hunt for the older barman, who was nowhere to be seen.

I stood over my opponent and dug my leather boot into his crotch. It was like stepping on top of a half-deflated volleyball. "Do you fold?"

He spit at me. I shifted my weight, applying even greater pressure. He groaned in pain, and the sound thrilled me. I wanted to strip him of his ego and dress him in shame. I wanted him on the brink of desperation, seconds from defeat, with nothing but the illusion of a choice.

He said nothing, holding on to the last shred of his masculinity.

I bent closer, my hair dangling inches off his face. "I said, do you fold?" I could smell the beer on his laboured breath.

"Fucking dyke." He reached for me, but I moved away. He was slow, unpractised. He tried again, thrusting his body off the ground. His nails scratched my neck, and it instantly burned.

"Say that again!"

"Fucking . . . dyke." He was still struggling to get up.

In that moment, this stranger embodied all my anger and hurt. I used gravity to my advantage and fell into my right fist. He yelped. I kneeled next to him and punched his face again and again. By the third blow, there was a loud thump as his head hit the hardwood floor.

Someone pulled me off, holding my arms to my chest. I thrashed about, trying to regain control. We fell backwards onto the floor. "Calm down!" It was the older barman. I felt his breath on my right ear. Teddy stared at me from across the pub, eyes wide, mouth agape. The Asad-lookalike lay still, except for his chest, rising and falling to the rhythm of his breathing. A pool of blood and spit collected under his mouth. The pub was silent.

My body relaxed into the bartender's and he held me on the floor. I couldn't remember the last time I'd let someone hold me. It felt disarming, intimate. I let my head rest on his shoulder. Tears rolled down my face, but I made no sound. He let go of my arms and turned my body toward his. "You've got to go now, okay?"

"Okay," I repeated, without fully understanding what it meant. I looked down at my hands. They were covered in blood, I couldn't tell whose.

"Go. Now."

I got up slowly, my ribs aching, and walked toward the bar. I put the napkin folded into a triangle into my pocket and I took the shot. The vodka burned on the way down, distracting me from the pain. I grabbed my coat off the chair. My knuckles burned. With some difficulty, I took out a £20 bill from my wallet and placed it under the shot glass.

I limped to the door, passing the table of men, no longer chanting. I pushed the door open and stepped out without looking back. I knew I would never be able to return to this place.

Outside, a downpour, not a single star in the sky. The fight replayed in my head: the push, the punch, the sidestep, the kick. I watched it as a spectator. I saw the sweat drip from my chin onto his face.

The coldness of the rain shocked me into the present. An older woman stopped to ask if I was okay. I nodded, struggling to catch up to the speed of reality. I wanted to stay put, to absorb the moment, but my legs began to move toward King's Cross Station. I saw myself in a shop's window—three red lines on my neck, hair tussled, coat unbuttoned, shirt covered in blood spatters. I stood still. There was nothing of myself in the reflection. An impersonator.

I put my hands on my head, to try to stop the thoughts from coming. Tears flowed down my cheeks. Would the man be okay? He seemed small now, defenceless. I replayed his head hitting the floor. Maybe it wasn't a thump. Maybe it was a bang, or worse, a crack. I fixated on the pool of blood. I couldn't tell where it had come from—his mouth, his nose, his head. Sirens wailed in the distance. It didn't seem possible that I'd done it. But I had.

I was a few feet away from the entrance of King's Cross Station when I heard my name. Two people were walking in my direction. The warmth of my tears fogged up my glasses. I squinted but couldn't make out who they were. Looking down at my shirt and hands, I ducked into the station and quickened my pace.

"Aki!"

I ran down the stairs. Rush hour was just dying down. Maybe I could blend in. I put the hood of my jacket over my head and tapped my Oyster card, following the crowd until I couldn't hear my name anymore. Once on the train, I savoured the memory of my anger, always bubbling underneath the surface, ready to make an appearance. The shove, the first punch, the feelings of triumph and defeat, polar opposites and yet each an end.

It was intoxicating.

CHAPTER 1

It's the quiet ones you have to watch out for, as the saying goes. Silence is not synonymous with apathy, but that's how the world reads introverts. We thrive in the spaces of what is left unsaid—in commas, semi-colons and ellipses. Behind poker faces, we are wildcards, teetering between perfect balance and complete chaos, a silence away from exploding. I say the world is right to watch out for us.

"Aki, how come you're so . . . unemotional?" Haru reached across, leaning close to me. The Lexus, a 2008 with the recently added black bird's-eye maple trim and voice-activated navigation system, was only a month old and still smelled new. Dad liked cars, so long as they were Japanese.

I leaned my forehead on the window, watching the opulence of West Vancouver disappear as we drove across Lion's Gate Bridge and saying a mental goodbye to West Bay. "Sorry, what?"

Mom lowered the volume of the radio, her hand lingering on the dial.

"Nothing ever fazes you, eh?" Haru was extroverted, popular, smart and intermittently sensitive with a rebellious streak. He enjoyed being the king of the contrary—breaking rules, skipping class and playing only contact sports, despite Mom's pleas for him to take up something like tennis or golf. He quit piano after a year because he didn't want to play the same instrument as Dad. And, according to all of us, he had poor taste in girls.

"I don't know that's true." I turned to face him. Only fourteen months apart, Haru and I had looked like twins until his first growth spurt at the age of thirteen. Sitting next to me, you could still tell he was nearly five inches taller, his legs hitting the seat in front of him. Of the two of us, he more resembled the Kiyama side of the family—almond-shaped eyes, straight, thick hair, fair, flawless skin and a robust build. I'd inherited the same thick lips and thin eyebrows but my curly hair and small frame came from my mother. And what my mother liked to call a half-monolid provided the missing ambiguity to my identity.

"You're moving to another continent, to a place where we have only ever vacationed, by yourself, but you look like you're just going downtown for a movie with friends. Are you scared? Are you excited? I can't tell."

I leaned forward and caught a glimpse of myself in the side mirror. Haru was right. My face was expressionless. I thought back to when I told my parents I wanted to study at LSE.

"London!"

Despite a couple of shopping trips cloaked as college visits, my parents, Mom in particular had always expected me to end up somewhere closer to home. UBC would have been ideal, but even the University of Toronto, where my uncle was a professor, would have done it.

"You said I could pick anywhere, so long as I got in."

"I know, but London?" My mom threw her arms in the air, exasperated.

"Maybe it will be good for her." Dad tried to steer the conversation in a less confrontational direction. "Aki is so quiet and reserved. Maybe going somewhere new will help her break out of her shell."

"You think this is a good idea, Yuto? I can't believe you!" She stormed out of the room.

"Aurora! Aurora, please!" Dad looked at me. "I'm sorry. I have to go after her." I sat at the kitchen table by myself, the fear of upsetting them not substantial enough to overshadow my thirst for freedom. I'd always thought of emotions as integers—some positive, some negative and some neutral. When I was feeling many things, like now, I imagined them cancelling each other out. Sure, leaving behind everything I'd known was disconcerting, and I knew I would miss my family. But without some distance I stood no chance of ever being more than I already was: the good student and daughter my parents expected—balanced, composed, pleasant.

Even after they agreed to let me go to LSE, I don't think my parents believed I would follow through, just like my first sleepover. They had expected me to chicken out and ask to come home and, when I didn't, they drove to the Pryces' house after eleven o'clock, got Sarah's parents out of bed and convinced me to come home.

"Haru, you could stand to learn a thing or two from your sister." Mom had been eavesdropping, of course, despite our low voices.

"Nah, I think I'm good." Haru laughed.

She smiled, showing perfectly straight white teeth. She didn't really want my brother to be like me. He was her, if she'd been a man, strong and unapologetic. She had emigrated from Colombia with her grandparents when she was only thirteen and often said she had lived a life of limited opportunity until she met my dad. In many ways, she was my antithesis—every emotion I hid, she expressed threefold. Maybe that's why we'd come to rely on each other so much. I was a testament to how good a mother she was.

"You could use some improvement, Haru." Dad looked at me through the rearview mirror and blinked slowly, his soft eyes framed by round glasses, a thick eyebrow hair pointed in a wayward direction. "Aki, you're perfect."

I smiled and stared at my hands before looking out the window again. Perfect. It was the worst thing anyone could be: everything to lose and nothing to gain, an infinite number of ways to disappoint.

I understood where these expectations came from. My dad, named Yuto because my grandparents wanted him to be courageous and calm, was a third-generation Japanese–Canadian, the youngest of four, still trying to prove to himself and my grandfather he was just as successful as his brother, an ethics professor. As the daughter of a struggling immigrant who'd always felt like an outsider and a hyphenated Canadian from a high-achieving family, being perfect was the pinnacle of achievement and a sure-fire way to blend in with West Vancouver society.

After we unloaded our suitcases outside International Departures at YVR, Dad and Haru headed off to park while Mom and I went to the British Airways check-in and found the Business Class line. A small Asian woman in her thirties waved us over.

"Good morning! May I have your boarding passes please?"

My mom set her Louis Vuitton purse down on the counter and began to look for the boarding passes I'd printed and that she'd insisted she keep together—first calmly, then frantically. "I can't believe they're not here. Why does this always happen?"

"Deep breath." I took the purse from her and opened an inside pocket, where I'd stored both our boarding passes and our passports. I handed them over to the woman behind the counter. "Here you are."

"London, eh? Are you going on vacation?"

"No, I am dropping off my daughter at university."

"Oh, you must be so proud."

Mom looked at me, eyes tearing up. I reached for her hand and smiled. "We will have a whole week together."

By the time Dad and Haru had found their way back, we were already waiting by the large piano near the international security check area. We ordered drinks at Starbucks and chatted about my brother's rugby match next weekend and how Dad had to take our dog, Terry, to the groomer this Tuesday for her biweekly bath. As the time approached for us to head to our gate, we got quieter, unsure of what to say.

We got up slowly and made our way to the security area. Haru hugged me first. He towered over me, his arms wrapping around my neck instead of my back. He smelled of CK One and spearmint chewing gum. "Don't go British on me, okay?"

I pulled away and looked at him. "And be even more emotionless? Never." Sarcasm was the only type of humour I did well, and even then, I was economical with it.

He laughed, then got serious again. "I mean it. Don't forget where you come from."

"I won't." I felt my heart tighten and, for what felt like the first time, imagined life away from my brother.

I moved to Dad next. He'd just hugged my mom goodbye and his eyes were brimming with unspilled tears. "Be responsible, Aki-chan. I am very proud of you." I leaned in and he gave me a one-arm hug before turning his face to wipe his eyes with a blue checkered handkerchief. I followed my mom into the security area, turning back one more time to see Haru patting my dad on the shoulder.

CHAPTER 2

We landed at London Heathrow on a Sunday morning. Over the years, we'd taken many trips to London as a family to visit two of Dad's high school friends, so the airport was comfortingly familiar. We took a cab into the city and dropped our bags off at a boutique hotel near Russell Square before looking for something to eat nearby.

"Shall we head back to the hotel after lunch?" My eyes felt heavy with jetlag, and I wanted to make sure I was awake for frosh week and all it entailed.

"We can't do that." Mom signalled for the check. "We only have a week, Aki. And you only brought two suitcases. I need to make sure you have everything you need."

From Russell Square, we took the tube to Oxford Circus and headed to John Lewis where Mom picked out matching bed sheets and bath towels for me, then a set of blue and white plates, eight glasses and a twenty-four-piece cutlery set. Despite my protestations, she also got me a mini fridge and a microwave—both prohibited items according to the residence guide they'd sent me a month back. We scheduled delivery for the next day, when I would be getting my room keys; Mom confirmed three times that they would bring the items up to my room.

"You have to use your Colombian ways to get what you want."

She flip-flopped constantly between wanting to fit in and standing out from the crowd. Less than an hour before, she'd happily flashed her Louis Vuitton bag at the security guard at a high-end store while instructing me on the importance of being seen as "one of them," by which she meant British and posh. As an immigrant, she considered assimilation both a threat and a reward, even when travelling abroad.

"I am not sure much of that was passed on to me." Asking for anything didn't come easily to me—neither did expressing discontent.

"It's there." Mom tapped my stomach. "The beast is just sleeping." She winked, then laughed.

The next day, while I devoured a full English breakfast, Mom went down an extensive list of everything we needed to get done. First, go to my residence, register and meet the delivery people from John Lewis. Then, head into LSE, grab my student ID and buy sweaters for Haru and Dad. In the afternoon we would go to a stationery store to get all the supplies I was missing and then Waterstones for my list of books.

"Actually, I was hoping to attend a couple of the frosh events today. You know, to meet people."

"Of course, how long do you think you'll need? One hour? Maybe two?"

"I don't know. I was hoping maybe you could take the afternoon to do your own shopping and we could meet here later."

"Oh. Yeah, of course." My mom took a sip of coffee and looked away. London emboldened me to sit in the discomfort.

We headed to the residence in silence. Mom seemed pleased with the location and the fact all rooms had been refurbished the year prior. I had my own room with my own small bathroom, and while she disapproved of the curtains and the carpet, the fact I'd be the first person to live there since the room had been renovated made it bearable.

"I'm so glad they will be coming in to clean once a week," she said over and over as she inspected the shower, toilet, sink, closets, cabinets and bed.

"I can clean too." I wanted to sound responsible but ended up sounding childish.

"Yes, and I sing beautifully." She looked at her watch, then at the door. "When will you be back at the hotel?"

"I don't know. For dinner. So, six, maybe seven."

"Okay, be careful."

I didn't need to leave straight away, but this felt like the natural lull in the conversation. "Will you be all right with the delivery?"

"Will *I* be okay?" she scoffed and smiled.

"All right. I guess I'll see you later," I said tentatively. Part of me wanted to stay here, in this empty room with her.

She stepped forward and put her arms around me. "You will do great." Her voice wavered, and I felt dampness on her cheek next to mine. She let go of me and moved toward the window. "Have fun. See you later."

LSE was smaller than I'd expected. In my university search, I'd been to UBC, McGill and U of T, which were all much larger. Houghton Street was packed with students, all around my age but seemingly less fearful and more eager. I walked past a blond woman introducing herself to a group of strangers, followed by a couple of men drinking beer outside the student pub. I missed the sign to the Old Building and had to circle back.

A tall man dressed in dark green trousers, brown dress shoes and a checkered button-down approached me with a map. He dressed differently than the West Coast athletic type, more manicured than I expected of someone my age, and I instantly assumed his privileged background. The man had the face of someone who'd just started to grow facial hair. He had Haru's hair, thick and shaggy, only his was much lighter. "Are you all right? Looking for something?"

"Uh, yes, I guess I am. I need to get my student ID."

"Hmmm, let's see." He brought the map closer to me and we examined it together. "Here it is!" He turned, green eyes hidden behind thick square glasses. "Right behind us. I'm Jamie, by the way."

"Thank you, Jamie. I'm Aki."

"I guess I should ask you the three fresher questions, according to this little book." He tapped the booklet he'd been holding underneath the map. "Name, check. Next, what's your degree?"

"International Relations. You?"

"Government." There was a pause. I realized he was also struggling to make friends. "Last question, where are you from?"

"Canada. You?"

"Boring old London." We stared at each other for a moment, then at the floor. "Well, I won't stand in your way. Off you go to get your ID."

I smiled. "Thanks, Jamie. I'll see you around."

I stood in line at Student Services for nearly ninety minutes in a seemingly endless sea of awkwardness, avoiding eye contact along with everyone else. I felt like I'd finally met my people. Afterward, I walked up and down the four streets that are LSE, making a stop at the library before heading to Clement House for my program's orientation so I wouldn't have to make too much small talk.

There were only a few seats left. "May I?" I gestured to a seat in the third row, between two women who were already chatting.

"Of course! I'm Ginika." Ginika was tall, Black and curvaceous with green eyes and hair braided and gathered in a loose ponytail— the only person in the whole room who actually looked like an adult.

"I'm Abby. Abigail, really, but no one can pronounce that the way it's meant to sound in Spanish," said the other girl in a thick Hispanic accent. She extended her arms and hugged me as I sat down. Abby was petite, even smaller than me, something I could tell even while she was seated. She was fair-skinned, and her nose and cheeks were covered in the kind of light brown freckles that disappeared in the winter months.

"Nice to meet you both. I'm Aki." I took out a small notebook from the backpack I'd been carrying.

"Jackpot!" Ginika put her notebook away. "Only one of us really needs to take notes, right?" I smiled and nodded.

After orientation, I found out the three of us lived in the same mixed residence for University of London students. We walked back together, even though I wouldn't be sleeping in my room until my mom returned to Canada.

"So where are you from, Aki?" Abby asked, after volunteering she was from Venezuela.

"I'm from Vancouver. Canada."

"No, where are you *really* from?" Ginika interjected, with a sarcastic tone. "You see, before London, I lived in Kenya, but I'm from Nigeria."

"Well, I was born in Vancouver. But my mom is from Colombia."

"So, you're Latina, like me."

"Not really. My dad is Japanese–Canadian." I paused, resisting the classification. "I guess that makes me mixed, but I don't like that term."

"I know what you mean. In Venezuela, I am white. Or that's how I am perceived. It's kind of the same here until I open my mouth. My accent gives me away. It's weird being singled out like that."

There was a pause. "You know, people like us have got to stick together." Ginika gestured to the three of us.

"What do you mean?" The three of us couldn't have looked or sounded more different.

Abby searched for the right words. "Did you notice that the people in orientation all looked and spoke kind of the same?"

"She means white and posh." Ginika laughed. "You can say it, you know."

"I meant more European."

"She meant white."

I looked at Abby and Ginika. "Caucasian? Caucasoid?"

They both laughed. "You're funny," said Abby. "I agree. People like us, from developing economies, have to stick together."

"Yeah, because if I hear one more stupid question about safaris, I will lose my shit."

"You know I wasn't born or raised in Colombia, right?" As much as I wanted to be part of the club, I didn't want to sneak in on a technicality.

"Well, you may not have grown up in a developing economy, but you certainly don't blend in. Look at this beautiful hair, these curls and the eyes—not white! And Abby, while she blends in with her looks, her accent gives her away. We're witnessing her first lesson in racialization." Ginika smirked.

"So, what you're saying is that between the both of us, we make a brown person?" Abby looked at me and winked.

"Sure, why not?" We all laughed.

Mom's week in London came to an end quickly. On the day of her departure, we checked out early and walked to my residence. I suggested we grab lunch somewhere, but she couldn't stop crying. Instead, I got take-out from a pub a few streets over. Two Sunday roast dinners: roast beef, potatoes, over-cooked vegetables, Yorkshire pudding, gravy and horseradish sauce.

When we were done, she opened my closet and asked if there was anything I wanted her to take back to Vancouver.

"What? No. That makes no sense. We just dragged all this stuff here from Canada. Why would I send it back with you?"

"I don't know. It's a pretty small space. Maybe you wait until December to bring the heavy winter stuff, so you have more space now for fall clothing."

"I don't want to have to take back a large suitcase every time I come visit."

"Visit? What do you mean, visit? Vancouver is still your home."

"You know what I mean. Now that I'm going to LSE, my life will be in London."

"How can you say that?" She took one of my favourite shirts from a hanger, a flannel checkered in blue and green.

"Please put that back." I got up and walked toward her.

"Will you even miss me?" Her eyes filled with tears again, but instead of eliciting compassion, they made me frustrated.

"Of course, I will miss you." I took a deep breath and sighed audibly. "There's no need for melodramatics."

"Why couldn't you stay in BC? UBC is a great school."

"All the kids I don't like are going to UBC. Plus, shouldn't university be an opportunity for me to branch out?" That seemed to appease her, but then I went on. "It will be good for both of us to have some space, to grow."

"What do you mean?" Her tone changed.

I knew I should have stopped. Maybe I could stop now. "I mean, I rely on you a lot. Maybe this will help me to be stronger on my own. That could be good, right?"

"What are you saying?"

"Nothing. Let's change the subject."

"What are you saying, Aki?"

I snapped. "I'm saying sometimes I feel suffocated. Living in West Vancouver . . . there is no air for me to breathe in that house. I need my own space, my own life. Away."

My mom looked shocked; I'd never spoken to her like that before. She laid the shirt she had been holding down on my bed and walked to the bathroom, without saying a word. I tried to think of something to say, but "sorry" felt cheap and fake.

CHAPTER 3

Mom suggested I needn't bother taking her to the airport, but I knew better than to fall for that trick. I ordered a cab and waited with her at Heathrow until it was time to go through security. We hugged, neither of us mentioning the scene in my room. To get back to the city, I decided to take the Piccadilly line all the way to the Russell Square tube station.

I had taken the tube many times before, but I was alone for the first time. It made me feel a part of something, as if I belonged in this city. I observed as commuters entered and left. A group of tourists from the States opened up a large map of the city and began circling all the attractions they wanted to visit. A young mother tried to break up a fight between her two toddlers. A businessman blatantly checked out a nurse who looked like she'd just come off her shift. None of these things seemed even remotely connected to my life back in BC, and that excited me.

I got back to the residence on Malet Street to find Abby and Ginika sitting on the chairs by reception. "Great! Here you are." Abby got up and picked up her purse. She was dressed in tight jeans, a cardigan and heels, which made her look a bit like one of the skinny moms from back home.

"We've been waiting for you. Want to grab dinner out?" Ginika stayed seated, her legs crossed. Her grey and red wool dress hugged her curves unapologetically.

"On a school night?"

Ginika laughed loudly, then covered her mouth. "We are at university, Aki. Not school."

"We can do whatever we want." Abby continued, "Your mom is gone, right?"

We headed to a Thai place a few streets over, by the London School of Hygiene and Tropical Medicine, and ordered papaya salad and spring rolls to share. Then three Pad Thai, with varying levels of spiciness: mild for me, hot for Abby and very hot for Ginika.

"So, what's home like?" Abby asked between mouthfuls.

"I couldn't tell you." Ginika took a sip of her cocktail. "I went to boarding school when I was seven. Here, in England." She looked at me, waiting for my response.

"Home is—" I struggled to find the right words. "It's, hmm. I'm, hmm. I'm lucky."

Abby laughed. "You sound a little conflicted."

"Home is just a lot." I looked down at my hands. "I can't say I fit in exactly."

"I hear you." Ginika pushed a loose braid off her face. "When you spend most of the year away, it's hard to feel like you fit in your life." She paused. "I'm the second youngest of twenty-three siblings, you know."

"Wait, what?" Abby put her fork down. "You have twenty-two brothers and sisters?"

Ginika laughed softly. "Yeah, my mom was my dad's fourth wife. He divorced one of his previous wives to marry her."

"Oh, wow. How old is he?" Abby looked a bit too interested, and I wondered if Ginika might not want to answer these questions.

"He passed away when I was six." She looked down. "I don't remember much about him, to be honest."

Abby opened her mouth to ask another question, but I interjected. "How about you, Abby? How do you like home?" Abby paused. I looked at Ginika, who smiled at me.

"I love home. Have always lived in Caracas." She smiled.

"Of course, you do." Ginika jokingly rolled her eyes.

We built a collective routine almost instantly. In the mornings, Ginika and I would wake up and work out, while Abby slept in. At seven o'clock, we'd meet at the dining hall and have breakfast together, before the fifteen-minute walk to LSE. We had the same lectures, though we were not in any seminars together. As days went by, the personalities of my new friends became clearer. Abby, no matter where and when you found her, was surrounded by people. Ginika changed her hairstyle, and sometimes eye colour, almost every week, and she knew where all the gyms and outdoor workout spots were. Me, I knew the library best, having mapped out the best study spots on each floor. We had lunch together nearly every day.

Two weeks into the term, Thea, a German girl in my program, asked me if I was into *The L Word*. I must have stared too long at her massaging the shoulders of the student sitting next to her. I had no clue what she was talking about. I looked at Ginika for support, but she shook her head. Nothing but *Sex in the City* played in her room. I leaned in and asked Thea about the show. She smiled and told me to watch it. "Let me know when you do. I'll quiz you."

At the end of our third week, Ginika suggested we all join the Athletic Union. "It would be great if we were all on the same team. Running—that would be the best."

"Running? No, thank you." Abby shook her head. "That's the most boring sport ever. What's the point of it?"

"Come on, Abby! Aki?"

"What? Me?" I put down my sandwich.

"Yeah, you. Won't you please join the running team with me?" Ginika pleaded.

"I am more of a tennis player." I paused. "Well, it's the family sport." We'd played tennis every weekend since I picked up a racket at age five.

Ginika sighed. "Didn't you say you wanted to try new things? Maybe it's time to give tennis a break. Plus, running won't hurt your tennis game. If anything, it will help!"

Running, not tennis? How would my parents feel about that? Then again, fourteen years was a long time to do the same thing. "Fine. I'll do it, but only if Abby joins the AU too."

Abby rolled her eyes. "Fine. But I will not run. It will have to be something else."

Ginika smiled, knowing she'd won the argument.

Later that night, when I spoke with my parents over the phone, I told them about our plans to join the AU. "Ginika is really invested. She wants us all to join the running team, but Abby is not having it."

"Running?" My mom's voice felt pointed, sharp. "Isn't there a tennis team at LSE?"

"Yeah, there is. But I don't know. Maybe it's time I try something else, you know."

"But you're so good at tennis." Mom sighed audibly. "I just don't want you to waste all those years of practice. We didn't send you to London to lose your ways, Aki."

Dad stepped in. "Can you join both?"

"I guess," I said tentatively. "It might be a lot though."

"Nothing is too much for you, Aki."

I could hear the smile on his face, feel the pride in his voice. "Okay, I'll look into it."

"Promise?" My mom dragged out the word.

"Yeah, I promise."

I lied to my parents for the first time in years, saying LSE didn't

take any first years. Mom was enraged and threatened to call someone, but I managed to talk her down by promising I'd join a tennis
club outside of LSE. I didn't do that either. I was scared and excited
by how easy it was to keep things from them.

On the night of initiation into the AU, all the fresh recruits met
outside the student pub for a night of games organized by our indi-
vidual teams. Abby, having joined netball—an absurd sport that
blended basketball and handball, with no dribbling nor running—
was one of a group of new recruits that had to challenge the existing
team after downing three tequila shots in quick succession.

We runners had to complete a relay. Instead of a baton, we were
required to drink a pint of beer before our teammate could go on.
Needless to say, Houghton and Portugal streets were soon covered in
vomit and stale beer.

Sometime between the wrap-up of the drunken games and our
stumble home, Abby, Ginika and I made our way back to the student pub. They were each interested in some other fresher who was
being initiated into the AU, and I didn't like the idea of walking
back to the residence on my own.

"So, have you watched *The L Word*?" Thea put her hand on my
lower back.

I laughed. "Yes, I have."

"So, what did you think?"

Maybe it was the beer, but I felt filled with courage. "I would like
to kiss a girl myself." The crowd around us pushed to get closer to
the bar. I fixed my eyes upon hers.

"What are you waiting for then?" Thea bit her lower lip.

I leaned in and kissed her. She tasted of beer, her mouth more
bitter than I'd expected. Eventually, she pulled away, and I smiled.

"Now you can cross that off your list." She turned to go, but
before disappearing into the crowd she looked back and caught my
eyes.

Ginika and Abby, both a few feet away, rushed to me. "Dude! What was that? Are you like . . . interested?"

"Was that like your first kiss with a girl?" Ginika squeezed my arm in excitement.

I nodded, eyes open wide, unsure whose question I was answering. I'd kissed boys before, two or three during high school, but Thea's touch was subtle and tender in a way I'd never experienced before. I had kissed a girl.

The next morning, the three of us lay on the floor of my room, each too nauseated to move. "That was fun, right?" Ginika turned her face slowly to look at me. Her braids were coming undone, and her eyes, now without the green contacts, were a deep brown.

I met her gaze, then stared into the ceiling. "Yeah, it was." I smiled.

CHAPTER 4

By early October, I started enjoying my runs. They took me across parks, alongside the Thames and through new neighbourhoods. I'd always been impressed by the architecture of the city, the sheer breadth and diversity of its building styles—Romanesque, Gothic, Baroque, Art Deco. The way the orange light hit the buildings at sunset.

I remembered one of my favourite teachers in West Vancouver saying London was a textbook definition of dignified degeneracy. I hadn't understood then, but I was beginning to now. And Londoners always seemed so sure of themselves. I knew I'd made the right choice: London was the place for me.

One Tuesday, after practice, as autumn leaves collected on the ground, I sat in Hyde Park, examining other runners' forms, hoping to learn something that would help me get closer to Ginika's speed. A woman came into view, running clumsily, wavy black hair bouncing. She was looking down when she should have been facing forward. Her knees were out of line, bending inwards. Her elbows weren't close enough to her body, messing up her aerodynamism. She definitely wouldn't have made our running team.

As she approached me, keys fell out of her pocket. She was too out of breath to notice, so I ran toward her and tapped her on the shoulder. She turned around. Thick eyebrows, dark eyes, wide smile, pointed nose.

"You dropped these." I smiled back and handed her the keys.

"Oh, thank you." Flustered, she grabbed the keys.

"You might want to put them in your jacket pocket . . . the one with the zipper."

"Can you tell this is the first time I've ever run outside of PE?" She smiled wryly, and my chest filled with warmth.

"Kind of." I laughed. "You've got to start somewhere, right?" I'd never seen someone so beautiful.

Two weeks later, Anaïs, from our Econ B class, invited us to a party at her residence in Southbank. We'd made friends with her after the third lecture, when she'd arrived wearing a pink fur jacket, a matching leather trouser suit and high heels.

Abby was instantly intrigued by the outfit. "Can I touch it?" She gestured to the jacket, as Anaïs made her way down the row of seats in front of us.

Anaïs nodded. "Don't worry," she said, looking at me. "It's not real." She turned to Abby. "I got it at Pull & Bear for half off, back in Leeds."

"Should I get one?" Abby looked at me, then Ginika. I said nothing and waited for Ginika to respond, expecting she'd be ruthless, but instead she said nothing.

"Not everyone can pull this off." Anaïs gestured to her outfit, moving her hands up and down the side of her body. We all laughed.

At the party, most of us were first years from LSE, and the big topic of conversation was the Lehman Brothers scandal. More than half of the university's graduates got jobs in investment banking and, being the precocious, neurotic teens that we were, we worried that three years would not be long enough for the world economy to rebound. In truth, almost everyone in that room had parents with connections and, financial crisis or not, would likely come out largely unscathed, but it felt good to talk business like we were adults.

Ginika and I started comparing notes on running. Ginika was going on and on about these new shoes she'd bought and how they were going to help her shave off three seconds off each mile. Only mildly interested, I half listened, then I saw the woman from the park make her way across the room. When she spotted me, she called "Keys!"

We spent the rest of the night talking. Ayesha didn't go to LSE and had little to contribute to the discussion on current affairs, let alone economics. Instead, we talked about how she was studying at the Chelsea College of Art & Design and growing up in Bradford, near Leeds. She and Anaïs had gone to school together, at Ruth Gorse Academy. I told her about how I'd moved to London from Canada, and she tried to guess where my ancestors were from. Ayesha told me her dad had colon cancer and that her mother was progressive, not a traditional Pakistani wife. I told her how my great-grandparents had immigrated to Canada, bringing my mom, hoping to secure a better life for one of their grandchildren. My *abuela*, my grandmother, had never left Colombia. She'd remarried and had three more children. Mom wasn't close to her younger half-siblings, but we did visit most years.

We talked about everything and nothing, and I shared more than I'd probably had to anyone my whole life. She opened up too. That night, I learned she was a non-practising Muslim who drank, smoked and kissed women.

After the party, I offered to take Ayesha home. On the way, we snuck into Regent's Park and found a place to sit near the boating lake. I put my coat down and we lay on it, looking up at the starless sky.

"When we were little, my mom would wake us up when the

night sky was clear." Ayesha turned her head to me and I felt the warmth of her breath on my cheeks. "It was crazy to me to think that the moon, the stars, they were all there, even if I couldn't see them."

I turned to her, our lips a few inches apart. The same warmth I'd felt in the park spread through my chest, but this time it was more intense—something I'd never experienced before. "I know what you mean." I paused, staring at her lips. "You need to bring the chaos of the city down, turn off the lights, to see it. That's pretty poetic, don't you think?"

"Look at you, LSE! And I thought all you could talk about was economics." She laughed.

"I'm more than just brains, you know." I looked up at the sky again.

"I'm glad I came to Anaïs's party tonight."

Ayesha held my hand in hers to keep it warm, and I was surprised by how seamlessly they just fit together. For the first time I felt like the protagonist and not just a supporting character in someone else's story. I wondered if this is what falling in love was supposed to feel like and how long I could make it last.

Ayesha and I were just different enough to arouse an unsatiable curiosity in one another. We hung out almost every day for weeks. Abby and Ginika didn't seem to mind too much, since they were pursuing their own romantic interests. Besides, we still kept to our scheduled meals, doing breakfast and dinner back at the residence. Ayesha took me to the British Museum, Tate Britain, the National Gallery, educating me in art, challenging my ideas of beauty. I studied her smile from the opposite side of the Rosetta Stone, sat next to her on the steps of the Tate Modern, challenged her to a sprint alongside the Thames. On cold, rainy days, she perched on my bed and drew while I read Plato, Aristotle, Cicero, St. Augustine. When she fell asleep, I put a blanket over her and traced her body in my mind, lingering on her neck and shoulders.

I'd never met anyone like her. Unlike Ginika and Abby, whose privilege I could relate to, Ayesha was different. She'd had a seamless life by all accounts, but without the ostentation I was accustomed to—no international trips every summer and winter break, no limitless shopping trips, no owning her own car at the age of sixteen or even eighteen. The more she shared about her life in Bradford, living in a three-storey terraced house with her parents, brother and paternal grandmother, the more I questioned the rules I'd grown so accustomed to following.

Ayesha had chosen to study art, not because it was useful or even something her parents wanted for her. She saw the world and everything in it as beautiful in its own right, rather than practical and strategic. With her, I gave myself permission to stop and ponder, I gave myself permission to breathe.

Despite the flirtatious looks and my all-around awkwardness when our bodies touched, it took me a whole month to admit to myself that I wanted something more than just a close friendship. I'd never been with a woman before, never allowed myself to entertain it as a possibility. It was a Wednesday, the day after Obama had won the United States presidential election. Abby, Ginika, Ayesha and I were part of a group that had stayed up the night before watching the numbers trickle in. Even though Obama wasn't going to be our president, it felt like we were on the cusp of something big. By the time it got dark, I hadn't slept in over forty hours. All I wanted was my pillow, but Ginika insisted we go out to celebrate with the others. We ended up at Zoo Bar, a club known for cheap drinks and covers. Even mid-week, it was packed, heat rising from the crowd.

As always, I stood at the bar, avoiding the dance floor until I found a seat by one of the speakers, the red velvety cover stained by what I assumed was alcohol, sweat and vomit. I sat on the edge, avoiding the stains as much as possible, scrolling through Facebook on my Blackberry.

Ayesha periodically came over to check on me. "Just one dance and I'll leave you alone," she pleaded, each time enunciating her words more clearly. She eventually coaxed me to stand near the rest of the group. I closed my eyes and opened them slowly, the strobe lights softening my focus. The crowd jostled my body back and forth to the rhythm of the music, and that seemed to please Ayesha. She danced near and around me, occasionally twirling, eyes fixed on mine. I wanted nothing more than to make the rest of the world disappear.

She was beautiful and it was only a matter of time until someone else noticed. A tall man in his mid-twenties approached her and, running his fingers through his hair, looked back at a group of men before leaning in and whispering something in her ear, something I couldn't hear. He put his hand on her shoulder.

I wanted to look away but couldn't, and Ayesha maintained eye contact with me. This was supposed to be my cue to leave. Did she want me to go away? Did she want me to stay? I only knew what I wanted, what I needed. I downed the rest of my drink and tapped the man on the shoulder. He turned to me—his green eyes expectant.

"Excuse me," I screamed over the loud, electronic music. "She's taken."

He leaned in. "Sorry, what?"

"She's taken," I yelled into his ear. He put both hands in the air and mouthed sorry. Then, he turned his back and walked away. Ayesha looked at me confused.

"What did you say to him?"

"I told him you're taken."

She smirked. "I am?"

I pulled her closer by the waist. "Yeah, you are."

She traced the outline of my face with her fingertips. "How is it that you make me feel like the only girl in any room we're in?"

"Well, that's the intention." I stared at her lips, then leaned in. They were soft. I bit them. She grabbed the nape of my neck and pulled on my hair. The world fell silent for a moment.

That night we slept together for the first time. We cabbed to her place, a modest, two-bedroom apartment a few blocks from Bayswater tube station that was owned by her grandmother. She lived with her older cousin. "Don't make a sound until we get to my room," Ayesha said as she unlocked the front door and we stepped into darkness. She pushed me ahead, trying to guide me in the direction of her room. I kept my arms out to make sure I didn't bump into a wall, or a piece of furniture. "Hurry up," she whispered. I took a step forward, my right fingertips brushing against a smooth surface. I felt an object shift, then a loud shattering noise.

"Ayesha! Is that you?" The crash had woken her cousin.

"Yeah. Just got home." Ayesha shoved me forward, toward the end of the hall.

"Are you okay?"

"Yeah, yeah. I just knocked over a vase. Go back to bed, Sana. I'll clean it up." Ayesha rushed past me and turned the light on in her room. "Just come in," she whispered in a fake angry voice. "What am I going to do with you?" She slipped out of her dress and pushed me on the bed. I kicked my shoes off and put my hands on her waist. She moved her body toward me. I undid her bra with one hand and cupped her breasts. They were bigger, rounder than I'd imagined. Ayesha lifted my shirt and slid her hand up my stomach. My whole body tingled at her touch.

We pulsated, at first to our own rhythms, one slightly faster than the other, then in unison. I felt everything—every touch, every breath, every sound. It was almost overstimulation, and for a brief moment I worried I would burst. No one had ever made me feel this way. I'd never let anyone this close. I knew then that I loved her.

The next morning, I left before Ayesha woke up. I wrote her a note and put it on the pillow I'd slept on. I told her what a great night I'd had and that I didn't want to cause any trouble with her cousin, but that we should go out on a proper date. I even drew a heart next to my name.

I shut the door of her room behind me and carried my shoes, to avoid making noise in the hallway. It was barely seven in the morning, but a timid November light was coming in through the large windows in the living room, making evident the mess I'd caused the night before. Pieces of broken glass were scattered throughout the narrow corridor, mostly in large chunks. It was a miracle neither of us had stepped on them.

The vase looked expensive in a way that the other furniture in the apartment didn't. I bent over for closer examination. From what I could see, it was hourglass-shaped, made of clear glass with speckles of blue and green. It shouldn't be left on the floor like this. Someone could get hurt. Ayesha could get hurt. I made my way to the kitchen in search of a plastic bag and found one under the sink. On the tip of my toes, back arched over, I grabbed the large pieces of broken glass first, followed by the smaller ones.

The bag was heavy, and I held it carefully against my chest as I left the apartment. Another resident gave me a dirty look. Maybe there were rules about which way to take out the trash. As I carried the bag to the station, on the tube, to my residence, up the elevator, into my room, the need to repair the vase grew. On an old issue of *The Guardian* with a headline about North Korea, I rebuilt Ayesha's vase with Loctite glue.

I began to fill all my free time with Ayesha. After lectures on Mondays and Wednesdays, I walked to the Strand and took the 87 bus to Chelsea College of Arts. On my nineteenth birthday, she took me to Tate Britain just to stare at Arthur Hughes's "April Love." It was one of her favourites.

The painting shows two lovers in an ivy-clad summerhouse with lilac outside the window and rose petals on the stone floor. The man is barely visible, his face obscured by shadows, head bent over the woman's left hand, the petals at her feet echoing the deep purple of her dress. She's sombre, and there's an undeniable air of melancholy to the scene: the fragility of young love.

Ayesha told me that when it debuted in the 1850s, Hughes accompanied it with an extract from *The Miller's Daughter,* Alfred Lord Tennyson's pastoral poem. Eyes closed, she recited it to me.

Love that hath us in the net,
Can he pass, and we forget?
Many suns arise and set.
Many a chance the years beget.
Love the gift is Love the debt.
Even so.

As weeks went by, I wondered how she felt about me and what we were to each other. We'd never set clear rules and we both continued to flirt with other people, sometimes in front of each other, but to my knowledge we weren't sleeping around.

One day, I lay on her bed while she smoked by the window. I hated the smell of cigarettes, but somehow, I didn't mind it on her. She looked at me and smiled, as she often did, with only one side of her mouth. I shifted on the bed and propped myself up. Hugging my knees, I looked at her. She was focused on something outside. "Ayesha, what are we doing here?" I said finally. "You know, are we dating or—"

"Why so serious?" She deflected. I wondered if this could be a phase for her, whether she assumed it was a phase for me too. "We are having fun—can't we just leave it at that?"

"I guess we can." I wanted to mean it, but my chest tightened at the uncertainty of our relationship. I wanted Ayesha all to myself, but to say it out loud felt needy and pitiful. Attempting to let her response roll off my shoulder, I got up and grabbed the lit cigarette from her hand. I tossed it out the window and pushed her on the bed. Using my teeth, I unbuttoned her shirt, to reveal the lacy purple bra I'd helped her buy. I bit her shoulder. I kissed her neck, pinning her arms over her head. Her breathing was laboured. She arched her head backward, eyes closed.

Then we heard the front door open. Ayesha jumped off the bed. "It's Sana. She can't see you! She's ultra-conservative." With my trousers down to my knees, Ayesha shoved me into her closet and closed the door. I could hear her cousin came into the room and they talked about their day, switching back and forth between English and Urdu. I crouched on the floor, thinking about the midterm essay I still had to finish on classical natural law theory. I took out my Blackberry and browsed the BBC site on my phone. I scrolled down the sports section—Filipino boxer Manny Pacquiao had defeated Oscar De La Hoya during a welterweight bout at the MGM Grand Garden Arena in Las Vegas the day before. Examining the photos on the small screen, I wondering what would compel someone to want to hurt another person on purpose.

Eventually, my eyes began to hurt so I went over Hobbes' *Leviathan* and his theory on the state of nature in my head. I had an outline fully formed when, an hour later, Ayesha snuck me out, while her cousin was taking a shower. On the stairs, she avoided eye contact with me. "Weird, huh?" Ayesha said, trying to brush over the tension. I clenched my teeth and took a deep breath.

We didn't talk or see each for a few days after that. It bothered me profoundly that she wouldn't apologize to me. I'd been shoved in a closet for over an hour, and she still felt like that was okay. Despite my feelings for her, it felt like Ayesha and I weren't on the same page. I wanted something more than what we had, and it felt like she might not be so sure. Ayesha tried to reach out, texting me and calling at least once a day, leaving messages like, "So, when will I see you again?" or "Did I do something?" She never acknowledged what had happened in her room, never explicitly apologized. It seemed that she hoped by ignoring it, things could go back to the way they were. But I wasn't happy with the way things were and so I dodged her attempts, day after day. Instead, I lay in bed and imagined her missing me.

We had friends in common, so I knew it was only a matter of time until I would see Ayesha again. Twelve days after the closet incident, Ginika organized an outing with the girls from the running team to The Penthouse, a club in Leicester Square overlooking London.

That day, I'd been busy Christmas shopping on Regent Street. After getting my dad a cashmere scarf and my brother a new leather weekender, I'd spent hours at Hamleys, where I'd been fawning over a train set for myself. Once I had everything I needed, I walked up and down the high street, the festive arches illuminating the crowds below, with no real purpose or goal, a cup of hot chocolate in hand. When my hands began to feel stiff and cold, I walked back to the residence. I wanted to come up with an excuse for not going out clubbing, but Ginika made it clear that I would not be forgiven for not showing up since this was the last outing before everyone went home for the holidays.

To ensure I wouldn't escape, Ginika, who wasn't keen on this holiday, agreed to walk through the Christmas market in Leicester Square with me before we met up with the rest of the group. At the third stall we visited, I reserved a German wooden Christmas incense smoker for my mom for pick-up the next day. It was a Santa with a pipe in its mouth and skis on his feet. Mom had collected these wooden figurines ever since I could remember, and it was a tradition to give her one every year.

It was 11:00 p.m. when we lined up for The Penthouse, and we could hardly see the beginning of the line. It was a fancier than Zoo Bar, the kind where they had a dress code, which included no T-shirts, no sneakers and no jeans, but it was nothing like the upscale Mayfair clubs Abby, Ginika and I visited at the start of term—the ones that reminded me of West Vancouver, if West Vancouver was a country club decorated in neon flashing lights. Besides the running crowd, Ginika decided to invite a few extras, including Anaïs, who brought Ayesha along.

When Ayesha and I spotted each other, we waved awkwardly. Then, I proceeded to avoid her while we waited in line, trying to make conversation with a group of girls from London Met. After thirty minutes, Ginika managed to get us in without paying the cover.

"You are the youngest daughter of Mazi Amadi!" the bouncer, a tall, broad-shouldered man said in a thick Nigerian accent. He looked over the ID Ginika had handed to him. "My father worked for your father for many years."

Ginika smiled politely and offered a £50 bill.

The bouncer shook his head, refusing the money. "No, no, no. The daughter of Mazi Amadi does not pay." He gestured to a woman inside The Penthouse. "Please give them your best available table and some champagne."

Abby turned to me in confusion. "What the heck just happened?"

"I think Ginika is more than just wealthy. Her family might be a big deal back in Nigeria."

That night our group was large—too large to reach a consensus about anything. We couldn't agree on which room to try first. Ginika wanted hip hop. Abby wanted techno. Ayesha wanted pop. I didn't want to choose, so I went to the bar to order shots for the group. When Ayesha pulled me aside, I pretended the music was too loud to hear what she was saying and walked away with the drinks. I knew there was no winning if I kept ignoring her, but it felt too late to change course.

I felt a tap on my shoulder. Two girls from London Met stared at me, while they sipped on Smirnoff Ice with J2O. They could have been siblings, similar in both appearance and dress, and they were taller than me with straight, blond hair and blue eyes.

The one to my right leaned in and yelled in my ear. "I've never kissed a girl."

I smirked. "Thank you for sharing that!"

I looked back at my group of friends. Ayesha stared at me, then walked between the girls from London Met and me, pushing me back. She grabbed Ginika, who was chatting up a man, and pulled her to the dance floor. They danced, their bodies too close to each other to be merely platonic. Logically, I knew Ginika would never do anything, but she'd hinted at being bicurious before and I struggled to control my jealousy. If Ayesha wanted a scene, I could play this game.

I pulled the London Met girl who'd just yelled into my ear closer, our mouths less than an inch apart. "May I?" I whispered through a smile. She pulled me in, coarse lips meeting mine. It felt like kissing a dry leaf, but that wasn't the point.

"You're a good kisser!" She handed her drink to her friend and threw herself in my arms. I stumbled backwards, surprised by the gusto with which this total stranger wanted to make out with me. Across the room, I met Ayesha's gaze. Jaws clenched, she turned away and left the dance floor. I left the club twenty minutes later with the London Met girl, walking past Ayesha on our way out.

I woke up the next day hungover and full of regret. I'd gone too far this time. Maybe it was the pounding in my head or the sudden realization that she might never speak to me again, but I panicked. I wasn't ready to let it go, to let her go. I'd given up too easily and needed to rectify the damage.

I got up and went on a cleansing run. I'd decided London is most beautiful on Saturday mornings, before most of its residents have awakened, and was counting on some fresh air to help me come up with something that would win her back.

When I eventually called Ayesha, she didn't sound happy to hear from me, but she agreed to meet me at Tate Britain. The museum was closed when I arrived, so I sat on the steps and waited for her. At 10:10 a.m. I spotted Ayesha walking down Millbank, her black hair bouncing to the rhythm of her gait. Her stride was as bad walking as it was running. She stood in front of me and waited for my reaction. The rule in apologies is the aggressor must make the first move, but this wasn't that simple. Ayesha had shoved me in a closet, then ignored the situation. Then I'd ghosted her, made it impossible for her to apologize and kissed someone else to boot. We were both completely inept at talking about how we felt.

I got up from the step and leaned in, but she didn't hug me. I guessed I deserved that. We went in the Manton entrance, on Atterbury Street, on the lower floor of the museum, and turned left toward the stairs. Once on the main floor, we turned left again, past the 1870 room, through the opening on the left to 1815, followed by 1810. I headed toward the room with the Pre-Raphaelites. I couldn't tell if she was following me out of habit or if that's where she intended to go too. There were hardly any visitors around, which made the museum seem bigger and more intimate. I stopped in front of "April Love." Ayesha and I stood in silence, staring ahead at the painting. I wanted to hold her hand or pull her closer, but something stopped me. I inhaled deeply and took out a book wrapped in parcel paper from my back pocket and handed it to her.

She pursed her lips and unwrapped it carefully: an 1890 edition of Tennyson's *The Miller's Daughter*. It had taken me days to find it. I recited the lines she knew by heart.

> *Love is hurt with jar and fret,*
> *Love is made a vague regret,*
> *Eyes with idle tears are wet,*

Idle habit links us yet;
What is Love? for we forget.
Ah no, no.

She held the book against her chest. Then, she grabbed my hand and smiled, but I could see she was tentative, still hurt. I knew I wasn't allowed any more mistakes.

Ayesha and I spent the next few days together, until I could no longer postpone returning to Vancouver. The thought of leaving her in England felt unbearable, but my family was already upset I hadn't returned home as soon as classes had officially ended.

We took the Piccadilly line to Heathrow. It was mid-afternoon and the tube was less crowded, so we found seats straight away, me with a large suitcase between my legs and a backpack on my lap. The heater blew hot air on my ankles, which rose up my pant legs. With our arms entwined and Ayesha's head on my shoulder, we made plans to Skype each other every day, doing the math to determine when my parents would be asleep and we wouldn't be interrupted.

"When will you be back?"

"First week of January, on the Sunday. I'll be gone for less than two weeks. It's going to fly by."

Ayesha looked up at me. "Will you go clubbing in Vancouver?"

"Are you asking me if I'm going to hook up with anyone?"

"I don't know. Maybe." She paused, straightening the running team hoodie I'd lent her. "Are you?"

"No. No, I won't." I smiled, her jealousy massaging my ego.

She put her head down on my shoulder again and whispered. "I am going to miss you." I saw a tear on her cheek.

I kissed her on the forehead. "I'm going to miss you too." An older couple sitting across from us stared and whispered something to each other. It was uncomfortable, but I didn't care enough to do anything about it.

Their judgment reminded me of how different my life would be for the next two weeks. Vancouver felt like a distant past, an alternate reality I wanted to keep entirely separate from London. Sure, I'd share stories about my classes and my friends, but I wanted, needed, to keep Ayesha to myself.

At the airport, Ayesha stayed with me until the last possible moment. We kissed goodbye by the security gate, and just as our lips parted, she leaned in and whispered in my ear, "I love you. You know that, right?"

I was still riding the high of Ayesha's words when I disembarked almost ten hours later.

CHAPTER 5

When I was thirteen, I came home one day from tennis practice to find my parents waiting for me in the kitchen. As soon as I walked in, I knew something was up. I put my bag down, and they gestured for me to sit, a sure sign of trouble.

"Is everything okay?"

"Aki, Mrs. Anderson from the tennis club called." Mom looked at Dad, perhaps wanting him to weigh in.

He was visibly uncomfortable. "Yes, she called earlier today."

"She saw you and your friend Cassie at the club." Mom shuffled in her seat. "You see, for us Latinas, it's okay to be affectionate, but people might misunderstand your friendship. Do you know what I mean?"

"Not really. What did Mrs. Anderson see?"

"She saw Cassie sitting on your lap," Dad said quickly, almost too fast for me to understand.

"Aki, we don't want people to talk. We don't want people to think you are, you know, a homosexual."

"What?" I felt offended, as if this was an out-of-line accusation.

"Just maybe no more sitting on each other's lap, okay?" Mom reached for my hand. "For your own good, all right?"

I nodded, then I got up slowly and left the kitchen. As I made my way into the living room, I could hear my mother say, "Could you ever believe that? Our Aki? A homosexual?"

Now six years later, here I was, the closeted homosexual heading home. The few times I'd allowed myself to ponder what my parents would think about this relationship, I'd been on the verge of a panic attack. I'd promised myself I would get it all—whatever this was with Ayesha—out of my system at university, then return home after three years and marry a respectable Canadian boy. It seemed like a good plan, at least in my head: I could be happy for now, and my parents' long-term goals for me would be fulfilled.

My mother and brother were waiting for me at International Arrivals, but not my dad. A private asset manager, he was, as always, working every possible minute up until Christmas Day. Haru hugged me; he seemed even taller than when I'd left home just a few months prior. His hair was shaggier than usual and he smelled like sleep and cigarette smoke.

"How are you doing, sis?" He held me by the shoulders and looked me up and down. "See, Mom. Nothing to worry about. Aki looks the same as when she left."

My mom laughed a bit nervously and jokingly hit Haru on the arm. "Unlike you, who now smells like an ashtray." She wore pressed beige chinos and a long-sleeved pink Lacoste polo, with a Burberry quilted jacket over it.

"I've told you already. My friends smoke. It's just my clothes. I haven't put a cigarette to my lips." Haru winked at me.

A family of four attempted to move around us, so I moved aside and mouthed sorry.

"They can wait. I haven't seen my baby in over three months!" My mom pulled me closer and inhaled deeply.

"I've missed you too, Mom," I said, hoping to expedite this public display of affection.

"You're embarrassing her!" Haru took my large suitcase. "Let's go home. I'm starving."

We drove to West Vancouver from Richmond, chattering. Haru

sat in the front with my mom on account of him being so tall and I sat in the back middle seat, as requested by my mother.

"So, how's college?"

"It's university, Haru."

Even though he'd been to London before, he assumed going to LSE was completely different than visiting family friends. He wasn't wrong. Haru wanted to know what it was like living in London and when he could visit me. "You. Me. London!" my brother looked at Mom, as if to say, "Will you get the ticket already?"

"How are those two girls you met in the first week?" Mom took over the conversation.

"Ginika and Abby? They're great. I'm glad we're in the same program." I wondered how Ginika was doing. She'd dreaded going back home, considering it only marginally preferable to spending the break alone in London.

"Have you met anyone? I mean, have you met any boys?" She caught my eye in the rearview mirror.

"No, not any boys that are more than friends." I tried to smile with my eyes. "I've been too busy with school to meet anyone." I was going to have to become proficient at this lying thing, but I knew my mom couldn't be mad at me for being a good student.

"Of course you have." Haru looked back from the passenger seat and rolled his eyes. "Still just as perfect as when you left."

"How about you, Haru? How's the love life?" I tried to shift focus from me. I still was only good for one lie at a time. Mom scoffed audibly.

"I know you don't like her, but that doesn't change how I feel about Becca."

"It should! I am your mother." There was silence in the car for the first time. Thankfully, we were just five minutes away from home.

I want to be supportive of my brother's relationship, but I disliked Becca too. She and Haru had begun dating two years ago. The two of them had nothing in common besides elevated hormone and popularity levels. Whenever she came over, she made no effort to talk to my parents or me and once I caught her being rude to Luzia. Luz was my mom's distant relative, maybe a third cousin, who my parents had sponsored to live with us. Luz had been our nanny and now helped Mom around the house.

Last spring, when Haru was still sixteen, he had confided to me that Becca had invited him to come over when her parents were out of town. I didn't want Haru's first time to be with her, especially if this was all an act to spite my parents, so I told Mom. We drove to Becca's house where Mom dragged Haru out of the Palmers' house by the arm. I'd never seen either of them that angry before. They screamed at each other all the way from the British Properties to West Bay while I sat in the back, window open to let out the noise.

"Any plans while you're here?" Haru filled the silence.

"Not really." We pulled into our driveway, Mom barely putting the car in park before stepping out. Haru and I sat for a few seconds, waiting for her to go inside. He turned to me and smirked, "Aren't you glad to be home again?"

The few days leading up to Christmas were spent recovering from jetlag. Mom was busy with Christmas Eve preparations, Dad was at the office and Haru spent his days on the phone with Becca, or trying to convince my mom to let him spend Christmas Day with her family. Their busy schedules gave me the breathing room I needed to acclimate to life back in West Vancouver. Instead, I stayed up until after midnight to speak to Ayesha and, while I waited, re-watched *The L Word*.

When I was fifteen, my mom, brother and I spent our summer break in Colombia. One night on this trip, my cousins and I stayed up channel surfing. A parental advisory warning came on, followed by a scene of two half-naked women moaning in the shower.

Gabriella and Maya put their hands over their eyes, while Fernando yelled to leave it on. I looked back and forth, then at the TV, feeling a strange sensation, like the time Cassie sat on my lap after tennis practice. I blushed in embarrassment.

It wasn't until I met Thea that I learned the name of the show. As soon as the box set arrived, I'd wake up early or stay up late after going out to a club just to squeeze in a few episodes. I'd lie awake on the floor and try to picture myself as one of the characters, any one of them. Then I'd start replacing the other characters with my friends.

Talking to Ayesha in the middle of the night was risky enough. Watching lesbian soft porn was asking to be found out. But the show felt like a tether to the London life I'd created for myself. Despite my better judgment, I brought all of the DVDs back to Vancouver with me. As the house grew quiet, I would lie in bed in my room, headphones plugged and watch episode after episode, waiting for Ayesha to wake up in London.

CHAPTER 6

On Christmas Eve, my parents threw their traditional party intended to show their friends, neighbours and family how perfect and happy we were. I didn't mind this event so much—I was used to pretending perfection—but Haru abhorred it.

"I don't get why we have to be here." He walked into my room.

"Why didn't you invite your friends?"

"Because they'd rather have an unsupervised party at Lucas's place." He paused. "Besides, can't they just entertain all these old people on their own?"

"Haru!"

"Even if you don't say it, I know you're thinking it." He stopped walking and stared at me. "They might not notice it, but you've changed."

I looked down. "What are you talking about?"

He stepped closer to me. "Look, we don't have to talk about it. You clearly have a lot on your mind. But our rooms share a wall, and I can tell you've been staying up."

"I'm just talking to my friends, you know."

"I'm not judging. I'm just saying that whatever you are saying to your friends, you're not saying to Mom and Dad. That's a first."

There was a knock on the door and Luz came in. She was shorter and slighter than Mom but the resemblance was there. "Are you both ready? Your mother is very stressed." She still had a thick Colombian accent, despite twenty years of living in Canada.

"Oh, Luz. It will be okay. In five to seven years, this ordeal will be over." Haru hugged her. Luz playfully resisted him.

We made our way downstairs where the whole ground floor was decorated in red and gold, as it had been decorated every December 24 as far back as I could remember. Mom moved about the living and sitting rooms with purpose, her tight, embroidered dress forcing her to take small steps quickly. I spotted Dad on the phone out on the deck. He waved, mouthing something I couldn't understand. The rule was phones off after the first guest arrives; he was squeezing every last minute he could, doing his best to reassure clients whose portfolios had tanked recently.

Ojiichan and Obaachan, my father's parents, arrived first, five minutes before the party's start time. Next were a few of our neighbours. By eight o'clock the house was packed. Hired waiters walked around with trays of hors d'oeuvres, and two bartenders took orders in the dining room, which had been converted into a bar.

I walked around smiling at people, hoping to avoid engaging in actual conversation. From a distance, I watched my brother charm a group of Dad's clients, making them laugh at whatever he was saying.

"Aki-chan." I felt a tap on my arm. My grandparents were sitting alone on a small loveseat in the sitting room. I crouched next to them. My grandfather, who was in his mid-eighties, had salt and pepper hair parted to the right, thin-rimmed square glasses and hands covered in sunspots. Obaachan was considerably shorter, her back arched forward from years of making herself small. I looked at the top of her head, her short straight hair permed into curls by chemicals.

"*Ojiichan, nanika goyoudesu ka?*" My Japanese was rusty,

especially since I hadn't studied it since middle school, but I still could communicate basic ideas.

He shook his head. "No, I don't need anything."

"Are you sure? We have *hojicha*. I can make it. You don't have to drink the cocktails."

"We are good." My grandfather straightened the vest over his button-down. "How is London? You know, I taught at UCL for a year."

I looked around and found an unused footrest. I carried it closer to my grandparents and sat down. "London is great. I am really enjoying LSE."

"Of course you are." He smiled wide. "You're like me. A creature of the mind."

I chuckled. "They do have an amazing library. Did you know it's the largest social sciences library in Europe?"

Ojiichan was born in Yamaguchi, the capital city of the Yamaguchi Prefecture. When he was still a teenager, he was conscripted into the army during World War II. Being from an upper-middle-class family, he was never sent abroad to fight, but the war introduced him to worlds beyond his sheltered one.

He met my grandmother, Hanoko, in April 1942 through an arranged marriage. She was from Salt Spring Island and had been sent to Japan to stay with relatives and learn Japanese. She was the only person in her family who had managed to escape the internment camps. At the time of their meeting, Hanoko was living with distant relatives, small business owners struggling to make ends meet.

Omiai, arranged marriage, saved Hanoko from poverty and Daisuke from ignorance. Post-war he studied Moralogy and became an academic. They moved to British Columbia in the mid-1950s, where my father and his three siblings were born.

"I wish your dad hadn't given in to the wiles of money." Ojiichan looked across at my father and sighed with disappointment. "So smart. Too smart for his own good."

I wasn't sure what to say. "Maybe he's happy."

Ojiichan looked at me. "A frog in a well knows nothing of the sea." Obaachan tapped him on the shoulder and, without saying a word, the two got up and headed toward my parents to say goodbye.

We spent the week between Christmas and New Year's in Whistler with the Lees, family friends who owned a timeshare there. Their daughter Karen had gone to high school with me, but we had very little in common, especially now that I'd moved away and made other friends.

"What's LSE like? Any cute boys? I just love that British accent!" Karen was tall and she used her height to kick ass in volleyball. Her thick, straight black hair had purple highlights. The shimmering glow of the fireplace made her cheeks look flushed.

"I don't know. Most people have a British accent, I guess." I leaned back in my armchair.

"Wow, that's the dream. We have a Scottish guy in my seminar." She moved to the edge of her seat, then leaned closer. "Not the same."

Haru stormed into the room. "Unbelievable!"

Karen looked at him, then me. "What? What's unbelievable?"

He ignored Karen and turned to me even though I hadn't asked the question. "Mom and Dad won't let me spend the weekend in the Village with Becca." He plopped down on the floor.

In the kitchen we could hear the parents chatting. Mrs. Lee was trying to persuade Mom to give skiing another go, but she refused. A few years back, Dad had convinced her to take lessons; she'd been the only adult in a group for beginners. That was the last time she'd been skiing.

"You mean at her family's condo?" Karen interjected, trying to insert herself into the conversation.

"Yeah. I want to spend time under the same roof as her."

Dad and Mr. Lee walked through the room, talking investments. He tried to reassure his client that he had everything under control, though Mr. Lee seemed skeptical of Dad's confidence amid the global financial crisis and in the wake of the Madoff Ponzi scheme.

"You mean, you want to get lucky." Karen had a smug look on her face that made me remember why I hadn't called her as soon as I got home.

"Whatever." Haru rolled his eyes and stretched out by the fireplace.

The next few days went by painfully slowly. Now that I was sharing a room with Karen, I couldn't talk to Ayesha. In the mornings, we headed to the slopes, while Mom found a café where she could read. Haru met up with some of his school friends from Collingwood and snowboarded. Part of me just wanted to feign an injury so I could call Ayesha in what would have been the middle of the night for her, but that would mean one-on-one time with Mom and inevitable questions about my life in London.

On the last day, while everyone else headed out to ski, Mom insisted we go to a spa together. Inside a steam sauna room, we sat a few inches apart, with white towels on our laps.

"I feel like we haven't gotten a chance to chat like we used to." She tried to catch my eyes through the fog.

"What do you mean?" Feigning ignorance felt easier than fabricating lies.

"This has been such a busy time." She paused. "I just want to make sure everything's all right with you."

"Yes, everything's good," I said it a bit too quickly.

"Feels like you're becoming someone else."

I didn't know how to respond, my feelings lost somewhere between fear of being found out and annoyance at having to explain myself. "How so?" I mustered in a neutral voice.

"You're distant. It feels like you're not here. Like you're not with us."

I took a deep breath, trying to resist the urge to lash out. "It's just different being home." I wanted to sprinkle my lies with as much honesty as I could muster. "I feel like my lives are split between Vancouver and London."

My mom sniffled, but I didn't look up. "It's hard to watch you grow. Even harder to not."

I scooted closer to her and put my arm around her shoulder. Then, half disingenuously, I said, "I'm still here."

CHAPTER 7

Ayesha met me at Heathrow. Even though we'd only been apart a short time, I worried about seeing her—how she would react, how I would greet her. I hardly slept on the flight over, but as soon as I saw her, her wonderful hair, her beautiful eyes, I rushed to embrace her.

"I've missed you so much. I can't believe I survived being in Vancouver."

She hugged me again, resting her head on my chest. "I'm so glad you're back. London isn't the same without you."

I was overcome with emotion and, though I fought it, I couldn't help but shed a tear. Ayesha was here now, within reach. I held her face in my hands, the heat emanating from her cheeks, then leaned in to kiss her. "Shall we head home?"

Back at my residence, we locked ourselves in my room and didn't emerge until Wednesday, when I had my first lecture.

"Wow, are you alive?" Abby joked on our way to LSE.

"You just wish you had someone to lock yourself in a room with," Ginika chimed in.

"How were your holidays?" I tried to change the subject.

"Amazing!" Abby beamed.

"Why do you always have to be so happy?" Ginika grunted. "I'm just glad to be back."

"Same here." We caught each other's eyes and smiled.

"Did you tell your parents about Ayesha?" Abby started walking backwards so we could speak face-to-face.

"Are you insane? Of course not!" Ginika jumped in.

"Why not?" Despite all the hints I'd dropped in the first term, it seemed Abby had not clued into my life at home.

Ginika shook her head in disbelief.

I laughed. "My parents are conservative when it comes to sexual orientation. My mom asked me if there were any boys in my life. Pretty sure I'd have to come out first, then bring up the topic of Ayesha."

"Are you going to?"

"You know, Abby, sometimes it's better to keep your curiosity to yourself." Ginika cautioned.

"It's all right," I paused, considering how I wanted to frame this. "Pretty sure I will never come out to them. I can't see a scenario where they are okay with it. Besides, my relationship with Ayesha is just that, something between her and me. No one else."

"That's right Now can we pick up the pace? I know you're not a runner, Abby, but we are going to be late!"

Our first lecture was in the Old Theatre, one of LSE's oldest lecture halls. A hundred or so bodies huddled in, the smell of damp and body odour rising to the balcony. Back in London, surrounded by my peers, I stood out in no particular way. I was one of the many diligent students who spent most of their time in lecture halls or the library in my case, reading up on the great Greek philosophers and famous historians, like Henry Thomas Buckle and E.H. Carr—white men I'd been conditioned to admire and whose narratives I'd learned not to contest.

It felt good to blend in once again. I looked at my watch, doing the math of how long it would be until I saw Ayesha again—another twelve hours. The man behind me inched forward and I felt faint breath on the back of my neck. I slid further down in my chair, my knees hitting the seat in front of me.

"A man has free choice to the extent that he is rational."

A middle-aged woman stood centre-stage, reciting lines from a book. This was GV100, Introduction to Political Theory. Our professor, who had a background in theatre, liked to personify famous thinkers when she taught. That day, she was St. Thomas Aquinas. Abby whispered something to Ginika, who snorted, throwing her head back. The professor walked forward and squinted, trying to locate the commotion. We looked down and continued to take notes.

I pulled out my phone to text Ayesha. Three missed calls from my mother in the last ten minutes. It was 1:30 a.m. Vancouver time. What was she doing up? Also, she knew I was in class. My mind went to Obaachan, and I imagined all the terrible things that could have happened to her. Mom called again. I made my way down the row, through the double door and out of the theatre.

At the foyer, the door to the streets was open. A cold breeze swept in, scattering pamphlets near the entrance. Two security guards chased the flying papers.

"Is every—"

"Is this true?" Mom yelled.

A pamphlet landed near my right foot. I crouched down to pick it up and watched one of the guards rush toward me.

"Is this true?" she repeated, even louder.

I adjusted the phone to my ear and handed the pamphlet to the guard, before turning my back and taking a step away from the Old Theatre. She was angry. The last time I remembered her this angry was the first time Haru came home smelling of weed. She'd never been this angry with me. I couldn't think of anything I might have done wrong.

"What do you—?"

"Is this true? Is this true? Is this true?" She gasped. "Is. It. True."

I opened my mouth to say something, to ask what she meant, but I knew she would cut me off again.

"I found the box," she finally said, her voice trembling.

Box? What box?

Shit. My heart froze. The back of my closet.

Hidden behind my underwear drawer was the box my special edition of *The L Word* DVDs had come in. A photo of seven naked women embracing each other, set against a dark background. The title in hot pink. Maybe if they had their clothes on, we could have both pretended the "L" stood for luxury, lipstick or liquor. Any other "L" word would have done.

I thought I'd been so careful. I'd forgotten all the times I watched my parents raid my brother's room or call the school to have someone keep an eye on him. There had never been any need to snoop on me. Still, I should have seen it coming. I imagined my mom finding the box—the disgust on her face. She would never forgive me for this.

"Is it true?" Mom paused. "Are you . . ." Her voice trailed off. "Are you?" She couldn't say the word her lips didn't want to touch.

"Yes," I replied, my tongue betraying my heart. I knew I wasn't ready for this. I wished I could take it back, but before I could say anything else, she hung up.

I stared straight ahead, my phone still pressed to my ear. The guard was rearranging the pamphlets at the entrance. I watched him as I replayed the conversation in my head, altering the dialogue but always ending up in the same place. There was no way I could have won that conversation, no chance I would not disappoint her. I made my way back into the lecture hall, forgetting to ease the door shut. A loud bang. The last two rows of the theatre turned around and stared at me. I stood for a bit until someone asked me to move. Then I found my friends and sat.

"She knows," I whispered to Ginika.

"What? Who knows what?"

"My mom. She knows," I repeated.

"Oh, fuck."

We listened to the rest of the lecture in silence.

I sat on the carpet in my room, with my back against my bed and my Blackberry pressed against my ear, trying to focus on what Haru was saying. He was having breakfast, getting ready to drive to school. He knew. I strained to hear him, the words slipping away before I could grasp them. On the other end, his voice sounded muffled, like maybe he was covering the mouthpiece with his hand, but I knew that wasn't it. It was the haziness of my mind. I held my phone tighter. Something about how he'd guessed something was up while I was back in Vancouver. Something about how he was there for me.

"Why didn't you tell me?" His voice came through loud and clear this time, and I softened my grip on the phone. I wanted to say so many things, but the options were overwhelming, so I settled for a grunt. "I could have helped. I would have prepared them," he continued.

"I . . . I don't know. I wasn't ready. I never wanted Mom to find out." My voice wavered, and I wondered if what I was saying was actually true. I'd left a huge clue for her to find. Maybe a small part of me wanted her to see the real me.

Cool air blew in through my open window, shuffling a pile of papers on my desk—the latest version of my essay for my GV100 class, which I'd started before I left London. I had planned on finishing it that night, but philosophy was the last thing on my mind. Sheets of paper swirled in the air, like they were dancing for me. I followed them with my eyes, waiting for chaos to descend.

I was no longer the "perfect child"—a nickname that, despite some genuine irritation and feigned modesty, I enjoyed a whole lot. At school, I was consistently at the top of my class. I played tennis competitively. I was the captain of the debate team. I was on the student council. I played the flute in a jazz band. I volunteered at a soup kitchen. I obeyed my parents' orders and fulfilled every one of their expectations. Not anymore.

My hurt morphed into anger. How could this one thing change so much about how they saw me? Why was their love conditional on their expectations? Fuck them, fuck this. There had to be another way.

Thinking about all the times I'd ratted him out, I couldn't believe how nice Haru was being to me now. I definitely hadn't done anything to deserve this level of understanding, and as I realized this, his empathy began to weigh on me. It made me feel guilty, so much so that I wished he would just be mean to me, just this one time.

"Aki?" I knew I hadn't spoken or listened in the last few minutes. I wanted to come up with the right words, but none came to mind. I had no answers for him, no revelatory anecdotes. I hadn't come up with a script that I could easily recite.

"Yeah, I'm here. I'm sorry. I just don't know what you want me to say." I felt frustrated that I couldn't push through this wall of indifference I'd built around me. I knew only three emotions—happiness, sadness and anger.

When we were young, Haru followed me around the house, copying my every move. I hated it. The whole reason we'd ended up in different schools, both private, was because my parents hoped a little independence would do him good, and it had been a long time since Haru had wanted to be like me. We'd spent years growing apart, becoming our own selves. Maybe I'd pushed him away. Maybe he'd realized he could be better, bigger on his own. Either way, this intimacy felt forced. We'd hardly spoken about things like this when I still lived at home. It felt like too big of a jump to start opening up about everything now.

Haru sighed, sensing my reluctance. "Okay, I'm not going to push it."

Terry barked in the background and my heart stopped at the thought of Mom finding my brother talking to me. Would she feel betrayed that Haru had called behind her back? Or had she asked him to do it, to check up on me? You could never be certain with my mom. There was some shuffling on the other side, as if Haru was walking toward the door.

"It's just the gardener. She still barks every time she sees him."

"How is she?"

"She's good."

"Have you been taking her on walks?"

"Uh, kind of? You know, we have a backyard." He chuckled.

"That's not the same, Haru. She needs to exercise."

"Funny thing, she's been sleeping in your room since you left for London." The idea that our dog would never have a clue about what was going on, made me feel momentarily better, like a small corner of my world would always remain unchanged.

Haru and I ran out of things to say. I had no trivial topics to bring up. He'd run out of ways to comfort me. Still, we stayed on the line in silence.

"I have to go soon," he said finally. Cabinet doors opened and closed, a glass clinked against the marble countertops, the fridge beeped—these sounds once so familiar, now felt distant and misplaced. Haru poured himself something, probably his favourite OJ, squeezed daily by Luz. "Mom is out at the grocery store. She should be back home in a few minutes."

I played with the hem of my shirt, undoing a thread and pulling it until I could stretch my arm out. I wanted to tell him how I feared for our family, how I felt I had disrupted the peace, how I didn't know how to make it better, how to fix things. But the words were trapped in my chest and the more I breathed the lower they sank, gravity pulling them down until I couldn't make out what they were anymore.

"They will come around." He tried to reassure me between gulps. "Mom's just really upset right now. It's been tough over here, even before today. Dad's clients have lost tons of money, and his business is being blamed for it. Mom says we're becoming social outcasts."

A beam of sun came in through the window, illuminating the sheets of paper on the carpet. I followed the light with my eyes, across the room to the pair of Air Jordans at the other end of the bed, my Christmas gift from Haru. I'd been planning to debut them at a special occasion, but none of that mattered anymore.

My dad called during his lunch hour. I wanted to say so many things. I wanted to reassure him I hadn't changed. But I'd learned silence from my dad. Even when I was little, we could sit for hours in the car, in our living room, at the dinner table, without saying a word. It's not that we would be doing other things. We just sat there, staring blankly ahead, subtly acknowledging each other's presence but not making a sound.

"What's going on, Aki?" His voice, low and measured, made me feel nostalgic, like it had been weeks since I'd heard it. There was concern in his tone and a hint of fear I hadn't heard before.

I wanted to explain that I was still figuring things out, that I didn't or couldn't confidently say what I was or who I liked. But that wasn't the language we spoke. I heard steps, muffled phrases and then a loud thud.

"We are alone now," he said. I visualized the Zen garden that sat on his desk. When he was stressed, he would carefully drag the small rake through the sand.

"Aki, our family has survived—thrived even—by blending in, not standing out. Being different has never worked in our favour."

His words were loaded, deep-seated in histories of otherness, of exclusion, of dispossession. I stood near my bed and let my body go, falling onto the duvet with a soft thud. I nestled my head on the pillow and inhaled deeply, the scent a blend of sweet and smoky. I tried to remember how weightless I'd felt the night before, when none of this had happened and it was just Ayesha and me in this room. Now it felt crowded, suffocating to be there.

My dad continued, "Don't be the nail that sticks out. Everything you do, every decision you make, is only possible because of all of the people that came before you and the sacrifices they made. The choices you make now must honour them, make them proud." He paused, and I remained silent.

There was a sliver of hypocrisy in his words. We both knew his father hadn't approved of his career choices, especially now that he might be on his way to becoming a failure. He let out a deep breath. I heard a knock, then a door opening. My dad walked out into the noise. In the background, pans and pots clinked against the glass top of the convection stove. I looked at my graduation gift, a Rolex wristwatch. It was just past eight o'clock my time. Mom was probably making lunch.

This was the most Dad had said to me since I'd moved to London. Actually, this was probably the most intimate conversation we'd ever had. Nineteen years of silence, and this was what he'd come up with. Not "I love you" or "We will work through this" but "Don't be the nail that sticks out." How could he choose a Japanese proverb over his daughter?

"It's not the right way, Aki-chan," he said, interpreting words that were not his own. He cleared his throat and I wondered if this might be the first time I'd hear him cry over the phone. I closed my eyes and focused on the sounds on the other end of the line. Cutlery being laid on the table. Unintelligible whispers. A can opening. "Some things are out of our control."

If Dad had taught me anything, it was to always be in control.

I'd grown up with everyone telling me I was like him—reserved, quiet, introspective. I'd always looked up to him, even when I didn't know what I was looking up to, but at that moment I wished we were better with words, better with emotions. I wished he wouldn't hide behind a proverb to tell me how he felt. I resented his reaction. How could he not see he was doing to me what Ojiichan had done to him?

Out in the corridor, a group of students ran to the dining hall, giggling and talking about upcoming exams. "I should go," I said finally. I wanted to continue, but I feared what I might say next, my sadness morphing into anger.

"We'll fix this," my dad said and he hung up without saying goodbye. I closed my eyes and imagined we were sitting around our dinner table. I pictured myself getting up and looking at him. He was smaller than I'd remembered. I tried to get him to look back at me, but he stared blankly ahead.

I stood up, put my phone in my pocket and looked around the room. Everything seemed out of place, like the world had shifted and, in the process, I'd lost myself. It was disorientating. I grabbed my coat off the chair and headed out the door. I ran down the stairs, brushing past Ginika, who lived a few floors down, and stepping outside, urging the cool breeze to calm my heart. It wasn't working. I closed my eyes and took a deep breath. Still nothing. I brought my hand to my chest and made circular motions, trying to slow down my heartbeat.

I'm sorry for being weak, I'm sorry for losing my way. I'm sorry for bringing shame to my family.

I needed to make this right. I looked around, searching for something that would ground me in reality and saw Euston Church, a few blocks away. My fingers caressed the large cross that weighed on my chest. It was really too big for someone of my size but my *abuela* had left it to me when she passed away three years ago. I'd taken to wearing it in London; Even though Mom wasn't religious, the cross made me feel closer to her.

I started walking toward the church, imagining an ear to confess to. A quiet place to be. Someone to forgive me. Built in Neo-Gothic style, Euston Church was made of Bath stone with a tiled roof. It was never finished, so its opulence was interrupted by imperfections, sections of exposed brick where there should have been stone. The main entrance on Gordon Street was closed. I tried the north entrance. All the doors were locked. I tried knocking. There was nothing but silence on the other side. No absolution here.

I circled back one more time and found a bench on Byron Place. I looked down at my watch. Almost 9:00 p.m. The time I usually checked in with Mom. I used to tell her everything but in the past four months, there was so much I hadn't shared—the running team, the copious amounts of drinking. Ayesha.

I dialled her number. Voicemail. I hung up without leaving a message and looked down at my feet. The tears built up and my vision blurred. I watched them drip onto my sneakers.

I looked at the church. *Why am I even fucking here?* When I was little, and we visited Medellín, I loved going to Sunday service with my grandmother. Mom and Haru weren't interested, but me, I accompanied my *abuela* to the big church near her house. It was the only place my quietness didn't annoy her, where I didn't get scolded for always being in my own head or not speaking Spanish well enough. On our walk there, *Abuela* would tell me stories from the Bible and quiz me on last week's sermon. I would snuggle up next to her at mass; my head fit perfectly under her arm. I would observe her fingers counting the beads in her rosary as she whispered prayers under her breath. She would often convince me to donate my allowance during the offertory. I felt like a good person then. I was surrounded by people in that church, and there my quietness was an advantage. I wasn't sticking out like the nail Dad was so concerned about. I'd gotten so used to imitating the person I was expected to be, rather than charting my own path, I'd become complacent. And now I was standing out.

Maybe they'd let me have this one thing if I excelled in everything else. Maybe this one digression wouldn't matter so much? Surely, the grading scale worked on a curve? But I knew my parents better than that.

I shook my head, clenched my fists and focused on my bouncing leg. Would they hide me from their life back in West Vancouver? I intertwined my fingers behind my neck and pressed my hands down. Would they hide me under piles of excuses about where I was and who I was with? Mom said hell was your own conscience, and I already hated myself for fucking it all up. I looked up at the sky. Dark clouds were moving in. It was going to rain soon. I wiped my eyes and started to walk. I needed a drink.

CHAPTER 8

"ID, please."

I looked up and around. I was at a pub on Tottenham Court Road, just a few blocks away from Oxford Street. I couldn't remember how I'd gotten there—my feet had done the work my brain couldn't.

"I said ID, please." A large man wearing a black bomber jacket was staring at me.

I emptied my right coat pocket into my left hand. Loose cards fell on the sidewalk. I crouched and picked up my driver's license, handing it over to the man at the door. While he examined it, I collected the rest of my belongings from the ground. He handed the driver's license back to me and gestured for me to go in. It was Wednesday, after nine o'clock, and the pub was mostly empty. A man in his fifties loosened his tie by the bar, gesturing for another drink. A table of tourists carefully examined their food, looking at the menu as if to verify it was what they'd ordered. A group of men in their twenties talked about football. I heard the name Carlos Tevez. "Under Pressure" was playing faintly in the background.

I looked around, surveying the place. It seemed familiar, but I couldn't remember from when. Then again, most pubs I'd been in since September resembled this one—a wooden bar with a few wooden stools, a couple of round tables with some chairs around them, the faint smell of rancid beer and bodily fluids. Two TVs faced each other. One right behind the bar, for the pub's customers, and one strategically positioned so whoever was working that night needn't miss a second of the match. On the board, a list of next week's games written in chalk.

I made my way to the bar and ordered two shots of vodka. £4. I drank one straight away and took the second over to one of the tables. I looked out the window and watched people rush down Tottenham Court Road, umbrellas over their heads. A couple got splashed by a black cab. The wind blasted the door open. One of the tourists let out a shriek. The football fans laughed. A whiff of air.

My phone rang. I placed it on the table and watched the call go to voicemail. Abby. I didn't want to talk for the tenth time that day about what had happened with my family. Surely, my friends could just share the information among themselves. I let my index finger trace the rim of the shot glass in front of me. Clockwise, first. Then, counter-clockwise. I closed my eyes and imagined I was rewinding a VHS tape. I moved my finger faster, faster until the vodka spilled on the table.

"Are you okay?" The bartender gave me a concerned look as he wiped the table with a dirty towel. I gave him a light nod. "You were here a few of weeks ago, with . . ." He cupped two nonexistent breasts and moved his hands up and down.

I scrunched up my eyebrows. Big boobs? I suddenly remembered the place. Ayesha and I had planned to catch a movie a few doors down. I stood out in the cold for almost an hour. When she finally arrived, I stormed off and walked into the nearest pub. She followed right behind me. We made up and she stayed over. It had been the beginning of December, right before she'd shoved me into her closet.

"Break-up?" he asked. I nodded. Break-up seemed relatable.

He brought over two shot glasses and a bottle of vodka. "To large knockers!" He raised his glass in the air. I felt obliged to do the same. The football fans banged their hands on the table and raised their beer glasses.

The bartender poured me another shot. I pressed my lips together and nodded. "It gets better," he said before he left.

The men from the next table sat down uninvited. "I'm Olly." one of them said. He pulled a chair from a nearby table. "This is James," he added, pointing to the stockiest of the three. James scratched his eyebrows, his greasy, curly hair rested above his blue eyes.

"Jack," the third one said, extending his hand. Jack was wearing dark jeans and a fitted knitted light blue sweater over a white T-shirt. He was more manicured than the other two.

"You like big knockers, huh?" Jack said.

"We like them too," Olly added excitedly. James gave him a reprimanding stare. There was something about James that reminded me of my first boyfriend—awkward, shy, probably a virgin.

I looked around the table, making eye contact with each of them. Olly laughed nervously. He was wearing a Man U jersey that was a size too small and a pair of grey sweatpants. James joined in, but Jack continued to stare intently at me.

"Are you, you know?" James winked.

This was the last thing I needed. I got up, downed the shot, put my phone in my pocket, grabbed my coat and turned to go. As I started to walk away, I felt someone grab my wrist. "He asked you a question," said Jack. I tugged at my arm, but he gripped tighter. He pulled me toward him. I fell into the table, then onto the stained carpet. Jack let go. They laughed. My vision blurred as I struggled to get back up.

I looked over at the group of tourists. They stared and whispered but didn't move. When I was a child, my mother told me stories of damsels in distress who were rescued by knights in shining armour.

"Every princess has a prince, someone to protect and look after her," she'd say.

What happens if everyone around you is a fucking coward, Mom? If no one was going to stand up for me, I was going to do it myself. I was no damsel. I leaned over and dug my teeth into Jack's jeans. He jerked his leg, hitting his knee hard on the wooden table. "What the fuck is wrong with you?" he said, pushing me back to the floor.

What the fuck is wrong with you? I pushed my body off the floor, wiping my mouth as I came up. I drew my right arm back and lunged it forward with the weight of my body. I felt each knuckle meet his left cheek as his head thrust sideways and backward. I punched him again. Then a third time.

Jack gritted his teeth, blood dripping out of his mouth, down his chin. He charged forward, hitting me right above the stomach with his left shoulder. I landed on my back, wheezing. Black spots danced on the ceiling as I tried to catch my breath. He towered over me, spitting on the ground, speckles landing on my face. He turned his back to me. I rolled to my left side and got up, kicking the back of his left knee. He fell to the ground, hitting his head on the edge of the table, crying out in pain while his friends shouted, "Get up!"

The bartender pushed us away from each other. "Enough! Back off!" Jack got up. He spat in my direction, pushing his chest against the bartender's hand. I put my coat on, circled the table and headed toward the door. Jack threw a punch but missed. The bartender held him back, using his body weight to keep Jack in place. "She totally hit you," one of the other idiots said.

I pushed the pub's door open into the pouring rain. A couple bumped into me. They looked back and mouthed sorry, as they continued to run toward the movie theatre. The nerves on my back contracted. Muscle spasms sent a shooting pain up my spine. My head pulsated, and I felt like I was about to be sick. I bent over, put my hands on my knees and tried to catch my breath. A droplet of sweat ran between my eyebrows, down my nose. I licked my lips and tasted vodka and salt. As I straightened, a cold breeze blew through; my coat opened up behind me like a cape.

I looked up at the streetlights and let the rain wash Jack's spit off my face. I closed my eyes and replayed the last five minutes in my head. My whole body tingled and, for the first time that day, I felt in control. My problems felt manageable, smaller. I let that feeling sink in until my phone rang.

"Sorry I missed your call. What's going on?" Ayesha's voice.

I tried to think of words that could make a sentence, but breathing was all I could concentrate on right now. "Can I come over?"

"Sure." I could hear her breathing on the other end of the line. "Are you all right?"

Wheezing, I replied, "Better now."

Putting away my phone, I flexed my hands, examining my knuckles, a thin crust of blood forming over each one, bruises already appearing. They looked as if they didn't belong to me. These hands were capable of more damage than I'd ever imagined. Would they take long to heal?

I hailed a taxi and caught my reflection in the windows. I was smiling, a wide, confident smile—the smile of someone who'd finally found her strength.

CHAPTER 9

Ayesha was outside her apartment building, waiting for me. I shifted my body slowly, my back still spasming from the fight. She held a black umbrella above her head and smiled as I stepped out of the cab. I walked to her and rested my forehead on her shoulder, letting out a repressed sob.

"Everything will be okay," she said, holding my hand in hers.

"You don't know that." I felt defensive. She had no idea what was going on. Even if she did, she didn't know my parents, couldn't appreciate how much I'd disappointed them.

"Let's get you inside." Ayesha waved at a neighbour as we made our way into her building. We stepped into the elevator and I rested my hand on the metal railing, revealing my bloodied knuckles.

"What happened?"

Wordlessly, I pulled my hand away and stuck it in my pocket. If I told her, I would actually have to admit it happened. When the elevator pinged, I pushed my body off the handles and walked out.

Ayesha sighed. My silence and general inability to communicate bothered her, but she never said it out loud, and I didn't have the strength to do the emotional work right now. Ayesha opened the door and gestured for me to go in first.

A woman was sitting in the living room, feet on the couch, a pile of sketchbooks around her. She smiled as she looked up from her laptop. "Ayesha—introduce us!" The woman walked over and extended her hands. Before Ayesha could say anything, she continued, "I'm Sana, her cousin."

So, this was the ultra-conservative cousin I had to hide from? She was breathtaking. Almond-shaped eyes. Wavy black hair with light brown highlights. Plump lips. I flinched as she gripped my hand. She turned it to reveal my bruised and bloodied knuckles.

"What happened?"

"Oh, this? It's nothing. I . . . I just punched a park bench. I've had a difficult day."

"Ayesha, can you get the first aid kit?" Sana continued to hold my hand, while Ayesha moved toward the bathroom.

The living room was small and modestly decorated with old wooden furniture and some colourful wall hangings with intricate patterns that I assumed Ayesha had brought from her home in Bradford.

Sana led me to the worn leather couch and moved her computer and sketch pads aside so we could sit. I looked across at her and smiled. Her silky, black robe parted in the middle, revealing black velvety leggings. I wondered what they would feel like.

Ayesha came in carrying a rectangular plastic basket. "This is everything I could find." She knelt next to Sana. They both looked at me, then at each other.

I shifted my hands and looked at her. I wondered if they could tell I was lying.

"I think hydrogen peroxide?" Sana said. "Do we have cotton?" Ayesha handed her a container filled with cotton balls.

Sana dabbed my knuckles, grabbing my hand tighter as I instinctively pulled away. She handed the used cotton balls to Ayesha, then applied Vaseline to my knuckles. "I read it somewhere that it's as good as an antibiotic." Sana looked up at me and smiled. "I think we're done here." She let go of my hand and it fell on her lap. The contact startled us both.

I looked at my gooped-up knuckles and brought my hands close to my chest. "Thank you." I had lost track of Ayesha, who was kneeling at my feet.

"Are we all good now?" Ayesha said picking up the basket with the first aid kit. "Let's go to my room?" I nodded and stood up, but Sana grabbed my arm.

"Come on! I never get to meet your friends, Ayesha."

I looked back and forth between them. Sana didn't seem as oblivious as Ayesha had made her out to be. The two cousins waited for a response from me. I knew not to play this game, so I waited for Ayesha to say no. It bothered me how she was never clear about what she wanted and, after all I had been through, reading her mind was not at the top of my list of priorities. Ayesha sighed and sat down in an armchair next to the couch. She took out her phone and looked at me like it was my fault we were still in the living room. Sometimes it felt impossible to please her.

I spent the next couple of hours talking to Sana, Ayesha rarely joining in. Sana interrogated me about my background and my major, and volunteered information about her family. I learned their moms were sisters, that she grew up just outside of Manchester and that she was older than me by two years. She spoke about fashion, of which I understood very little, and how one day she wanted to be a designer. The night was not what I had expected. If anything, I thought meeting Sana would be painful. Ayesha had told me she didn't know about us, but she was meeting me now and didn't seem to be freaking out. Either way, the whole closet thing began to feel like an overreaction.

Around midnight Ayesha began to drift off, her head bobbing until she closed her eyes, her face smooshed against an armrest. I told them I should probably go. Sana walked me to the door, Ayesha reluctantly following behind her.

"Ayesha, I like your friend," Sana said, looking at me. Ayesha mustered a half smile. I knew I was going to pay for this later. I hugged them goodbye, making sure to linger a bit with Ayesha. Then I kissed her on the cheek and squeezed her hand. Even if this hadn't been the night she imagined, it had saved me from hours of self-pity and pain back at my residence. I wanted her to know I appreciated being there with her, especially her.

It had stopped raining by the time I made my way out of their building. A walk would have been nice, but my body ached from the fight. I got a night bus at Queensway. At the residence, Abby was sitting on the steps outside with a couple of girls from UCL. She looked beautiful, as always, even though she was wearing pajamas under her coat. Abby reminded me of Haru. There was an innate confidence about her—you could tell she'd been popular in high school. So much so that even though she was slightly shorter, all our friends assumed she was taller than me.

"Would it have killed you to answer the phone?" she said jumping up. I opened my mouth to say sorry, but she continued. "It's all right, Ayesha texted me you were with her."

It felt like everyone enjoyed being on my case. I started to go up the steps toward the main entrance. "Breakfast tomorrow?" Abby asked. I nodded. "Then we can go over the unit on general equilibrium?" she yelled before I went in. I gave her the thumbs up and turned away.

My room was dark and I avoided turning all the lights on for fear of what I might see. Half-illuminated by the streetlights, I undressed in front of the mirror and turned around to check for bruising on my back. I couldn't see anything, but it still hurt when I lifted my arms.

As I got ready for bed. I thought of what Dad had said to me, "Don't be the nail that sticks out." It felt arbitrary that he and Mom got to decide what constituted sticking out.

It felt like I'd lived entire weeks in one day. I opened and closed my hand, the sore knuckles grounding me in the present. Being out was proving to be a catalyst in a chain reaction I couldn't have predicted. It felt like the molecules inside me were rearranging. I'd begun to morph into something else entirely.

CHAPTER 10

A knock on the door woke me. Eyes still closed, I felt for my phone on the bedside table—6:14 am. Who the fuck would need me this early?

I lay still, hoping whoever it was would go away, but the second knock was even more forceful and accompanied by a stage whisper. "Aki!"

"Hold on." I rolled out of bed, body aching, gravity exacerbating the soreness of my muscles. I braced myself against the wall with my right hand, while holding my lower back with my left.

Ayesha was standing in the hallway, dressed in the same clothes as the night before, clearly upset. "Can I come in?"

I moved aside and felt around for the light switch. "Hmm, yeah. Come in."

Ayesha made her way across the room, then turned to face me. "What the fuck, Aki?"

Shit. "What do you mean?" I stalled.

"Exactly what happened to you yesterday?" She struggled to keep her voice low. "And why do I have to find out in a text from Abby?"

The last thing I wanted was to go over the whole situation with my parents. "Then you know what happened. My parents found out I'm gay. But don't worry, they don't know about you."

"And what happened to your hands?"

I crossed my arms, averting her gaze. "I told you. I punched a tree out of frustration."

She let the silence sit, as discomfort settled under my skin. "Yesterday you said it was a park bench."

"Same thing." Why did it matter?

"No, Aki. Not the same thing." Ayesha walked toward me. She paused, then continued, "You don't have to do this alone."

I felt irritated by her kindness—I wanted to feel strong and impenetrable, not comforted. Ayesha's attempt to be exactly what I'd hoped her to be all along made me feel vulnerable. I stepped back and pressed against the door.

"Let me be here for you." Ayesha extended her right hand.

"I told you. I'm fine." My voice was sharper than I'd expected.

She let her hand fall to her side. "Okay, then." She walked toward my desk, and took off her coat, placing it on my chair. She removed her shoes, followed by her jeans, then made her way to the bed. "I'm tired," she said finally.

Ayesha scooted over, making room for me in the twin-sized bed. "It's here for you whenever you want it," she patted the space next to her, then lay her head on the pillow. I was glad she was willing to be the bigger person.

I lay down with my back to her. She inched closer, placing her bare legs between mine and putting her right arm over my waist. She burrowed her face into my shoulder, and we fell asleep without saying another word.

Later that morning, my phone buzzed. A text from an unknown number. "Hi, Aki. It's Sana. I got your number from Ayesha. We should hang out again soon."

I re-read the message. Why did Ayesha give my number to her

cousin? She clearly wasn't happy we'd spent the night talking. Was this a test? Or maybe I was reading too much into it.

"We should! How about coffee sometime?" I typed, then hit send.

A week later, I stood outside Russell Square station waiting for Ayesha, reading the news on my phone. A bearded man approached me, offering me the latest edition of *The Big Issue*. I gave him a twenty-pound note and told him to keep the change. Droplets of rain were starting to fall. I looked at my watch. Ayesha was late—again—by seventeen minutes. Small pools of water began to form near my feet. I ducked into the Tesco Express and bought a bag of Jelly Babies.

When I emerged, she was standing under an umbrella across the street, looking for me with her phone in hand, ready to dial. I waved and signalled for her to wait until it was my turn to cross. When I joined her, she said teasingly, "You don't have to wait if there are no cars. You know that, right?"

"It's still jaywalking," I replied, irritated.

Ayesha's smile disappeared. She turned her face away from me and sighed.

"I'm sorry. I'm just in a bad mood." But we both knew it was more than that.

We crossed Russell Square in silence, walking alongside each other, but not holding hands. Instead, I made way for other people to walk between us, moving closer, then further away like an accordion. I knew the distance was something I had created but I couldn't push through it.

"Is everything okay? I feel like you're avoiding me, dodging my calls," Ayesha said finally.

I turned to her and clenched my jaw. "I probably am." Everything seemed to be too much effort at the moment: my parents, who still weren't taking my calls; my friends with their annoying concern and attempts at sympathy; the never-ending list of course and reading assignments; the running team; Ayesha. Everyone wanted something, and I had nothing left to give. I'd been sucked dry.

She waited for me to continue, but I didn't. "Okay . . ." Her pace slowed until she stopped in the middle of the SOAS University of London courtyard, a shortcut we took from the station to my residence. A group of students were staring at us and I wanted to keep walking. We were less than five minutes away from the privacy of my room.

Ayesha didn't budge. I turned to her. "It's not you. I'm just dealing with a lot right now. I'm trying to figure it all out, you know?"

Ayesha looked at me and extended her hand. "I understand it's a lot. Just don't disappear, okay?" I nodded even though I knew I might not be able to keep my promise. More and more I was feeling the urge to escape, to run away as far as I could, but it didn't seem right to tell her that. Instead, I grabbed her hand and we walked the rest of the way to my residence.

We slept together, and it didn't feel any different than the other times. My bruises had turned from purple to yellowish green, but they were still sore to the touch. She traced my knuckles, gently caressing the scabs on them. I nestled my head between her neck and her shoulder and burrowed my face in her hair. I breathed in deep, then deeper, until all I could smell was her—a mix of argan oil and cigarette smoke. I let my body relax into hers and her warmth became my own. I felt safe then, lovable even. But I felt it might be our last time.

Despite Ayesha's best efforts, the distance between us grew. In the days and weeks that followed, I grew increasingly annoyed at her concern. When I was with her, I felt I could only be the version of myself that was helpless, pitiful, struggling. I resented her attentiveness and began to feel suffocated.

I knew all I had to do was talk to her again, let her in a bit, but I was digging a hole I couldn't crawl out of. Much as I wanted her, I couldn't bring myself to make the effort. Days would pass between my replies to her messages. I asked for raincheck after raincheck until she began to draw back too. "I'll give you the space it feels like you want," she texted one Saturday afternoon. That night, I drank myself to sleep, unable to muster a reply.

CHAPTER 11

In the weeks that followed, the once-daily calls with Mom were replaced by brief checkups from Haru, before he went to school. Somehow a seventeen-year-old had taken on the role of my parent. "Have you been eating properly?" he would ask hesitantly, after inquiring as to how I was and where I'd been that day.

"Yeah," I answered, wondering how long we had to pretend this was normal. I knew Haru probably had a script—one Mom had given him—but that didn't make the conversations any more bearable. It just emphasized the size of the rift with my parents. How long until they would be willing to repair it?

Perhaps because relationships were on both our minds, Haru opened up to me about Becca and how he felt about her. After I'd ratted him out, Haru had kept most things about her secret. I knew they were in the same grade and had birthdays just a few weeks apart, but I couldn't understand what attracted Haru to her. Sure, she was good-looking, as far as beauty standards went—large blue eyes, wavy blond hair, slender and nearly his height. But she was rarely complimentary and seemed to resent Haru going out with his friends.

"The only positive thing from all of this is that Mom and Dad have allowed Becca to come to the house again," Haru said, pausing for my reaction.

"Really?" I replied neutrally. Becca had been banned from the house after Haru had been roughed up by her older brother. My parents had come home to find Luz carrying a bag of frozen peas up to his bedroom.

"Yeah, she's coming over this weekend."

"Have you told her that Mom and Dad are pacificists?" I played with the corner of a piece of paper where I'd written the outline for an essay, folding and unfolding it a few times until it was creased on both sides.

"Come on, Aki."

"Seriously though. If you want her to stand a chance at winning them over, she better be extra nice. And her brother better not show up at the house." I tried my best not to sound judgmental.

"Okay, okay," he said, exasperated. "Just try to be happy for me?"

"Sure, I will. Try, that is." Even if Haru couldn't see it, it was only a matter of time until he would outgrow her. That much I knew, or at least hoped for.

I imagined coming out had made me human in Haru's eyes: fallible, imperfect and, most importantly, capable of making my own choices. For all the reasons my parents didn't want me to be the nail that stuck out, Haru probably did. I understood now that, together, we could distract attention from each other's shortcomings and create some breathing room around familial expectations. We could be partners.

"How are they? Dad and . . ." I asked, trying to change the subject.

"Dad's managing. I mean, it's hard to tell how that man is feeling, but he says the worst is over. I don't know what to believe, but he seems to have kept most of his clients. Mom is her usual dramatic self. She's convinced our life in West Vancouver is over—that no one will want to associate with us for a while."

I retained enough perspective to acknowledge that Mom's reaction wasn't just to my coming out. The potential loss of wealth and social standing were inevitably mixed in with what she likely felt was our family's fall from grace. I still called her every day. The phone usually went to voicemail—the silences between rings were excruciating, my hope crushed with every beep. On the rare occasions when she picked up, she had hundreds of excuses up her sleeve: I'm driving. Someone's at the door. There's a call on the other line. I'm making lunch now. She never made time for a conversation and she never promised to call back later. There were many days that I didn't want to call, but I feared what absolute silence might do to us. I feared the crack would become a break, and a break would be irreparable.

After four weeks of not speaking, my mother finally called as I was walking home through Regent's Park, after running with the team. As she often did these days, Ginika had left to meet up with her new kind-of boyfriend, Kwaku, a Ghanaian Econ student who played basketball. I'd come to enjoy these solitary walks, when my muscles ached enough to distract me from my thoughts.

My heart pounded as I stared at "Mom" on the screen. I had forgotten what to say. I'd become unaccustomed to her voice, her way of speaking. "Hello?" I said tentatively, my voice cracking.

"Hi, Aki."

"How are you? How's Dad?" I tried to sound like this was one of our normal calls, but it felt forced, rushed.

"We are very disappointed. What happened to you? You know what, don't answer that."

"I . . . I understand."

"I don't think you do."

I stopped in the middle of the path and felt a runner brush past me. "Out of the way!" I switched to the grass, dampness wetting the tips of my shoes. Mom began to speak but I couldn't focus on her words, my thoughts creeping in from every corner. Something about them trying their best. Something about who was to blame.

Something about how they could never tell their friends. I sunk to the ground, trying to grab at the emptiness around me.

"Aki!" My mom's voice jolted me back to reality. "Are you even listening?"

"Yeah, I'm sorry. I'm listening."

"Your father and I have done everything we could to give you and your brother a life full of opportunity. Why are you so ungrateful?"

I tried to think of an answer that would satisfy her, but the question was rhetorical. I knew that.

"This, this choice of yours is wrong. It's not natural. It's not good."

My conservative parents had always pretended gay people didn't exist—at least not within their circles. On the weekends, when we went shopping downtown, walking along Robson toward Stanley Park, my brother and I would make a game of counting how many same-sex couples got the double take from my parents.

I knew better than to bring the subject up, but one evening, during dinner, I did anyway. It was half past seven and Dad had just arrived home from work. As usual, he'd gone up to his room and changed into one of his many checkered pajama trousers, but he was still wearing his work shirt, the top button undone. Dinners at my house were always an event—two hours of uninterrupted family time, with no distractions allowed.

Mom ran the show. Dressed in the cream-coloured apron my brother and I had given her for Mother's Day, she brought out dishes from the kitchen—Japanese rice, pinto beans, fried cassava, karaage chicken and freshly made arepas.

"You know Eva?"

My parents nodded in unison and looked at each other. Even though they'd never met her in person, Eva had sort of become a recurring guest at our dinners, with me constantly bringing her name up in stories. Eva was a Swedish girl who was bi. She was a year younger, but we had Spanish together. She had once asked if I was into women; without skipping a beat, I said no. She laughed, "It's not an insult, you know." I apologized and we became friends. Mom had often asked when she would meet this new friend, if she had seen her in passing and whether she knew her parents.

"She's dating a girl from West Van."

"Like a friend?" Dad asked. My mom looked up and stopped mid-bite. She didn't like not knowing my friends.

"No, I think like more than a friend," I said, not raising my eyes from my plate. "Like boyfriend and girlfriend, only her boyfriend is actually a girl." The room fell silent. I took a bite and looked straight ahead, past Mom sitting on the opposite side of the table, to a wall-mounted photo of our family by the Eiffel Tower. Haru looked at me, eyes wide, eyebrows raised, with a slight tilt on his head, as if to ask where I was going with this.

"What's the point of this? Why are you saying this?" My mom put down her fork, the rice and beans spilling back on her plate.

"I . . . I don't know." She didn't blink, her eyes fixed on mine. I saw an argument coming but carried on. "I thought I'd share what's happening in my life."

"What do you mean happening in your life? What are you trying to say, Aki?" Mom was becoming exasperated, little bubbles of saliva collecting on the side of her mouth. She patted her hands down her apron, like she was searching for something.

"Nothing, she's just a friend who is dating a girl. I thought it deserved to be mentioned, you know."

"No, I don't know," she said firmly.

I should have changed the subject. Instead, I continued. "What's the big deal? It's legal to marry someone of the same sex now—you know that, right?"

"What is the big deal? The big deal is it's wrong. Yuto, did you hear what your daughter just said?"

"What do you think Adam and Harry are?" I continued, referring to the neighbours a few doors down. "You don't think they're room-mates, do you?" Haru kicked me, his slippers softening the impact.

Mom gripped the sides of the table, as if she was going to get up. Her apron had come undone and dangled a few inches from her body. "They will burn in hell. And so will you."

"For what? For believing it's their business to date whoever they want? That's why I'm going to hell? Besides, we're atheists, aren't we?"

Dad fiddled with his cloth napkin, his eyes shifting between his plate and hands, like he was trying to form sentences in his head. "Let's calm down," he said finally.

But it was too late. Mom proceeded to lecture me about right and wrong, good and bad. How it was unnatural for two women or two men to be together. What they'd given up so we could have every opportunity in life. I knew better than to insist. When she was finally content with what she'd said, I told her I understood and apologized. I never brought up the topic again.

Mom's voice, softer now, brought me back to the present. "Maybe we need to bring you home. Together, we can fix this."

I lay on the grass and breathed in the crisp air of London. It was February, and the ground was cold and damp, but I didn't care. Hope and anger sat on my chest, wrestling for undivided attention. "What do you mean, fix?"

"Maybe you just need to be reminded of who you are, who we are. Maybe we should bring you home, back to Canada."

"Who I am!" I felt my blood quickly rise to my head, heat eman-ating from my ears. What did she know about who I was? My hands trembled; the phone fell on the grass. Her words no longer made sense to me. I knew their anger and disappointment came from love. They wanted to spare me the pain and hurt of being the nail that stuck out, but I didn't want salvation. I was not—could not—be who she wanted me to be. How could she not see that?

"I can't do this. I can't do this now," I said, then hung up.

I lay on the ground, stiff, my ponytail pressing into the back of my head. How could they not understand how much they'd hurt me? I closed my eyes and tried to let go of the weight of it all—guilt, shame, resentment—but it clung to me, gripped tightly at my heart until I was consumed by it. I attempted a few deep breaths, but every time I exhaled my lungs got heavier, the air denser. I felt my chest crush underneath the weight of my unrelenting thoughts, my unprocessed emotions. I felt my body sink further into the ground and hoped the earth would engulf me, bury me under piles of dirt.

CHAPTER 12

Even if I was no longer the perfect daughter, I could still present as a normal friend, a regular student. I worked out with Ginika at the University of London gym in the morning: thirty minutes of warmup, followed by thirty minutes of weights rotation, ending with forty-five minutes of running. Ginika, Abby and I still walked together to LSE every day, I still attended my lectures and seminars, I handed my assignments in on time, I attended every running practice.

But the part of me that should have cared was absent and the pretense was exhausting. I began to skip my meals at the dining hall every few days, making my way down all the pubs along Torrington Place instead, preferring the company of people who didn't know me or care about what was going on with my parents and who didn't give two fucks about how I was feeling. I'd stumble home just short of midnight and pass out in my bed, wearing the same clothes I'd spent the day in. On the nights I ate in, I replaced socializing with locking myself in my room and resuming my martial arts training.

When I was seven, Mom used to take me to her Taekwondo lessons, in an old wooden building, with large, exposed beams and blue mats run by a small, second-generation Japanese man in his sixties. Wearing a white-and-black *dobok* and a full salt and pepper beard, he led the group, which mostly consisted of men and women ten years older than Mom, through a series of high kick drills. At the end of each lesson, they sat down, legs crossed, to meditate. I begged to join in, but she said I was too young—it was too violent a sport for such a young girl.

So, I waited patiently to reach the age of violence. My first real experience with martial arts came at fifteen, when I finally convinced my parents to let me take some lessons, supposedly to help my tennis training. I wasn't allowed to pick any martial art, however. After much back and forth and consultations with Ojiichan, my parents decided on Aikido. They especially appreciated the philosophy of redirecting the attacker's force rather than opposing it, causing as little injury as possible.

After some research, I found a small dojo in East Van, where a Japanese instructor offered evening Aikido lessons. I needed someone to practise with, and with none of my friends interested in martial arts, I had to put up an ad at school for a partner. A few days later, a boy in the year below me agreed to join the class too. Johnathan was about my height, with ginger hair and shy green eyes. We had French together in school, and he appeared harmless—a seemingly good choice for an Aikido partner. Each Thursday, after school, Mom drove us rode to the dojo on East Hastings.

We trained in a bare-bones room that doubled as a dance studio on most other days of the week. Classes began with stretching, followed by training on how to fall, and finally, some defence moves.

At first, Johnathan was a necessary nuisance useful for warm-up and exercise drills when a partner was needed. But one night, when we had to take the bus because Mom couldn't pick us up, he tried to kiss me. At the next class, I asked our sensei if I could focus on drills we could practice individually. Johnathan stopped joining me after that, though his parents continued to pay for the lessons. I trained for almost thirteen months until sensei decided there weren't enough students to keep that class time open. That year practising in a dance-studio-turned-dojo was the only experience I'd had with fighting. Until now.

On YouTube, I watched videos of judo, karate and Brazilian jiu-jitsu, studying practitioners of mixed martial arts—Anderson da Silva, B.J. Penn, Chuck Liddell. My interests moved from the philosophy of politics to the philosophy and practice of the Aikido greats—Morihei Ueshiba, Michio Hikitsuchi, Hiroshi Kato. I wondered what my parents would think now of the way I'd applied the aikido lessons I learned as a teenager. I was sure it would disappoint them, but I doubted a fight would have stood out among the other ways I was letting them down.

Every night I replayed the fight in the pub on Tottenham Court Road, word by word, blow by blow. And the fact that I couldn't talk about this with my friends made the desire to fight again even more intense.

The balance of absence and presence was enough for my friends to wonder whether something was the matter, but not enough to do anything about it just yet. To keep it that way, I eventually gave in to Abby and Ginika's demands to go clubbing in Southwark, a part of South London we didn't visit often. On our way home, I picked up a pamphlet outside another club, advertising their special events for the month. The following Saturday, Valentine's Day, they would be having a Latina night. Three floors and five rooms playing salsa, reggaeton and samba, it boasted. There'd be cheap drinks and lots of machismo, I thought as I folded it and slipped it into my pocket.

So I decided. That would be the night. During my solitary preparation, I developed some rules for myself in anticipation. Picking a fight wasn't going to be about letting loose; there had to be a method to it. Rule number one was basic. If I wanted to keep this a secret, I would have to fight people I didn't know. The club in

Southwark fulfilled my second rule: never fight at a place my friends or I frequented.

That Saturday, I was heading out of the residence tingling with excitement and anticipation when I bumped into Abby and Ginika in reception.

"Aki, we've been looking all over for you!" Abby was carrying a few grocery bags from the Tesco Express nearby.

"We haven't seen you all day," Ginika said between mouthfuls of prawn cocktail flavoured chips. "Want to hang out? Abby and I were thinking a quiet night in, watching *Sex and the City*."

"Can't. I need to head to the library to finish up a paper."

"You? You're not done with it yet?" Ginika looked suspicious. "I find that hard to believe." Abby nodded in agreement.

"Turns out someone in my seminar chose the same topic."

"Oh . . ." Ginika said slowly.

"Oh, what?" Abby sounded confused.

"Aki here doesn't want to be compared to someone else."

"Is that too much to ask? How many things can you say anyway about Franz Ferdinand?" Before the conversation could continue, I walked toward the door. "See you tomorrow," I said, without turning back. I knew that as long as they saw me the next morning at breakfast, things would be fine.

It was still early, just after ten o'clock, when I walked the short distance from the tube station. I wanted to arrive before the action really started so I could scout out the place. It wasn't so much a club as an abandoned warehouse with unfinished concrete walls and floors. The DJ box in each of the rooms was set in a corner, on top of a makeshift stage made of cheap slabs of wood. But there was space, lots of space, which meant they expected a lot of people.

I walked to the bar on the main floor and ordered two shots. "Give me what's cheapest." Except for a couple smooching in the corner, it was only the bartender and me. The lights were dimmed, and I squinted to make out her features. She was about my height and build, with dark straight hair and light-coloured eyes, maybe hazel or green. She wore a tight black shirt, dark jeans and a name-tag that said Anna. She looked me up and down before asking for my ID. I handed it over and resisted the urge to hit on her. Anna poured two shots of tequila, my least favourite spirit. I took one at the bar and walked off with the other. There was a burnt aftertaste in my mouth. That's what I got for asking for the cheapest shot.

I found a quiet place on the second floor and waited for the club to fill. Movement was slow at first, but things seemed to pick up after 11:00. The clientele was mostly Latino, a good mix of couples and singles. People were mostly speaking Spanish, most of which I could understand.

I watched men hit on women and women hit on men. I observed couples dancing. I saw eyes wander, followed by an argument. Sometimes I walked around, cutting through the middle of the dance floor, heat emanating from the crowd. Fishing.

It was almost 1:00 a.m. when I spotted him. I was coming off the stairs to the main floor when two women brushed past me. "¡Que asco!" one of them said, looking back at a man in the middle of the dance floor. He was clearly English, in his twenties, with light brown curly hair. His tight white T-shirt and jeans made him look like the brute the women had described.

It was also clear he was drunk—his body swayed without rhythm or stability. And he wasn't there in peace. He tapped on men's shoulders and yelled things like, "que buena," as he gestured to their girlfriends. He loudly mispronounced words in Spanish and mocked the music the DJ was playing. Near him a group of men, maybe friends, laughed while sipping on their beers.

The man approached a group of women and tried to copy their dance moves. They looked uncomfortable, huddling closer together, moving with smaller steps, trying to create distance. He circled them, shouting, "*Hola, chicas,*" over and over again. They dodged him and laughed—the nervous, uncomfortable laugh of those who feel trapped. "Go Fred," one of his friends yelled, and Fred shifted closer. I looked around to see if anyone else had noticed what was happening. Aside from a couple of glances and a few eye rolls, no one seemed to think this was out of the ordinary. Here were some damsels in distress.

I made my way toward the dance floor. This room was the biggest in the club and packed full, except for an area on my left, where people were avoiding a giant puddle of puke. The DJ was playing Daddy Yankee's "Gasolina." It must have been the fifth time I'd heard it that night alone. I hated that song.

By the time I'd arrived at the club, I had thought of rule number three: never choose someone smaller or weaker. Fred wasn't big, but he was maybe half a head taller than me.

Fred ticked all my boxes. Besides being sleazy, he wore his privilege proudly. His mockery conveyed a sense of superiority that sent a shooting anger up my chest. Rule number four: fight someone who deserves to be put down.

I couldn't resist the temptation any longer, so I tapped him on the shoulder. Fred turned to me, half surprised, half amused that someone was reacting to him. "*Hola, chica,*" he said, reaching for me. I moved aside.

"Leave them alone. They're not interested in whatever you want to offer." One of the women looked at me, a flash of relief in her eyes. Fred scoffed and moved in closer. A stench of cheap alcohol emanated from his body.

"She wants some!" one of his friends yelled. Fred looked back and gestured something that I couldn't quite make out before reaching for me again. He went for my shoulder, but I swatted his hand away. He laughed, and I remembered a guy who'd been to our first AU party back in October who had tried to plant a kiss on Abby's face. I'd been on the other side of the bar, too far away to do anything. I didn't know what I would have done then, but I knew now. "Don't touch me."

He threw his head back, laughing. A crust of spit had formed around his mouth. The sight of him repulsed me. I remembered how I'd felt when Jack had grabbed my arm at the pub.

"Come on, can you believe her?" Fred was looking for sympathy from one of the women he'd been harassing minutes before. They had started to move away, blending into the crowd. "And now they're gone too," said Fred, licking his lips. "It's just you and me." He winked and I felt my jaw tighten.

I looked at him, my blood rushing to my head. My heart pounded, my fingertips tingled in anticipation. The fifth and last rule, I decided, was perhaps the most important: give the opponent a chance for redemption. I wasn't unreasonable—everyone should have the opportunity to de-escalate.

"Look around you," I said. "You're just making everyone uncomfortable. Don't you think it's time for you and your friends to leave?"

Fred leaned in and whispered, "Playing hard to get, huh?" I felt the warmth of his stale breath on my ear. He put his right arm around my waist and pulled me closer to him. His chest was damp with sweat; being close to him made me feel dirty. I put both my hands on his forehead and pushed him away.

"Feisty!" He had a smirk on his face.

I lunged forward and punched with my left first. As my fist met his right cheek, a knuckle at a time, my body remembered that same pleasurable pain it had felt before. I closed my eyes momentarily, bent my legs slightly and advanced, hitting him with my right, my full weight behind the blow. His head thrust sideways and spit flew from his mouth. He was disgusting.

Fred stumbled back a few steps and held both his hands to

his face, shocked but drunk enough to be numbed, maybe a bit bemused. He smiled. The second punch had broken the skin on his left cheek. Blood ran in a straight red line to his upper lip. He wiped his mouth and licked his lips. I tightened my jaw.

Fred straightened his back and swaggered toward me, his unblinking eyes transfixed on mine. I tensed, put my hands up to protect my face and waited for his counterattack, but he just leaned in and said, "It hurts so good." His breath was warm and humid, almost palpable.

"You got it, Fred," one of his friends hollered. They were hooting, laughing. "You get 'er," he called.

I wanted to obliterate him. Them. Rage almost overwhelmed me but I assessed my options. How to bring him down. He was too close and facing the wrong way for me to hit him in the knees. I could have kicked him in the crotch, but that was a cheap blow. Unworthy. I needed to get him to take a step back, so I raised my right leg and brought it down on his left foot with all the force I could gather, my Timberlands leaving a dark grey print on his shoes. The impact reverberated up my ankle, calf and thigh, like accidentally stepping into a pothole at full speed. Fred jumped back on one right foot, turned. Before he could recover, I kicked the back of his right knee and he fell to the ground, half groaning, half laughing. I kicked him in the ribs, once, twice, three times. His laughter dissipated as he curled in pain. It wasn't funny anymore.

Sweat trickled down my face, dripping onto the floor. I looked up, hearing nothing but my uneven breath. It felt as if half of the room was staring at me. I opened and closed my hands, sensing where my skin had broken and moved toward Fred's friends. Not one of them had come to his defence. I walked determinedly, eyes on my target. They looked at me and whispered, and before any of them could say a word, I hit the one who had said I wanted some, striking his nose in an upward movement with my palm open. As my hand met his face, I felt a crunch. "You have no idea what I want," I said. He grabbed his nose, now bleeding onto his shirt, with both hands.

I turned around. The music kept on playing, but for a moment the room seemed quiet. The crowd moved to the rhythm of my breath, tired but even. Fred was still on the floor, rocking his body from side to side. I absorbed the scene and tried to single out every feeling pumping through my chest. A receding anger. An intermittent elation. A growing sense of control. As I identified them, I imagined putting each away for safekeeping, small treasures I'd collected.

I made my way to the exit door. Slowly, I regained full feeling in my body. Adrenaline dissipated and the pain grounded me in the present. My right hand throbbed. So did my left. I wiped my bloody knuckles on my trousers. I took a couple of steps forward, still limping from the pain shooting up my calf. The muffled sound of salsa music crept into the night. I stood in front of the club for a few minutes, feeling the cold London breeze kiss my cheek. The world was the same, but I felt different.

CHAPTER 13

I stood at the northwestern corner of the intersection at Oxford Circus, trying to pick Sana out from the crowd. It was the Tuesday after my second fight, and my knuckles still felt tender to the touch. I didn't want to explain to Sana what had happened, and I couldn't use the "punching a park bench" excuse again, so I'd made sure to wear gloves.

When I'd replied to Sana's first text, I had no idea where it would lead—unrequited lust on my part, at most. Ayesha and I hadn't spoken in almost three weeks but I didn't notice any spark or interest on her part. Still, after coffee, she asked if I wouldn't mind walking her to the London College of Fashion. Maybe she was lonely.

Sana began texting me every day, asking me how my day was going, telling me about hers. She started dropping by my residence unannounced and asking me to take her out. I'd meet her in the foyer, and we would walk to a nearby cocktail bar or a restaurant. She would reach for my arm when I said something mildly funny and sip her drink while maintaining eye contact. Once she grabbed my arm near Tottenham Court Road Station as the crowd intensified. We walked like that for several blocks, even after the sidewalks cleared. I couldn't tell if she just liked the attention, or if she was actually interested.

When Sana was "in the neighbourhood" at the end of February, she showed up wearing a perfectly fitted black dress that hugged her curves, a change from her usual colourful dresses paired with equally colourful coats or jackets. She'd told me that playing with colour was her favourite thing about getting dressed. I could see that—since meeting her she had never repeated an outfit. I had some reading to finish for the following day and an early running practice with Ginika and the team, so suggested a quick dinner in a small French bistro nearby.

She ordered the coq au vin and I had the ratatouille. We shared a bottle of wine while we talked about the situation in Gaza. Our conversations often veered toward the political, and we could spend hours discussing current affairs. Sana explained she'd been working on a conceptual assignment for one of her classes that involved creating a clothing collection inspired by the January 7 airstrikes carried out by Israel on Gaza City. "I am drawing inspiration from something that happened a couple of months ago, and taking that whole idea of what you wear says a lot about who you are to the next level. How do your clothes demonstrate your values?"

"And political views?" I added. "Clothing is inherently political."

"There's no one else in my life I can talk to about politics. My brothers don't care to hear my opinion. And my friends from college are interested in the colour of the season, not the latest update on the war in Iraq."

I raised my glass. "I'm glad to be of service."

"Seriously. It's nice to meet someone who is really listening. I wanted to get to know you sooner, but Ayesha . . ." She took a breath. "Well, she didn't seem super happy that night I met you."

"Hmmm." I didn't know how to respond.

"I must admit, I was happy when you stopped hanging out. It gave me room, you know, to get to know you." She licked her bottom lip. "I feel seen and appreciated when I'm with you."

"So," I said, wanting to steer the conversation away from Ayesha, "to what do I owe the pleasure of your company today?"

Sana rearranged her hair and took a sip of her wine while maintaining eye contact with me. "I don't know. I guess I felt like seeing you."

"I must be very interesting. It's the third time this week."

"You aren't half bad," she said, winking.

The waiter interrupted our conversation to offer dessert. I thought about how I'd soon get back to Plato's *Apology*—I still had about a hundred pages to read.

"When am I going to see your room?" she said after ordering crème brûlée to share. "You've never invited me up. I'm curious to see what you hide behind this quiet exterior."

"I guess I like to remain a mystery." I looked at my watch, calculating how long it would take to finish my reading. Maybe there was enough time to do it tomorrow morning, between practice and class. "Maybe I can fit you into my schedule."

We walked back to my residence in near silence, her eyes occasionally meeting mine. It was clear something would happen—if not now, eventually. It was also clear this would be another secret relationship. When we arrived at the residence, I nodded to the security guard at reception, and we waited for the elevator. Sana moved closer and I felt the heat of her body on mine, almost palpable.

As soon as my bedroom door closed behind us, Sana plunged forward throwing the entire weight of her body against mine. Her dress brushed against my hand and I struggled to grab at her. She smelled of Chanel No. 5, the scent complex with sophistication. I stumbled, taking a few steps back, and fell into the door behind me. Sana pinned me in place and whispered, "I've been waiting to do this all week." I stood still, mouth agape, wondering how we had gone from arm-holding to this.

That night, when Sana orgasmed, it was loud and dramatic, like something out of a porn movie. She panted for minutes after we were done. With her head on my chest, I wondered if she'd really enjoyed it. The hair-pulling, the scratching, the screaming my name. I wondered how much of it was true and how much was just for show.

I began to experiment with it, sometimes kissing her just as she was about to come. But even then, she managed to scream through the kiss, the eerie sounds of her orgasms trapped in my mouth. I couldn't help but compare. Sex with her was so different. With Ayesha, it was varied—sometimes quick and intense, other times slow and patient, depending on the mood. With Sana, it was always primal, rough. There was no nuance, and in our lack of harmony, I felt detached. Our reactions were so divergent that it seemed impossible we were experiencing the same moment. I figured time would help us sync, but the disconnection lingered.

Eventually I gave in, gave up. I figured she would be one of those passing relationships and I shouldn't try too hard for a connection, emotional or otherwise. Every time we met, I pretended it was the first—a one-night stand that looped indefinitely.

"Miss, we're here."

I was in a cab, parked outside the building where Sana and Ayesha lived. The last time I'd been here was the night of my first fight, when she and Ayesha took care of my bloodied knuckles. More than two months ago. I'd pushed Ayesha away and now I was back at her apartment to meet her cousin, something Sana kept insisting on. She seemed unaware of how difficult the situation was for me—I couldn't let go of Ayesha for good and being here was a painful reminder of the distance I'd created and couldn't overcome. Or maybe that's exactly why she'd been so persistent. The more time I spent with Sana, the more I wondered about their relationship. I guess living together didn't necessarily make them close.

I took a deep breath, paid the driver and stepped out. There was still time to chicken out. My phone buzzed—a text from Abby asking me what I was up to. Ginika was at a bar with some folks from the AU, and Abby wanted to join them, but she didn't want to go alone. Before I could answer, my phone buzzed again. This time it was Sana. She wanted to know how long I would be. I resisted the urge to take a raincheck and walked toward the entrance.

Sana opened the door to her apartment wearing nothing under her sheer red nightgown. "Perfect timing," she said. I stood at her doorstep, remembering the last time I'd been here. "Come in, silly." She pulled me in, carefully peeking out to make sure no one else was around. "Is everything okay?" She caressed the back of my neck.

I smiled, even though being there made me uncomfortable. "Yeah, I'm just a little tired. Long day at the library."

She held my face in her hands and kissed me. "Make yourself at home. I just need a few more minutes." Sana disappeared into her room, leaving the door half open, the light in her room providing the only illumination. I watched her through the reflection in her mirror, moving about, tidying things up. It looked like she'd laid half her closet on the bed.

"Where's Ayesha?" I called, moving down the corridor.

"She is out with Asad, her older brother. He's visiting from Bradford."

"Will they be home soon?" I was already regretting my decision to be there.

"No, they only left an hour ago. I imagine they'll be out for a while, getting dinner and whatnot." I let out a sigh of relief; Ayesha was a slow eater. Maybe I would be able to sneak out before they finished the main course. I continued to walk down the corridor, drawn toward the vase I'd broken when Ayesha first brought me over. I closed my eyes.

"I'm ready now!" Sana's voice shocked me into the present. I looked down at my hands. I was holding the glued vase, letting my fingers feel the crevices underneath them. I gently put it down and readjusted it on the dresser, trying to make it look untouched. The light from Sana's room accentuated the cracks. I should have bought Ayesha a new one.

I heard footsteps. Sana was walking in my direction, down the corridor. "What are you doing, silly? Come." She extended her hand toward me. I reached out and we started walking toward her room. She walked in front, guiding me through the darkness.

Sana thrust her hips up and down, unaware of her surroundings, while I tried to keep an ear out for Ayesha and Asad. When her moans became too loud, I peeked at the door, half open, every so often. It felt silly to worry this much, but since we had started seeing each other, it hadn't felt like something I could enjoy. There were too many complications for it to be seamless, healthy.

Eventually Sana came, her head tilted backwards, neck bent. She gripped my shoulder, her nails digging into my skin. In the process she'd screamed something like "Fuck me harder." I couldn't make it out, her legs pressed against both sides of my head. I couldn't hear or see anything. She let go. I looked up and she chuckled. I crawled up next to her and kissed her forehead. Without the pressure of her legs, a high-pitched ringing played in my ear on a loop.

"What the fuck!" Ayesha's voice startled me.

Sana sprang up, grabbed the sheets by her feet and covered herself. I stood up, half naked, and looked back and forth between them. Ayesha hadn't changed out of her studio clothes. Her jeans were stained with blotches of paint and the skin-tight black top she wore had a small hole near the sleeve. Her expression was one of disbelief and shock. Sana was whispering, "Shit, shit, shit, shit," under the blanket.

"I can explain." I took a step toward Ayesha, who took a step back. I ran phrases through my head. It's not what it seems. It didn't mean anything. I wanted you. Whatever I said wasn't going to be enough. I knew that. I just stood between them, trying to take up as little room as possible.

"How long have you been seeing each other?" Ayesha looked at me, eyes unflinching. A half-open brown leather bag dangled from her right hand, some of its contents had spilled on the floor—a packet of gum, some tissues, a couple of tampons.

"A few weeks." I opened my mouth to explain, then paused. If I tried to play it down, I would offend Sana. If I tried to give it meaning, I would hurt Ayesha even more. "After the last . . . uh . . . after our last time." Sweat trickled down the back of my neck and my knees shook involuntarily. I hated feeling out of control.

Ayesha turned to the shape under the covers and said, "Three months ago, she said she loved me." She paused and waited until Sana had pulled the sheets down from her face. "Did she tell you that?"

I felt my heart sink. Somehow hearing it made it worse. In my one-night-stand fantasy, I could pretend Sana was a random occurrence, someone I could have met at a bar who looked like Ayesha. But that wasn't the reality: I'd broken every basic rule of whatever this was between Ayesha and me—friendship, relationship, basic human decency, you name it.

Sana sat up and looked at me, then back at Ayesha. "I didn't know. I promise," she said pleadingly. It was true I'd never told her, but she must have had an inkling that first night we met, when she and Ayesha played nurse.

Ayesha's eyes met mine, and I watched shock turn into anger and then into hurt. She took a deep breath. "Asad is coming up in a few minutes. He went to buy some beer at the off-licence. You should leave before he gets here, for our sake as much as yours."

I tried not to make eye contact with either of them as I moved across the room, gathering my belongings and dressing myself.

Ayesha moved out of the way as I walked toward the door. "I'm sorry," I said, knowing the words meant nothing.

I closed the door to the apartment behind me and waited for the elevator, examining my reflection in a nearby mirror: dark circles under my eyes, hair frizzy and unkempt, hickeys down my neck from Sana's last visit. I'd been eating less and less and now my cheeks also looked sunken. I looked smaller than I'd remembered.

Raised voices filled the corridor. "What the fuck, Sana! She was my friend." Maybe I should turn back, try to explain. I had half turned when the elevator doors opened to reveal a tall Asian man, holding a six-pack of Carlsberg. Asad. I could see his resemblance to Ayesha. I cast a nervous glance at the closed door, relieved the volume was muted for the moment.

He followed my gaze. "Hi," he said, extending his free hand. "Are you a friend of Sana's? I'm Ayesha's brother, Asad."

"Hey," I replied instinctively. "I'm Aki."

Ayesha's voice, angry and hurt. "You're my cousin!"

"Everything all right in there?" Asad moved past me toward the yelling inside. He gave a half shrug. "Girls, right?"

I rushed into the elevator just as the doors began to close, grateful to escape, and walked home: an hour alongside Hyde Park, down Oxford Street and up Tottenham Court Road.

CHAPTER 14

I stood outside Queensway station and waited for Ayesha. After days of not returning my calls, she had agreed to let me explain what had happened with Sana. Part of me expected she wouldn't show up, but I had to try.

I looked at my watch—it was March 17, St. Patrick's Day, just past 5:00 p.m. I watched people come out of the station in rhythmic bursts—a mix of businesspeople heading home and the college crowd dressed in glittery green heading toward the bars and pubs. The sun was sinking toward the horizon. I had promised to go for a run with Ginika and a few of the girls from the team in a couple of hours, but maybe it was best to cancel. My recent unreliability meant I was on the verge of suspension, but Ayesha was more important and I didn't want to rush our conversation. Then again, maybe she would stand me up. I checked my watch again—5:03. I took Kant's *Groundwork of the Metaphysics of Morals* out of my backpack and started on the second section, skimming through it. I was a few sentences in when Sana tapped me on the shoulder.

"She's not coming, Aki."

Startled, I dropped the book on the ground. "What?" I felt disoriented.

"Ayesha. She's not coming." She paused. "Asad walked in when we were arguing. She tried to conceal it, say it was about a friend and how I'd stolen you from her. But Asad could tell it was more than that."

Was Ayesha all right? I wanted to ask. I stayed silent.

"He was angry. Asad prides himself on being progressive, but this was too much for him. I've never seen him like that, so upset."

I shuffled awkwardly, shoving my book back into my backpack.

"Ayesha is afraid of what will happen, afraid Asad will tell her parents."

"Uh, okay." Fuck. I didn't know what to say. I thought back to how my parents reacted. What had I done?

"How are you?" Sana leaned in examining the expression on my face.

I took a step back. "I'm fine." I turned around and walked into the station, disappearing into the crowd before Sana could say anything else. Two days later, I attacked Asad's lookalike in a pub near Holborn Station.

My first three fights mirrored Isaac Newton's three laws of motion.

One, a taste. "An object will not change its motion unless a force acts on it." Were it not for my parents finding out I was gay, were it not for the man at the bar pushing me down after an all-around shitty day, were it not for the immense lack of control I felt, I would have never shifted direction. I needed an external force to impose change and alter my path. Timing and circumstance led to my first fight.

Two, direction. "The change of motion of an object is proportional to the force impressed on it." If the world around me hadn't felt so hostile, if I hadn't felt so out of control, perhaps the story of the fighter would have ended with the first. But the late-night YouTube videos showed me a path to regaining some of what I'd felt I'd lost. The fight at Southwark was a rite of confirmation, a commitment to this new version of myself. I was ready to rise to the challenge and become someone else.

Three, retribution. "To every action, there is always opposed an equal reaction." I learned I could do more than absorb hostility. I could punch back, match my opponent's blow with the same power. When I found myself at the pub near Holborn and saw the man who looked like Asad, I wanted to achieve balance, to right what I felt was a wrong. And since I couldn't do it with Ayesha and Asad, that man had to do.

"The next station is Victoria. Change here for Circle and District lines, National Rail Services and Victoria Coach station."

I'd escaped into King's Cross Station, and now stepped out of the tube, head down, body crouched over, trying my best to not call attention to myself, occasionally raising my head to make sure I was going in the right direction.

Victoria Station was once two stations, operated by two companies and designed by two different engineers. It wasn't until 1923 that the two halves were integrated, opening up archways in the walls that once divided it. But instead of feeling like one cohesive structure, it feels like two separate things forced to be one, despite its deceptively open space. There are few walls to lean on, few places to hide.

What had I done? I'd broken my own rules. The fight was close to LSE. I'd been to that pub before. That man didn't really deserve it. And I'd never given him a chance to escalate. What started out as a bid for control was the total opposite.

I moved quickly, dodging people as I navigated through the openness. I looked around and searched for a live departure board. I needed a place to go. Anywhere far away from here. Several feet above me, I scanned the list of destinations. It was 21:38. The next train to Oxted was in thirteen minutes. I could make it if I ran.

The train was full, but not packed, mostly men and women in business attire, probably going home after a long day of work. I searched for at least two empty seats. I was afraid someone might stare, or worse yet, engage. As I walked along the train, I tried to clean up a bit. I wiped the blood off my knuckles onto my trousers and, facing one of the doors between cars, I readjusted my hair against the reflection. I did a lousy job. I needed water to make it better.

In the train bathroom, a rectangle-shaped mirror hung above a small sink. It looked greasy, like someone had tried to wipe it with a dirty cloth. I pulled back my hair and tied it with a black elastic on my wrist. My dark brown eyes looked hazy behind the maroon frame of my glasses. I moved closer and examined my face—my lips pale, the scratches on my neck now swollen. Maybe it was the train jostling about or the drinks from the pub, but I suddenly felt heat rise from the pit of my stomach to my head. I rushed to the toilet, retching, but nothing came up. Instead, tears ran down my face. I sat on that piss-stained floor, the smell of cheap disinfectant filling the air, without being able to tell why I was crying.

The next morning, I skipped the workout with Ginika and breakfast in the dining hall. Knowing the conversation my physical state and the fact I had not come home the previous night would start, I feigned sickness and stayed in my room all day. Texts and calls went unanswered. But I couldn't avoid them forever.

"Aki! Aki!" Abby's voice was punctuated by loud knocks on my door.

I continued to lie on the carpet, hoping she would go away.

"Stop that!" Ginika sounded annoyed. "Aki," she said softly. "Is everything all right in there? We're worried."

I cleared my throat. "Yeah, all is good. Just feeling a little under the weather." I opened and closed my hands. My knuckles were still swollen.

"Where were you? I mean, where were you last night?" Ginika's voice was muffled by the heavy door.

"I just went for a long walk and ended up at an all-night cafe." Lying was getting easier with each day. Soon, it'd feel just like telling the truth. "I got back around 4:30 a.m." Even if they were suspicious, neither of them would be able to verify that.

"Aki, Abby here." They whispered something unintelligible to each other.

"You can't say that!"

"Fine, Ginika." Abby paused. "Aki, are you coming down for dinner? Can we get you anything?"

"Thank you, but I'm not really hungry. I think I just need a good night's sleep."

There was a long pause. "Okay, then," Ginika said slowly. "Call us if you need anything."

"Yeah, Aki. We're right here."

"I'll see you tomorrow," I said preemptively. The bruises wouldn't be gone, but maybe I would be able to come up with a plausible excuse by then. The longer I spent in my room, the more suspicion I would attract. Reality, no matter how dire, is easier to manage than someone else's imagined problem.

CHAPTER 15

A week after the fight near Holborn Station, Sana came to see me. I was still holed up in my residence, my knuckles encrusted in dried blood, my ribs still sore to the touch. I lay in bed, throwing a tennis ball at the ceiling and catching it mid-air.

My phone was buzzing on the floor, the sound muffled by the carpet. This was the third missed call from Sana in the last five minutes. The phone rang again. She wasn't going to give up. I picked up but said nothing. "I came to check on you. I'm in your lobby."

I let the silence grow. "Aki, are you there?"

I could have told her I was coming down. I could have said I would sign her in. But I didn't. I hung up the phone, put some gloves on and headed for the door.

Sana must have known me better than I gave her credit for, because when I stepped out of the elevator into the lobby, she was patiently sitting in one of the Godawful green armchairs tucked away at the corner. She didn't seem upset or distressed; she seemed to know that I would eventually come to get her. Even her outfit screamed optimism: a floral dress of hot pink and orange, with a baby pink overcoat. Little droplets of rain had collected on the shoulders.

I smiled at her. Her eyes softened and I saw what I thought was a glimpse of pity. I signed her in, noting down her name, the time she arrived and my room number. One of the less likeable security guards behind the reception desk looked at us and then winked at me. I tapped my access card and guided her through the double doors near the lobby. "Let's take the stairs. I don't want that guy staring at us while we wait for the elevator."

My room was the neatest it'd probably ever been. Days in hiding had forced me to be creative about my projects. After I finished a couple of weeks' worth of reading on modern philosophers and the Cold War and researched the situation in Somalia, I'd organized my belongings. It started with the books and my desk, followed by the clothes and shoes in my closet. It ended with the area near my bed, reorganizing the photos on the wall, removing—but not discarding—the few that were left of Ayesha. I couldn't bring myself to throw away the photos I had of her. There was still too much left to process and understand. I hid them in a drawer in my bedside table, with the hope of one day being able to put them up again.

Sana took off her coat and laid it on my desk chair while inspecting the books on the shelf. A few weeks ago, she would have continued to undress. Now, she walked toward me and touched my cheek. "Let me see," she said, holding up my hands and removing my gloves. Her cold hands felt like relief. Sana walked around me— she moved my arms about, lifted up my shirt, gently pressed against my bruises. She examined me like I was a patient and she was the doctor, only it wasn't meant to be sexy.

"I had an accident with the weights at the gym."

Sana looked unimpressed.

"Really! It looks worse than it feels." I pulled my hands back and hid them behind my back.

"Have you seen someone? Did you go to urgent care?"

I shook my head, staring straight ahead.

"You should have." She paused and moved in front of me. "But you already know that."

Sana sat on my bed. She rubbed her hands together and looked up. In her gaze, I saw pity turn to sadness, and she looked like she might cry. For the first time since we'd met, I considered that she might actually have genuine feelings for me. It never occurred to me that it might be more than sex.

Outside, a group of rowdy residents leaving to watch a soccer match between Arsenal and Hull City at a nearby pub. The loudest one screamed for the rest to "hurry the fuck up." I turned my face away from the window, moving toward Sana and the bed. She watched me, her eyes fixed on my feet. I sat next to her and held out my hand. Sana put her head on my shoulder and squeezed my arm. She nestled her face on my neck and kissed my knuckles, then my lips. I pulled away, holding her by her shoulders. I didn't want any more trouble.

"It's okay," she said putting her hands over mine. "I know it's the last time."

Her voice was soft, but it lingered. The damage had been done. What did I have to lose? Sana kissed me again. My arms relaxed. I unzipped her dress and brushed it off her shoulders, folding it and putting it down on the floor. She lay down on the bed, expectant but passive. I lay next to her and traced the outline of her collarbone. We had never been this careful with one another.

She didn't pull my hair or scratch my back. She didn't scream. She just held on to me tighter and tighter until her body stiffened and twitched. Then she let go. I thought I heard a repressed sob but didn't ask. We didn't talk or look at each other afterward. We just cuddled—her head on my chest, her fingers tapping my stomach, our legs entwined. When the sun came up the next morning, the light glimmering purple through my cheap residence curtains, I watched her pick up the carefully folded clothes on the floor and dress herself. As she looked around, her eyes not focusing on anything in particular, I realized she might be saying goodbye to a place she'd grown accustomed to.

Sana kneeled down and put her forehead against mine. "Take care, Aki," she said and walked toward the door. I turned to the wall—I don't know if she looked back. There was a soft, barely perceptible click that reverberated in my ear. At each moment it grew louder and sharper, morphing into unknown shapes until it blended with other sounds.

My body still felt warm from her touch. I closed my eyes and imagined Sana walking down the corridor, into the elevator, out the lobby, down the stairs to Malet Street. I pictured her strolling down Tottenham Court Road and hailing a cab, because Sana could be extravagant. I saw her walking into her building and up the stairs to her apartment. I felt the coldness of her doorknob and the softness of the Persian rug in the entrance hall. And once I was done imagining her journey home, I promised myself I'd never think of her again.

CHAPTER 16

By the end of March, my dual life solidified: university student by day, reckless mess by night. My friends were there, but I avoided conversations that didn't involve practical matters. They wanted to know what really happened with Ayesha, and why I never brought her name up anymore, but the last thing I wanted was to revive the night she caught me in bed with Sana.

"Are you guys taking a break?"

We sat on the floor of Abby's room surrounded by piles and piles of clothes, unable to tell whether they were dirty or clean.

"Not really." I turned to Ginika. "How are you and Kwaku doing?"

"I don't know. We are still seeing other people." Ginika gestured with air quotes. It seemed like Kwaku was stringing her along, but she apparently had no interest in anyone else.

"I've heard enough about Kwaku! The dude needs to make up his mind," said Abby. "Besides, stop changing the subject, Aki. Why haven't we seen Ayesha?"

"Things just didn't work out, all right?" I heard the aggressive tone in my voice. "I'm sorry. I didn't mean to say it that way."

"I don't get it. You two were so in love until your parents found out." Ginika elbowed Abby. "What? I can't say that now?"

"She just means, you two looked good together." Ginika tried to save face.

"Yeah, well, we are not together anymore. Now, can we change the subject?"

To myself, I began to justify my actions, to concoct stories. Ayesha and I were never official. We hadn't agreed on the boundaries of our relationship. Her outing wasn't my responsibility. They shouldn't have been arguing about it when they knew Asad was bound to arrive. I told myself it wasn't wrong to sleep with Sana. We were all adults. Nobody owned anyone. In fact, I had every right to do so.

In the past I'd been worried about too much, carefully treading around my parents' feelings and thoughts—how they saw me and whether I met their expectations. Now, all that mattered was what I wanted. I wanted to fight again. And I wanted other women.

It began with Ahn, a half-Vietnamese student I'd met on my first day at LSE at a mixer for freshers. She wasn't really in my group of friends but the International Relations program was small compared to something like Economics, and sooner or later gossip travelled to the whole class.

Ahn, who lived just a few blocks away near Gordon Square, must have heard I was struggling because she began to visit daily, bringing me food and spending time with me. I would have preferred to be left alone, but she was pushy and hard to turn away. Ahn was a couple of inches shorter than me, so when she examined my face, she tilted her head up slightly. Her brown, almond-shaped eyes always glimmered in the light.

"Have you ever considered you go for the wrong people?" she said one day, unpacking a paper bag of Thai food.

"What do you mean, wrong people?" I inhaled deeply. The aroma of peanuts and oyster sauce permeated my room.

"You know, like Ayesha and her cousin."

I sat on my bed in silence. Ahn turned to me, but instead of looking in my direction, she stared at the floor. She made circular patterns on the carpet with her feet. I moved toward her and grabbed her face. It felt smaller in my hand than I had imagined it would. I leaned in and felt Ahn melt into my arms. Her lips were full and soft and tasted of peppermint Chapstick. I picked her up and she wrapped her legs around my waist. When I put her down next to my bed, I undressed her, starting with her black tank top and nude bra, then kneeling and pulling her cargo trousers to her ankles.

Ahn tried to undress me, but I pushed her hands away. "Not tonight," I whispered.

I went down on her for an hour, maybe more. She came once, twice, three times, and with each I felt lighter but stronger. I decided sex, like fighting, was a tool to cope with the chaos around me. It was about power and about all the things I could still control. It had nothing to do with intimacy—I'd wanted to let Ayesha in, but couldn't. I didn't want to feel like I'd failed again.

After Ahn, there was Rose, Heather, Jenn. Students who became proverbial notches on my belt. We'd go out, we'd drink, and I'd end up in one of their rooms. I had learned my lesson about attachment, so I was careful to never give the impression I wanted something more than sex. I always left in the middle of the night and never talked about our sexual encounters in the daylight.

I went out on my own, to cafes, bars, clubs. I took to saying yes to most women I met. There was Giulia, a second-year drama student who was into vampirism and BDSM. We met at an inter-university LGBT event. I told her I'd be open to anything, except blood. Face painted white, she drew the curtains of her bedroom and cuffed my hands to the bed. Giulia grazed her teeth against my neck, her black and red embroidered corset rubbing against my stomach. "You'll be mine for eternity," she said, wiping her mouth as if she'd drunk my blood. I didn't call her again.

There was Isabel, half Brazilian, who I met online. She took me to my first lesbian club in Soho and said she couldn't tell whether I was into women. Isabel flirted with half of the people there, but we left together. We had sex in a small hotel in the West End because she lived with her mom and I had stopped bringing women back to my room, having discovered nudging someone out was much harder than taking off in the middle of the night. Despite her swagger, the sex felt average. I awoke in the middle of the night to find her trying to sneak out. She started to apologize and explained she had a girl-friend, but they were going through some stuff. I stopped her and said I wasn't looking for more than a one-night stand. We left the hotel together.

On my way home, a drunken man tried to hit on me. "Hey, sexy." His words were slurred. "Want to come home with me?" He was heavy-set, with brown hair and a scruffy beard. His receding hairline made it difficult to tell how old he was, maybe late twenties, maybe mid-thirties, maybe early forties. Too old to be hitting on a teenager.

I could have let it go, but he continued to stumble after me. I made a fist, turned and punched his smug face. He fell on his back. "Take yourself home, asshole!" I spat at him.

He groaned. "Why did you do this? I just wanted to take you home."

"Shut up!" I kicked him. "Next time you have the impulse, think twice before following a woman at night."

The punch was just enough to whet my appetite, but not enough to satiate me. Meaningless sex and a drunken creep just wouldn't cut it. I was headed back to Vancouver in a few days, and this was my last unravelling. I walked down every alleyway on the way back to the residence, until I came across two men, each about twice my size, brawling outside the backdoor of a pub. I ran toward them and threw indiscriminate punches until I was knocked unconscious. I wasn't out for long, but when I came to it, the two men were both gone. I touched my split lips. The blood was already dry. My head throbbed. I sat up slowly, then rose to my feet, and slowly made my way home.

CHAPTER 17

My alarm sounded. I let it exhaust itself. Only fifteen hours until I would be back in Canada. Less than a day until I saw Mom, Dad, Haru. The wall near my bed was covered with photos of BC. I turned to it, finding the photo of my family, trying to recall the people we used to be.

Growing up my parents used to tell me many stories. Some were read. Some were made up. Some were true. Of all the stories she told, Mom's favourite was about how she met my father. As she recounted falling in love with the man she'd once served at a café, she always emphasized that my father was the only person for her. "He saved me," she would say. But I knew it couldn't have been Dad's charm alone that brought them together.

Mom was warm, loyal, sometimes overbearing. She valued honesty and spoke her mind always, often to her own detriment. Still, she cared, deeply, unabashedly. She had a way of disarming people and making them feel safe. She was the only person I'd ever felt comfortable saying "I love you" to; I hadn't said it or heard it from her in four months.

I sat up and grabbed the pile of neatly folded clothes at my feet. A pair of oversized distressed jeans, a white T-shirt and a black hoodie, with a white Nike swoosh in the middle. None of those items would have made it into my wardrobe a few months ago, especially the trousers with the holes in them, but I was experimenting with this new me and playing into all of the stereotypes. Last, I grabbed my graduation watch from the bedside table and clasped it on. I needed to leave soon.

The room was clean but a bit of a mess, with an assortment of books spread on the carpeted floor. One of the residence maids had come to clean it the day before. I could tell she'd been there because the philosophers were no longer arranged in chronological order, or maybe she'd perceptively paired St. Aquinas and Aristotle. All of the items I needed to take had been neatly laid out the night before. Dad had taught me how to prepare for a trip when I was only five years old, and I still followed his travel routine. I walked to my desk, avoiding the books on the floor and took my backpack from the chair. In it, I packed the laptop and a few notebooks. Then I checked my Canadian and Colombian passports and slipped them into a side pocket.

My phone buzzed with a text from Ginika. "You can do it. xoxo" I couldn't believe I was going home for the first time since coming out.

"Are you sure you need to go?" Ginika had asked during dinner a few nights prior.

"Maybe you can conveniently miss your flight," Abby suggested with a smirk on her face. "Like maybe the Piccadilly line broke down or something."

"I think not going will be worse in the long run." I played with a lone pea on my plate.

"It will go by quickly." Ginika tried to reassure me, but there was little confidence behind her words.

Maybe it was because the trip wasn't a sign that things were getting better as much as a reluctance to admit they were different. My parents and I had always assumed I would go back after Lent term and we were committed to maintaining a semblance of normalcy. I wondered what that would look like once I actually landed, especially given we had hardly spoken in the last few months.

I looked at my watch. I would need to leave soon if I was to catch the Piccadilly line to Heathrow. I walked to the mirror for one last look. There was so much my parents didn't know about me anymore. I'd lost some weight since I'd last seen them. My eyes were sunken, with dark circles. I took off my glasses and considered opening a bag of makeup my mom had sent me to college with, but it probably would have made myself look worse. Instead, I pulled my hair back and tied it in a ponytail. I looked down—my knuckles were mostly healed. None of the other bruises on my back and sides were visible.

Mid-morning light crept in through the half closed curtains. High up on a shelf above my desk were my *L Word* DVDs, seasons one through five. I was still waiting for season six to come out. I looked around my room. I was going to miss this safe space. Ten days away felt like an eternity.

"Welcome home," the immigration officer said, sliding the passport back to me. I grabbed it off the counter and mumbled a thank you. I looked up: my suitcase was going to be on Carousel 5. I probably could have survived with a backpack and a carry-on, but I'd anticipated a lot of alone time at the park, so I'd brought home a large stack of books.

My case was one of the last to slide down, and most other passengers were gone. I knew it was mine because of the ribbons my grandma had attached to it the last time we visited her in Colombia before she died. She had urged me to get a suitcase in a brighter colour—maybe yellow—but I was stuck on grey. As I clumsily dragged it off the carousel, the books seemed heavier than I remembered. I took a deep breath. No matter how long I delayed it, it wasn't going to get easier. I straightened up, patting my jeans and hoodie, before walking toward the large exit sign.

After clearing customs, I entered the in-between space that led to the arrivals hall and the unseen outside world. I urged the corridor to elongate by taking smaller and smaller steps. I stopped short of the door sensor, took a deep breath and stepped through.

My parents were waiting outside, holding hands for what I assumed was moral support. From a distance, they looked smaller than I had expected. Dad was wearing his weekend outfit, a pair of beige chinos with a teal-coloured long-sleeved polo. He was slightly hunched over, his shoulders arching forward. Mom had lost some weight since Christmas. She also wore chinos and a polo, but her trousers were navy and her shirt was short-sleeved. No Haru. Why wasn't he there? Why was he making me do this alone? I walked cautiously toward them. I didn't know whether to expect a hug, a kiss, or maybe an awkward pat on the back. They stood still, waiting for me to make my way, neither taking a step in my direction. I could see my mother eyeing my outfit up and down and was sure her expression was disapproving. It was official: I was no longer the same daughter that she had dropped off in London the previous September or had said goodbye to after New Year's.

When I finally reached them, I didn't know what to say. Somewhere in the walk over, I'd forgotten how to string words together. We exchanged awkward hellos. Mom gave me a half hug and I tensed at her touch. It felt warm, too warm, the heat burning through my hoodie and marking my bruised skin. Dad extended his arm toward my suitcase and grabbed the handle, avoiding contact altogether. I moved around a lot, fidgeting with the straps of my backpack, searching for distractions, avoiding eye contact. Maybe if I didn't really see them, they wouldn't see me and we could pretend all this wasn't really happening. We began to walk in an awkward silence toward the parking lot.

"How was the flight?" Dad asked, finally, once we got to the pay station.

"Not too bad. A little turbulence when we were landing."

"There was a wind warning last week."

I looked toward Mom. She didn't seem to be listening at all. Something about the way she looked vacantly ahead made me feel guilty, as if I'd broken her, and for a brief moment I wanted to fix it, to make it better, even if it meant going back in the closet. I thought about how realistic that could be, whether one could, in fact, go back into the closet. I hadn't seriously entertained the idea before.

I must have been lost in thought because my parents were now walking toward the car. I hurried behind them. I figured the awkwardness maybe warranted a bit of physical space between us, so I stayed behind, but only a little.

My father lifted my suitcase into the trunk of the Lexus with a strained grunt. He made a joke about lugging rocks from London, an attempt at relieving the tension. Mom mustered a fake smile. I tried to laugh, but no sound came out. He closed the trunk and shook his head. Then, he made his way around to the driver's side. Mom slid into the passenger side and I sat in the back, behind her, my usual place in the car. The interior was impeccable, as always—were it not for the fact that the new smell had worn off, you might think it was purchased last week. Since we were little, Haru and I knew not to eat or drink inside my father's car. He appreciated cleanliness.

Dad put the radio on a pop music station and increased the volume, maybe to prevent the need to make more awkward conversation. Katy Perry's "I Kissed a Girl" came on. When we hit the chorus, Mom rushed to turn the radio off, glancing at Dad with an unimpressed look. I rolled down the window and pretended not to notice.

I looked out into the horizon, rows upon rows of houses hidden by tall hedges along the Granville corridor. Once, this stretch had felt like coming home. Now it just felt nostalgic, like a place I no longer belonged to. I wondered if I ever had.

We cut through downtown and Stanley Park. When we came off the Lions Gate Bridge, I knew we were close. Marine Drive, right turn on 31st, watch it become Mathers. Then we were home. I prayed Haru would be there to alleviate the tension that had grown with each minute until it felt like there was no room for me to be. He wasn't.

My parents and I endured an awkward meal and some uncomfortable chatter, then moved to the family room, each of us sitting on our own brown leather sofa, pretending to watch another episode of *The Waltons,* one of my mother's favourite shows from her childhood. My whole body felt enveloped in a thick blanket of shame and guilt, and even though I tried as best as I could to come up with something to say or do, I was paralyzed. When Terry jumped up, yapped in excitement and rushed toward the door, Dad and I turned our heads to the entrance hall while Mom's eyes remained fixed on the television.

"You're in already?" Haru poked his head into the family room, his black puffed jacket still on. "Sorry I'm late. There was a lot of traffic downtown—an accident or something." His eyes were red, like he'd been crying, his lips pursed. My mom mumbled "okay," but didn't look away from her show. Haru was late by almost two hours and this should have been enough for a scolding. But, in light of my transgressions, acute tardiness no longer seemed like a punishable offence.

Haru took off his coat and laid it on the sofa next to me. He extended his arms for a hug and I half stood up to meet his embrace. I let myself relax into him. "Are you okay?" he whispered in my ear. I shrugged. My brother gestured with his head toward the door. "We're going up," he announced to my parents.

"Put your coat away," Mom said.

"How did you even see that?" Haru huffed.

My brother and I grew up sharing walls, not rooms. For the year before I left for college, Haru allowed no one to enter his bedroom. Well, no one except Luz. He disliked cleaning more than he disliked having his privacy encroached upon. So, when I walked into his room, I was surprised to find that the posters of scantily clad women had now been replaced by posters of Gothic-looking men, whom I could not recognize.

His desk was cluttered, but his half-open closet looked impeccable, his clothes organized by colour, shades of black, grey and white. He moved some books from his bed and told me to sit. Then he turned on the speakers, connected his iPod and put on some heavy metal music. I widened my eyes and shifted on the bed. Was I really that out of touch with my own brother?

"It's just so they won't hear what we're saying." He looked at me and smiled.

"Is everything okay with you? I mean, you look like you'd been crying earlier."

"Don't worry about it." He paused, hoping I would respond, but then continued, "Becca can be a little possessive sometimes, that's all."

"What kind of possessive?" I asked.

Haru sighed. I tried to make eye contact with him, but he walked away from me toward the window. "It sounds like I should be worried."

"Really—it's all good. We had a fight and I had to convince her not to end things." Another pause. "Anyway, it feels like you need to talk more than I do."

"I don't know about that. I feel like I'm talked out, to be honest."

"Things have been weird at home. They have really loosened the leash on me. So, thank you," he joked. I feigned a smile. "In all seriousness though, you just have to know your truth and stick to it, you know? Don't say something just because you think it will please them."

"Believe me. I've done nothing but disappoint them."

"Yeah, well. They've got to deal with that because what they're disappointed about is outright ridiculous." Haru paused and changed the tracks on his iPod to something with a little less screaming. "Maybe we should go out with my friends next weekend, get you out of the house."

I cocked my head to the side. I had never hung out with his friends and he'd never hung out with mine. Then again, anything to get me out of the house. "Yeah, that'd be nice." I looked at my brother, who suddenly appeared so mature.

"Turn that music down!" Mom yelled from the bottom of the stairs.

Haru increased the volume, before bringing it back down. He laughed to himself, then looked at me. "I've got your back. You know that, right?"

"I do."

CHAPTER 18

For the first few days, we all tried to pretend nothing was the matter. Sure, maybe I was a bit distant, but I'd always been bookish and an introvert. Yes, Mom was in one of her moods, but that wasn't unusual. And Dad, well, he was working late entertaining clients, like he usually did. It seemed the situation had stabilized and he was doing his best to keep the momentum going. On some level, we figured out that if we could avoid each other for long enough, we could make it through the ten days without more damage to our relationship. But our feelings were festering.

When I woke up on the Tuesday after Easter, I knew something was off. Haru and Dad were at the kitchen table, getting ready for school and work, but Mom was nowhere to be seen. We ate our breakfast in silence, and when it was time, Dad and Haru left together. I stayed seated, knowing a confrontation was brewing.

My parents' bedroom was on the third and top floor of our house. I didn't know if Mom was awake, so I went up the steps slowly and carefully. When I reached the top of the stairs, I crouched over and tiptoed my way in. It didn't feel fair that I would have to reach out, when she had given me the cold shoulder for months, but I'd always been the one to apologize first.

I sat on the floor, with my back against one of the sides of the bed. In the past, I might have climbed in next to her, but it would be more difficult to talk if I could see the look on her face, knowing it was me who caused it.

"Are you . . . okay?" I whispered, afraid that my words might bring down whatever crept on our metaphorical roof. She grunted and turned away from me. It felt like the room was too small to hold us both.

"Is this . . . because of me?" It felt weird to take the responsibility for it out loud, like I thought myself overly important. Mom didn't respond. Instead, she rolled over to the other side of the bed. I sat on the floor for a minute, then two, then five. It felt like it would never end. I counted to a hundred twice, in my head, hoping for anything that could tear the space between us. Eventually I got up and started to walk away. I looked over my shoulder. "Fine. I will leave you alone then," I said, half angry, half hurt.

When I was inches away from the door, she finally rolled over. "Was it me? Was it us? Did I do something wrong?"

I turned to her and saw despair. Was she afraid she would be judged for my shortcomings? Was she worried I would be shamed and exiled by her friends? I wanted to say no, but also yes. No, it wasn't her fault that I had turned out gay. No, she hadn't forced me down this path. But yes, she had done so much wrong. I had never heard a supportive or comforting comment when sexuality came up—not when I innocently showed affection to a friend at the tennis club, not when I brought up Eva, and especially not when they found out about me. She had taken all that I was and simplified it to this one thing, this one thing that was an unforgivable transgression in her eyes. I was lost, someone who couldn't see the light, someone who could not, would not, be forgiven.

I wanted to say all those things, but she was my mom and she was hurting, and it felt like my job to make the hurt go away, so I walked toward her and sat on the bed. "No, it wasn't you. You didn't do anything wrong. It's me. It's just who I am."

We didn't talk. I made her coffee and buttered toast and took it up to her room. Then I let her sleep. I walked back down to the kitchen feeling tainted, dirty. I had pretended, again. I had betrayed myself and I knew it. This once gigantic house now felt cramped. I grabbed my bike from the garage and zipped away, out of my mother's grip.

I biked to Eagle Point in Lighthouse Park. It was mid-morning and the park was mostly empty. Children were at school, grownups were at work. Birds were chirping, the wind was blowing, the occasional runner stopped by before continuing on to Point Atkinson Lighthouse. I sat with my back against a rock and inhaled.

Of all the things I missed about BC, besides my family, of course, this park was at the top of the list. It was the place I went to when I needed to process my emotions. I'd gone there after my first month in high school, which ended with me celebrating my birthday on my own. I'd gone there after some kids at school had created a Myspace page listing all the reasons why "Aki is gay" and circulated it to my entire class. And I'd gone there after I told my parents I'd be going to LSE for college. Whenever life would get too much, I would disappear there, sometimes for hours.

The wind knocked my bike over, urging me back to the present. A bird pecked the ground for a bug or remnants of food. I picked up a small rock, rolling it in the palm of my hand, and looked ahead at the open space before me. The sky was blue, with a few well-placed clouds, but the sun wasn't shining down too hard. I slid my body down, trying to find a comfortable position among the small rocks and coarse sand. There was a race in the skies and I watched the clouds move.

In the distance, I could hear three or four dogs barking at each other, one of them more high-pitched than the others. I thought of Terry and how I should have brought her to the park, but I also

knew Mom might want to have company around. I wondered if she
was up and whether she'd know I was gone.

The kernel of guilt in my chest expanded with every thought. I
tried to focus on the things I could see, hear or smell, to remain
in the moment, but this nagging feeling kept on pulling me back
into my head. I placed my hand on my chest and felt my heart
race, faster and faster until all I could make out was one continuous
thump.

The bird pecked closer, encroaching on my personal space.
It looked at me, cocked its head and pecked again. I sat up and
waved it away, but it came back and pecked closer. Was I giving off
a friendly vibe? My frustration grew. I wanted nothing more than to
whack the damn thing out of my sight. Instead, I got up and shooed
it away. The bird jumped a few paces backwards, waited and inched
forward again. That's when I lost my shit. I ran toward the asshole,
arms flailing. "Fuck you!" A runner passing by laughed at the scene.
I didn't appreciate having my anger mocked. My hands closed into
a fist and a familiar jolt coursed through my body. I yelled "What
the fuck are you looking at?" and for a split second I entertained the
possibility of getting on my bike and chasing him through the park
for a fight.

But I wasn't in London, and I couldn't come home bloodied and
bruised—it would be too hard to explain away. So instead, I took
a deep breath and marched furiously toward a tree at the edge of
the path. Without hesitation I punched it, once, twice, three times,
until my right and left knuckles were bloodied and dirty. A droplet
of sweat ran from the nape of my neck down my back. My hands
tingled and burned. I would tell my parents and brother I fell off
my bike. I looked back and saw the bird approach me again. The
fucker was mocking me, but I wasn't going to give it the satisfaction.
I got on my bike and pedalled home.

CHAPTER 19

Two nights before I headed back to London, I went out with Haru's friends. Anything felt better than staying at home. After an awkward dinner, Haru and I picked up Becca in the silver Toyota Camry he'd gotten for his eighteenth birthday, a few months back. I switched to the back seat when we got to Becca's house.

"Oh, hey." Becca slid into the passenger seat and faced Haru.

"Hey," I said, even though I knew she wasn't talking to me.

"Oh. You're coming too." She didn't look at the back seat. "That's great."

We drove through Stanley Park to Coal Harbour, where Grayson, one of Haru's friends from Collingwood, was hosting a party at his family's newest investment property—a 2400-square-foot condo at the Shangri-la. Though most owners had taken possession of the units in 2008, when construction was completed, the tower was largely uninhabited, which made it the ideal place for a party.

Haru, Becca and I rode the elevator to the forty-sixth floor in silence. As soon as the doors opened, she jumped off and headed in the direction of the apartment. It was clear they'd both been here before. I trailed behind them, regretting my decision to come after all. If there was anything I didn't need in my life, this was it—a lavish party for seventeen- and eighteen-year-olds in one of the most expensive buildings in Vancouver. I had avoided most parties when I was in school, and a part of me feared Collingwood students might be as cruel as the kids I went to high school with.

Haru and Becca stopped in front of door 4601 and knocked. Music seeped out into the corridor, and it was clear we would need more than a knock to get the attention of whoever was inside. Haru took out his phone as Becca stepped forward and tried the door-knob. The door opened to a large room with about twenty of Haru's friends. The apartment felt spacious and bright but also sterile, as if no one had ever intended to live in it. As we moved into the room, a boy about Haru's height walked toward us. His hair was blond and curly, and his eyes were a mix of blue and green. He wore a white Prada crew neck with jeans and held a bottle of Smirnoff Ice.

"Hey, man." He and Haru bumped fists. "Make yourselves at home."

"Thanks." Haru turned to me. "This is my sister, Aki, by the way."

"Welcome, welcome." Grayson extended his right hand. "Cold beers and Smirnoffs in the fridge. There's also a bar cart over there by the dining room."

Another boy made his way toward us. "There are also three rooms for more private entertainment." His jet-black hair obstructed part of his eyes.

"Lucas, don't be crass," Becca punched him in the arm. "Let's go get a drink, Haru." She grabbed my brother's arm and pulled him toward the kitchen.

I stood there, watching them walk away. Grayson opened his mouth to say something more—probably a gesture of awkward politeness—but before he made any sound I walked over to the floor-to-ceiling windows in the open-concept living room. Music in the apartment was loud and I had no desire to get to know any of Haru's friends. It was close to ten, and the only things visible were city lights against the backdrop of the harbour. I began to see our life in Vancouver, and by extension, my experience in London for what they were—examples of blissful ignorance and blatant privilege.

Two drunk teenagers bumped into me. I looked to my left, where I saw a door to a small empty balcony. I stepped out and closed the door behind me to create a physical distance between Haru's friends and myself, to be someone else. I wanted, needed, to be the outsider. This couldn't be my reality anymore.

I spent most of the evening on the balcony watching the city lights disappear as Vancouverites went to sleep. At around 1:30, Haru knocked on the glass door and gestured for me to come inside.

"We gotta go. Now." He looked flustered.

"Is everything all right?"

"Yeah, yeah. Becca is leaving."

"What do you mean she's leaving? Aren't we driving her home?"

"This girl was asking me about rugby, and Becca flipped. Anyway, we need to go now."

"Okay, okay."

"Hurry, she's already headed for the elevator. I gotta catch her before she leaves the building."

Haru rushed to the door, and I hurried behind him. Once we were inside the elevator, I asked him for his car keys.

"You can't drive, Haru. I can smell beer on you."

"I only had a few."

"I don't care—give me the keys or I'm calling Mom and Dad."

Haru threw the keys at me. "Fine. Why can't you ever be on my side?"

I wanted to be angry at Haru, but I saw the desperation in him, the fear of losing someone he cared for. I didn't like Becca, but I disliked seeing my brother in pain even more. "I'll drive you both home."

The elevator door opened to the lobby, where Becca stood pouting, tears streaming down her face. "You were totally flirting with her!"

"Baby, I'm so glad you're still here." Haru tried to hug her, but she hit his chest. "I'm sorry."

"Why do you do this to me?"

"There's no one else for me, Becca." He extended his arm, reaching out to her. Becca gave in.

"Let's go. I'm tired, and you both should get some sleep," I said, trying to remind them they weren't alone.

I led the way to the car, while Haru and Becca embraced and walked at the same time. Just as we turned to the street where the Camry was parked, we heard a commotion. Half a block over, two police officers yelled at a homeless man sleeping in a doorway. "Move!" They ripped the cardboard boxes the man had used to build a shelter. "You can't stay here." I stopped and turned toward them. The homeless man collected the remnants of his home from the ground.

"Aki!" Haru and Becca were standing next to me. "What are you doing?"

"Let's go, Haru." Becca pulled my brother. "Homeless people make me uncomfortable."

If it were possible to hate Becca more, I would have, but I was at my limit already. Stuck between who I thought I ought to be, and who I hoped I could one day become, I remained paralyzed. A coward. A silent witness to a crime no one cared about. I thought about the underage drinking taking place a couple of blocks away on the forty-sixth floor. I wanted to tell myself that if they knew, these police officers would have left this man alone to apprehend West Van's teenage elite. But that's not how justice works.

CHAPTER 20

I returned to London feeling drained and disconnected. When we were separated by continents and oceans, I could pretend the distance was only physical, but lying on my childhood bed, it had been hard to keep fooling myself.

The trip had reinforced my fear that I'd become bad, that despite whatever else I might do, I would never be enough again. I kept going over those thoughts, questioning what it meant to be a good person and whether there was any hope left for me, especially when I thought of the night at the Shangri-La. Why hadn't I tried to intervene when those two police officers harassed the homeless person? What good was fighting if I couldn't step in when it actually mattered?

A couple of days after my return, Abby convinced me to go to an Athletics' Union party for all the University of London colleges. I wasn't in the mood to go, especially since I had been suspended from the running team. Plus, it was all very heteronormative, and I felt I had a better chance of meeting someone at a random bar in Soho. But Abby wouldn't shut up about Lyam, a French guy she'd met a few months earlier she hoped to see him there. She didn't want to go by herself.

"I promise, there will be plenty of women there."

"Gay women?"

"Come on, please! I know someone I can introduce you to."

"I know enough women." Abby's expression made her opinion clear. "Can't you get Ginika to go with you? Someone, you know, that's actually in a team."

"She's going to spend the whole night with Kwaku. I need some emotional support." Abby adjusted her black sequined dress, pulling it up to show off her legs. Once she was satisfied, she cocked her head from one side to the other in front of the mirror, using her fingers and some product to create volume in her very straight, dirty blond hair. "Please?"

"Fine, but I reserve the right to leave after the first hour."

"Thank you, thank you," she said jumping up and down. "If all else fails, there's always the rugby team."

I threw one of her pillows at her. "I hope you're joking. Those girls scare me."

We took almost an hour to make our way to the party, on account of Abby's choice of footwear. Even though the heels she had on made her just slightly taller than me, they were also unstable and she had used my arm for support most of the way. Wanting to get back to the residence as soon as possible, I devised a plan.

"So here's how this is going to go . . ."

"Okay, okay. You sound so official."

I rolled my eyes. "When we get there, you will look for your Frenchman. I will get us drinks and find you."

"Can I have something with vodka?"

"Abby! Let me get this out." Abby pretended to zip her mouth. I took a deep breath. "I will meet said Frenchman and ask him an appropriate number of questions to make sure he isn't a creep. Once I've been able to ascertain that, I will head home. Okay?"

"Fine, fine. But once you meet my friend, you're not going to want to leave!"

As expected, we arrived fashionably late, three hours after the venue had opened. By then, the abandoned Gothic church where the party was taking place was overpacked. So much so, it took me twenty minutes just to reach the first-floor bar. When I found Abby, she was with a woman instead.

"Aki!" She waved at me over excitedly. I sensed she was up to no good and considered walking in the opposite direction, but we'd made eye contact. Plus, the person she was with had started to look in my direction too. I navigated my way through the crowd, trying to spill as little of our drinks as possible. When I was within reach, Abby pulled me in, undoing my whole balancing act. Half of the contents of one of the cups splashed on the floor by my feet.

"Aki, there's someone I want you to meet. She's on my netball team." Abby grabbed me and the woman by the arm.

"Hi, I'm Patience." The woman extended a hand. She was a few inches taller than me with light brown eyes, a face painted with freckles, and front teeth that overlapped a little. Her curly hair was half-braided in a ponytail. Compared to Abby, she looked underdressed, in jeans and a white T-shirt.

"Hi." I offered my wrist since I was still holding the two drinks. "Aki."

"You guys should talk," Abby said grabbing her cranberry vodka. "You have a lot in common." Before leaving us to find her Frenchman, she pointed to Patience and mouthed, "Gay."

Patience studied sociology, or maybe it was anthropology. I couldn't hear much of what she was saying. After an hour of screaming over the music, we both agreed it was too loud and decided to go outside for a bit. Walking in circles around the club, Patience, who was half-Jamaican, half-English, told me about how her biological dad had left her mom after discovering she was pregnant because he didn't want a half-Black child. She talked at length about how she loved her stepfather, but how she'd always been curious to confront the man who'd abandoned her. Since moving to London from Hastings she'd tracked him down. Many times, she'd wanted to reach out, but she hadn't built up the courage yet. "I don't know what I'd say. I don't know what I'd want out of it. I just know that I want something."

Of all the people that I'd come across since moving to London, Patience was the farthest removed from the world I'd grown up in. I learned that night she'd never travelled outside of England, let alone the U.K. She didn't speak other languages, like Ginika and Abby. She was at LSE on a needs-based scholarship and worked three days a week as a receptionist in a health clinic to supplement her income. She lived in a rundown flat with three other roommates.

For all our differences, Patience, like me, was discovering herself. She knew about the dangers of sticking out. "I know what you mean. Growing up Christian, it's hard to reconcile my faith with who I'm attracted to." She slowed down and looked at me. "You know, apart from Abby and a couple of people on my netball team, no one else knows."

"Not even your LSE friends?"

"Not really. I'm afraid if I start telling people, somehow it will slip to my parents. My mom and stepdad don't know I like women, and I need it to stay that way." She paused. "I mean, at least for now."

Talking to Patience felt easy, like I didn't have to explain myself over and over again. I felt seen and heard for the first time in a long time. Perhaps I was just the closest gay around, but I think she appreciated talking to someone who understood what it meant to be the nail that stuck out. We talked about the things that made sense to us, like the importance of family and humility, but also what we struggled to understand, like how it felt our stories were predetermined by rules we hadn't agreed to. Being with her, I felt like a good person.

It was early morning when I walked Patience to her bus stop. She lived in Brixton, a south London neighbourhood with a reputation for street violence. I offered to pay for a cab, but she insisted the night bus would be fine.

Ginika, Abby and I were too drunk to walk home, so we took the tube. When we got off at Goodge Street, the KFC near the station was closing—a woman a few years older than me was taking out a large, clear bag with day-old fried chicken and chips and three homeless men were arguing about who would get first pick.

"Ooo ooo, I feel like chicken." Abby tripped and nearly fell on her face.

"No, you don't." Ginika pushed her forward, in the direction of our residence.

I looked back at the homeless men. They were arguing loudly, cursing each other while pulling the plastic bag until it tore open. Chicken and chips fell to the ground and they rushed to grab it. I wanted to stop staring but couldn't.

"Aki! What are you doing? We need to get Abby back to her room. The bitch is fading!"

I shook my head and ran across the street less than a second before the light turned red. Ahead of me, I watched Ginika hold up Abby, who stumbled down the street. I looked back one more time. The three men were partially lit by the KFC sign. I had this feeling in my gut like I was dropping a few feet in the air.

CHAPTER 21

"Are you all right, Aki?" Ginika and I were stretching at the foot of the stairs leading to the main entrance of our residence. Conversations with my friends seemed to have become a routine daily check-in on my mental health.

"Yeah, I'm good." I switched legs, holding up my left foot behind my back.

"You've been awfully quiet. Even more than usual."

"Just a lot going on in my head, I guess."

"I'm here you know, if you need to talk."

I gave Ginika a tight smile. "Let's go. I need to get back in an hour."

Ginika and Abby still held me to the same routine: workouts in the morning, breakfast together, then the walk to LSE. Our friendship was the thread that tethered me to a semblance of normal student life but I couldn't help but resent them a little for not looking the other way.

They must have felt Patience was a positive influence on me because she became a regular at our dining hall, with invitations to come back night after night. I hadn't made up my mind yet whether I wanted to pursue anything more than a friendship, so our interactions became big question marks, balancing between harmless flirtation and sexual innuendo.

Patience introduced me to Brixton and a different side of London, a side that was vibrantly different from the drab grey I was accustomed to. She took me to places in Zone 2 and 3. We ate at a Trinidadian roti shop near Willesden Junction. We studied at the Peckham Library before going to a Black hairdresser where Patience had her hair braided. We went grocery shopping in Brixton Village Market. All the times I'd visited London, and since starting at LSE, I'd never left Zone 1. It had never occurred to me to do so. Why would I? According to my parents, leaving Zone 1 would be like getting a glimpse of the London no one wanted to see. Why had I allowed them to tell me what I should and should not see?

For perhaps the first time in my life I saw how wealth and privilege didn't necessarily translate into control. Patience was free, and I was still learning what freedom meant. Patience breathed life into a city that was beginning to lose its colour to me. With her, my world began to expand again, just like it had when I left West Vancouver. And as I allowed her to take centre-stage in my story, our friendship evolved too.

At the beginning of May, the four of us planned a visit to a pub Ginika had been hankering to try near where Abby and Patience would be playing netball. We agreed to meet near Liverpool Street Station. I left the residence at five o'clock and, wanting to avoid rush hour crossed Russell Square and walked down Southampton Row to catch the No. 8 bus on Procter Street.

I climbed to the upper deck and took a seat a couple of rows behind a couple of skinheads in oversized hoodies mocking the passenger in front of them. "Can. You. Understand. Me?"

The old man shook his head, waving his hand as if to say, "No, thank you. I'm not interested."

"Of course, he can't understand you. Look at him! He's not from here," his friend chimed in, arm raised, pointing a finger down over the top of the old man's head.

When the person sitting right behind these two yobs got up and went downstairs, I moved closer. The reflection in the bus window revealed that the old man was Asian. He had a square face with thick lips and round, dark-rimmed glasses, was neatly dressed in a button-down shirt with a navy sweater on top, and smelled like cabbage and daikon, just like Ojiichan did on Sunday mornings.

When the old man pressed the button for the bus to stop, one of the skinheads got to his feet and blocked the aisle. The old man half got up, gesturing with both hands for the young man next to him to move. "Excuse me." The old man's accent was thick. The young man didn't budge. "Excuse me," he tried again.

"I. Can't. Understand. You," the young man yelled. He and his friends laughed.

The bus came to a stop near St. Paul's. The young man continued to stare the old man down while the rest of the passengers sat in uncomfortable silence. I stood up and pushed the yob in front of me. He fell backwards, landing awkwardly on an empty seat diagonal to him.

"What the fuck!" he shouted. A middle-aged Black woman sitting nearby gasped and held her purse to her chest, gesturing to her children to look away.

"Look at her," one of his friends said. "She's his bastard grandchild."

I extended my hand to the old man, pulling him toward the aisle then pushed him ahead of me, using my body as a shield. Once he was past them, he let go of my hand and rushed down the steps.

I needed to get off the bus too. These three men were exactly the types to escalate the situation. As I turned to leave, a large hand shoved me from behind. My head jerked and my right cheek hit a metal bar, hard. I fell to my knees, and as I tried to straighten my back I saw a droplet of blood fall on the metal floor.

"How did you like that, cunt? Getting hit out of nowhere?"

I turned to face him. "As much as I liked you intimidating that man." I tensed my jaw, closing my right fist. The bus began to move. I lurched forward, using my lack of balance to my advantage and drove my fist into a torso. I could smell the stale beer on his hoodie. Someone screamed.

I raced down the stairs made for the area near the driver reserved for strollers and wheelchairs. As soon as we reached the next stop, I started running, in case the hoodies were coming after me. By the time I got to Liverpool Street Station, I was nearly half an hour late. Patience was the first to spot me. She smiled and waved, but as I got closer, I could see their expressions change.

"Oh my God, Aki!" Ginika ran up to me before I reached them.

"What the fuck happened?" Abby took my arm.

Patience stood a few steps back. "You're bleeding, Aki."

"I'm sorry I'm late—"

"Who the fuck cares?" Abby seemed exasperated.

"It's really nothing. I just fell on the bus and hit my face on one of those metal poles." At least there was some truth to that.

"Maybe we should sit down." Patience pointed to a bench under a large sign.

"Really, I'm fine." I wiped my face to show the blood was dry. "I'll just go clean myself up in the bathroom and we'll be on our way."

I followed the signs to the toilets across the station but heard Ginika say behind me. "We should just go home, right?"

I returned a few minutes later with a fresh-ish face. I'd tied my hair back in a ponytail, and though my right cheek was swollen, there was no more blood. Before any of them could say anything, I walked toward the exit to Bishopsgate, leading them out of the station. Once outside, Ginika took over, leading us up and down narrow streets until we came to a small bistro-like pub lit by warm, yellow lights.

Patience scanned the menu posted by the door. "I thought you said we were going to a pub, Abby."

Peering in, I could see that calling this a pub was a bit of a stretch. All tables had linens and there were no bar seats.

"Is this not a pub?" Ginika moved closer to the door to see the menu. "Ooo, sign me up for the Pan-Seared Steak with Garlic Butter!"

"It's £35!" Patience waved emphatically at the menu. "Am I the only one that thinks that's absurd?"

Abby said, "I can spot you. It's all right." She reached for Patience's arm, but Patience recoiled.

"That's not the point, Abby!" She walked away from the door. "What am I even doing spending time with you? Our worlds are clearly so different."

Abby and Ginika looked at each other, unsure how to respond.

I tried to fill the silence—awkward Aki to the rescue. "Did you know that pub is short for public house, meaning a drinking establishment that is quite literally open to the public—no memberships allowed."

"What?" All three of them looked at me, confused. Abby laughed. "You're so weird, dude."

Ginika shook her head lightly, but Patience stuck to her guns. "Pricing can be an indirect way of maintaining this idea of membership, so this is clearly not a pub."

She had a point. "What do you say, Patience? Lead the way to a real pub?"

Patience resisted a smile, but slowly the corners of her mouth bent upwards. "I guess as the only British person here, I best educate you then."

"Have you ever been called a bastard?" I was lying on the carpet in my residence room the Saturday after the fight on the bus. Despite my attempts at distracting myself, the episode had really stuck with me. I'd never experienced that kind of overt racism before. In my private school bubble, wealth, if you had enough of it, was more important than race.

"What?" Patience was sitting on the chair by my desk, browsing the music I'd downloaded on my laptop, creating a playlist for the evening.

I sat up. "Someone called me a bastard on the bus, because I look kind of, but not really, Asian."

"As someone who actually is a bastard child, I wouldn't care too much about random people on the bus." She made her way to the carpet next to me.

I looked at Patience, at the colourful birds printed on her T-shirt. To be a bastard meant to be impure, debased, to be less in value. That definition was the antithesis of her. My room phone rang. Reception had my delivery order—vegetarian fried rice with some bok choy for me and sweet and sour chicken on egg noodles for her.

We ate with our backs resting on the side of my bed watching *When Harry Met Sally*, which I'd downloaded from the internet. She had never seen it before. After the movie, she turned to me and said, "What a white, unrelatable movie for a queer brown person!"

I hadn't foreseen the criticism. "What do you mean?"

"Come on, Aki. Show me one brown person in the whole movie. One!"

I tried to think back to the scenes we'd just watched. There was none.

"Show me one queer person. One!"

There wasn't anyone either.

"For someone who's so concerned about being called a bastard, you should really focus on what you can control. Why watch these movies that weren't made for you or me?"

"I don't know," I said tentatively. I didn't know, and that made me utterly uncomfortable. Here I was thinking London had helped me be in control of my narrative. I'd been telling myself I no longer allowed my parents to drive my story, but my mind was still moulded to someone else's standards. What else could I not see?

I must have been lost in thought for a while, because Patience's next comment came at me out of nowhere. "When did you know you were ready, you know, for sex?" She'd moved a bit further away, but I could still feel her warmth.

I cocked my head to the right. "I'm not sure I did. It just happened."

"Do you think I'm ready?" Her voice was soft, almost a whisper. I knew Patience was a virgin but I didn't expect her to be so forward about it, especially since we hadn't kissed yet.

"That's a question I can't answer for you."

Patience looked at the window, then at me. She fidgeted with the hem of her T-shirt. "I think I'd like to try it." She leaned in. Her lips were dry but tender. I could feel her uneven breathing. I leaned in harder and took control, slowing the pace. Patience relaxed into me.

Sex with her was slow and tender. There was some pain, but she said it was bearable, even when her face scrunched up. There was also surprise. Patience had never had an orgasm, and as her body stiffened then relaxed, her eyes widened in astonishment.

I felt conflicted. I wanted to fall in love with Patience—she was beautiful and kind and seemed ready and willing to share her world with me. But no matter how much I tried, I couldn't shake the thought of Ayesha. I didn't deserve Patience's affection, and it was only a matter of time before she realized it.

Still, with Patience, my life seemed to get back on track. I made an effort to attend every class, every lecture. I did my readings and started a small study group. I also ate better, slept more, hung out with my friends. I even convinced the running team to let me practice again, though I still wasn't allowed to compete. And I didn't pick any fights. It was the closest I'd felt to me in a long time.

CHAPTER 22

The next morning, I awoke to Patience watching me sleep. I arched my neck back, looking up at the window. It couldn't be past seven o'clock. "Are you okay?" I mumbled, rolling toward her.

"On Sundays, I go to church." She paused and looked at the wall of pictures behind me. "Do you want to come with me today?"

I tensed. Church? During a visit to Colombia and my *abuela* was still alive, she'd demanded that Mom send Haru and me to catechism. "Do you want your children to go to hell?" she asked in a loud voice.

"Hell is not a place; it's a state of mind," Mom had whispered to us, a half-smile on her face. She'd been raised Catholic but considered herself an atheist. They argued for days until Mom finally relented. To spite my grandmother, however, she chose a Christian fundamentalist church. "There are many ways to win an argument, *mis hijos*," Mom told us the first Saturday. Once a week for a month, we drove thirty minutes through a quiet residential neighbourhood to a two-storey concrete house painted yellow. My mind, half-awake, would count the parked cars on our drive there: 345, 346, 347.

Sunday School made me anxious, like I was being carefully watched and graded against a rubric that wasn't clear to me. It wasn't that I couldn't memorize the verses or that I didn't know the answers. I was afraid of calling attention, embarrassing my family, making my mom look bad. I had no desire to be the top student in the class, but I knew the danger of being labelled the quiet kid, the one who needed prodding to speak. I did the bare minimum and flew just under the radar.

Of all the things that made me uncomfortable in Bible study, what terrified me the most were the aura readings. At the end of every session, our instructor, a short, balding man in his forties, lined us up by age and called out the colour of our souls. If you were a good Christian, if you prayed often and committed no sins, your aura would be golden yellow. If you forgot to pray every once in a while, if you weren't always good to your parents or your siblings, but you wanted to do better, your aura would be grey. But if you were a bad Christian, if you committed sins and didn't repent for them, your aura would be black.

Even though I wasn't a Christian, I worried a black soul would put my mother's parenting skills under scrutiny. Despite projecting indifference at every criticism my grandmother threw at her, I knew she cared about what people thought of her, especially Abuela. I knew a black soul would mean Mom would be blamed for leaving Colombia and her parents, but most importantly for being a bad mother and not raising her children as Christians. I wanted nothing more than to show her I was on her side, to prove to her how much I loved our family and how perfect we could be.

The mentor called out the colours loudly as he walked down the room. Every week, standing halfway down the line, I looked at Mom and felt my whole body shake in anticipation. *Please, not black. Anything but black.* I held my breath as he called out my colour. "Yellow!" Once my turn was over, I relaxed. I had passed another week; we'd fooled them again.

"It's okay if you don't want to. I won't be offended."

Church was my *abuela*'s rigid Catholic belief system. Church was where bad auras materialized. Church was my mother saying gays would burn in hell. Surely, Patience's church couldn't be much different. "No, no, no." I stopped, worried I'd said too many nos. "I would love to," I said slowly, pronouncing every syllable.

Patience smiled and nestled her head against my shoulder. I held her tight, maybe too tightly because she eventually wiggled away.

Patience's church was in East London, forty-five minutes away. I let her lead the way, first on the tube, then on the bus, not paying attention to where we were going, too preoccupied with the thought of being met by the same anger and disappointment my mother had shown me in the past few months. Patience talked and talked, describing the previous week's sermon and explaining how she'd found this church by accident while running errands. I half listened and nodded, while I read a series of texts from Mom about the swine flu, how she'd stocked up on Tamiflu and would send me some, and how I should not leave my room in the meantime. On the bus, I saw people who looked like they might be going to church, the dressed-up kind, and imagined how they might react if I showed up at their place of worship.

When we arrived, I was surprised to see that it didn't look like a church, but more like an old two-storey office building, with a reception area on the ground floor. A small group of people gathered outside—young families and couples, only a few people in their sixties or older. We entered through the front glass door, and Patience nodded to a few people before we took the stairs at the back to the second floor where there was a large open space with a small stage and a podium at the front. Metal folding chairs were set up in long rows that went to the back of the room.

Patience chose two middle seats in the third row. I would have preferred something at the back, where I could make a quick, discreet exit, if necessary, but I couldn't say that to her. The room filled slowly. A young family sat next to us. I wiped my sweaty palms on my trousers and straightened my shirt.

"You look good," Patience said. "Don't worry." She touched my leg with her knee and smiled.

Pastor David was a tall white man in his thirties, with a soft voice and an unrelenting smile. His sermon was about acceptance, or at least the parts that I could focus on were. My mind was still anxious, running through scenarios where our little excursion didn't go well.

"And let us consider how we may spur one another on toward love and good deeds, not giving up meeting together, as some are in the habit of doing, but encouraging one another—and all the more as you see the Day approaching. Hebrews 10:24-25." Pastor David read from the Bible, looking up intermittently at his congregation. I looked around, searching people's faces for a reaction to his words, while Patience stared ahead, unaware of or ignoring my gaze.

When the service was over, she told me to wait while she went up and greeted a few people she knew. I folded a pamphlet the family had left on a seat, making it first into a boat, then a frog. My dad had taught me origami, and once how to make a female crane, the body fuller, the wings smaller, than the typical male one everyone knows. I unfolded the paper one last time and tried to remember the steps, but it had become fragile after being transformed into one too many things and ripped.

"What are you making?" a child asked me. I looked up at a boy no older than five standing a few feet away from me. His curly blond hair bounced as he shifted the weight of his legs back and forth, his green eyes transfixed by my hands. I looked around, but couldn't see his parents.

"Well, I was trying to make a crane, but the paper ripped."

"Can you make an airplane? I know how to make an airplane."

"Charlie, don't run off like that!" Out from a group of people standing at the far right of the room, a woman in her mid-thirties marched in our direction. She was carrying a large bag and pushing a stroller with a baby in it.

"It's all right. Everyone here knows him." Another woman said, right behind the first.

"Still, I have to teach your son to not wander off like that. What if he does it in a place where people don't know him?"

"My son? I thought he was ours." The second woman touched her partner's hand and smiled. Then, she approached Charlie and kneeled down to his level. "Don't run off, okay?"

I sat there in shock. I had constructed this idea of what going to church would be like, who I would meet there. I had sat through the sermon watching the congregation intently, and in my anxiety, I had missed so much. I looked around and saw other queer people, churchgoers. Maybe there was a place where I didn't stick out, a place where it was enough just to be me.

"It's an inclusive church, Aki," Patience said when I asked her about it on the way home.

"Inclusive as in . . ."

"Inclusive as in the pastor is gay."

"Oh," I replied attempting to connect the dots in my head.

We went together the next Sunday. The experience certainly wasn't negative, but it still didn't feel like the place for me. I wasn't Christian and I didn't see myself becoming one, though I appreciated being welcomed and accepted in a place I'd only ever expected the worst from. After a couple of weeks of excuses, Patience stopped asking if I wanted to come along.

My excuses weren't entirely fictitious. Finals season had started at LSE. My degree, like most others, relied on essay-based exams that accounted for 100% of my final grade. As a first-year student, it felt like a lot of pressure to put on this one day, but no one else around me seemed to complain, and I didn't want my friends to think I was any less able to hold my own, so I stayed quiet. Like most other students, I was most of my time at the LSE library. The spiral stepped ramps were sometimes so congested it might take three minutes to go between floors, instead of the usual thirty seconds. Even the usually deserted rooftop dome, my favourite part of the library, was busy, and the light-filled atrium had become packed with people taking breaks or squeezing in a quick bite.

Patience, as a second-year, had already gone through the process once, although, because of her dyslexia, she took her exams separately from her cohort and on a special computer. Still, she was the second-top student in her class. She confirmed what others had told me: the trick was to come in really early (or late if you had been out the night before), put a few things down, go eat and start working around 7:00 a.m.

A group of us sat together and took turns going out for lunch at Pret A Manger or the Starbucks nearby. In the afternoon, the crowd would intensify, and latecomers would circle the library floor like vultures, waiting for an exhausted early-riser to leave. When my friends left around eight or nine, I stayed and waited for Patience, often walking up and down the ramps and through the metal stacks making note of how many books had been taken out and how many were still left.

Patience liked studying through the night and I could function on two or three hours of sleep, so it was the perfect combination. We would grab a quick bite somewhere near LSE, often at a Sainsbury or Tesco, eat on one of the stone benches outside the library, and return to our seats around 11:00 p.m. By then most people had left, and the few that stayed snored, sometimes in sleeping bags under the desks they'd reserved for fear of losing their study space the next day.

Most nights, Patience and I worked solidly for three hours before taking a break. We left the library around 2:00 a.m. and walked through a deserted London. These strolls made me miss Lighthouse Park, and the walks we took as a family on Saturday afternoons. At night, with Patience, it was hard to ignore the pain of my parents' emotional and physical distance. I tried to imagine what they might be doing, eight hours behind in Vancouver—Dad might be at a business meeting, and Mom would be out with her friends. London felt melancholic at night, like I'd be perpetually yearning for a happiness that wouldn't return or that perhaps was never there to begin with.

Patience and I often ended up strolling through the cobblestone-lined streets of Covent Garden, talking about how we'd been raised—what we believed in, what we weren't so sure about. I asked her whether she thought her family would be okay with her coming out. Patience was not ready yet to tell her mom and stepdad, though she considered it at times. I wondered if I would be considering the same thing, had my own family not already found out.

"My brother would be fine with it, I think. And I'm sure my parents would be too." We sat on the curb by a pub on Covent Garden Square. A streetlight illuminated Patience's freckled face, but around us the buildings were dark.

"Then what's stopping you?"

She picked at her bracelet, flicking each coloured bead at her wrist. "I guess I'm scared. At the end of the day, I don't know how exactly they will react." She turned to me and paused. "They're all I have."

As finals loomed, Patience suggested a visit to the National Gallery. She said we needed a break from studying, and that relaxing might help us focus better. I wasn't too fond of the idea—I hadn't been to a museum or gallery since Ayesha—but she was insistent.

Pollen floated around me in menacing clouds, but I took another Claritin and waited for Patience in Covent Garden. After a quick lunch at a bakery, we walked down to Trafalgar Square, stopping at Snog, a small frozen yogurt shop, on the way. I was teasing her about netball—"It's basically basketball and handball combined. Just pick one!"—and she surprised me by not countering. I looked at Patience and was surprised at the panic in her eyes. "What's wrong?"

Without answering, she pulled me into New Row. "Patience, what is it? What's going on?" She didn't answer, speeding up and pulling me by the arm. When she had finally outrun what she'd seen, we stopped and stared at each other.

"That was my stepdad. I didn't know he was in town." Her tone was painfully familiar. Being pulled into an alley was better than being shoved into a closet, but not by much. I watched the frozen yogurt melt, unable to take a single bite, while Patience walked alongside me in silence. The National Gallery was nearly empty, and our footsteps echoed. We walked for half an hour, maybe less, without attempting conversation. Then I faked a headache and went home.

I knew it was over. I started to study in my room when I could, and found a desk tucked away on the third floor of the library that I could use when I needed course books. A couple of nights later, after an unproductive session with Plato's *Republic*, I itched with anxiety and had to get out of my room. I'd lost both Ayesha and Patience, and the idea that I could make my parents proud and still be true to myself became more ludicrous by the day.

Morning was threatening to come when I found myself outside Tower Hill station at 5:00 a.m. A couple of drunken men mistook me for easy prey. I shot them down before they even had a chance to say anything and, when one of them reached for me, I took it as permission to speak the language of violence. A blow across the first one's face. A kick to the back of the other's knee. Three, four, five consecutive punches to the first one's stomach, until he was left retching. And a knee to his friend's chin. Less than ten minutes was all it took to bring the two to their knees.

The fighting intensified. Outside a bathroom in a packed club. Under a viaduct south of the river. Every night, I went out. Every night, I came home with more bruises. I stopped caring whether Abby, Ginika or anyone else saw the cuts and scratches.

"Aki, what's wrong with your knuckles!" Abby was looking at my hands at the dining table.

"I don't know," I said nonchalantly. "I guess I must have hurt them."

My friends looked at each other. Here it comes, I thought.

"Aki," Ginika paused. "Should we be worried?"

"About this?" I raised my fists up to my face, my knuckles facing them. "It will heal."

By Sunday, six nights in, my body felt broken. I knew I needed to stop, but only the fighting made me feel in control. Still, with each brawl, with each blow, the release I felt was diminished. Like an addict, I became trapped by the things I wanted but couldn't have. Chasing a high that would never come. Doing the maximum to ensure the minimum release. Afraid of what might become of me if I didn't.

One evening, in an attempt to avoid Abby and Ginika, I took a solitary walk to Covent Garden I walked slowly from our residence, making my way in and out of alleyways, up and down narrow streets, hoping for something that would keep my mind and body satiated. I was a few blocks from the station when I spotted a man pissing next to a homeless man near a large dumpster behind a restaurant.

"Hey! What the fuck do you think you're doing?" I quickened my pace. He turned to me, as he continued to pee. "Stop that! Can't you see someone's sleeping there?"

"Who cares?" the man slurred his words. "He's just a dosser."

I charged forward, hitting his left side with full force. The man wiped out; I fell on top of him with a thud. Before he had a chance to rise, I got up and kicked him in the groin. Once, twice, three times. The homeless man, now awake, scrabbled for his dirty shopping bags and fled.

"Stop! Please stop," the drunken man pleaded, but I couldn't stop. I kept on kicking until I heard my name.

"Aki!" A familiar voice. I turned. A figure stepped into the alleyway. My eyes adjusted to the streetlamp shining in my direction. "Aki, is that you?"

The man shuffled underneath me, crawling away.

"Patience?"

"What the hell is going on?"

"What are you doing here?" She lived nowhere near here.

"I'm meeting my stepdad for dinner. He's in town again for work." She paused. "Aki . . . what the fuck!" Patience gestured to where the man had been on the ground, trying to process what she'd just witnessed.

"I better leave then. Wouldn't want him seeing me with you," I said bitterly. I walked in circles, hands to my head. Patience shouldn't have been here. This wasn't meant to happen. Why did she have to walk through this alley?

"Aki, you're scaring me." Patience reached her arms out to me. I stepped back.

"You should go." I tightened my jaws and took a deep breath.

"I, I am . . ." She looked around. There was no one in the alley but us.

"Just go!"

Patience hurried away. I closed my eyes. The streetlamp turned darkness into a solid wall of orange. I opened my eyes slowly.

Patience tried to reach me all the next day. She called, texted and even left voice messages. "Aki, please, please talk to me." "Why are you like this? Why can't you let me in?" "I have to tell someone what I saw. Aki, call me back."

She tracked me down at the library, just after midnight. "Can I sit?" she said gesturing to the empty chair next to me. I nodded, even though I didn't want to.

She looked intently at her hands, then mine, and struggled to make eye contact. Maybe she had come here to make sure things were over, but we both knew they were.

"I don't get it, Aki," she started. "These last couple of months have been good. I mean, I've had fun." She fiddled with a piece of paper in front of her, one of my essay outlines.

"It's okay," I said, looking at the books in front of me. "I know what you want to say, and I'm cool with it."

"What the fuck happened in that alley? What the fuck happened that night you showed up with a busted cheek?" She paused. "Aki, look at me."

I turned my face. Pools of water collected on her lower lids. "I don't know what you want from me." There weren't many people in the library at this hour, but I hated making a scene, even to a small audience.

"How about some honesty? What is going on with you? I feel like I don't even know who you are." She reached out for my hand, but I recoiled.

"You don't." I stared at her.

"I can't do this." She looked down.

My heart tightened, but I keep any emotion out of my voice. "Okay." I turned back to my books and picked up a pen.

Patience got up and straightened her T-shirt. Then, she leaned closer, "I thought you were a good person. I guess I was wrong."

She didn't look back as she walked to the elevator. Her words echoed inside my head. I remembered the words my parents had said to me over the last few months. I recalled every moment of inadequacy, of what felt like failure. My breath quickened. A sinking feeling and then the sounds around me muffled. My vision blurred and I fell sideways, to the floor. I felt my head hit a table leg. Someone rushed toward me. I saw fuzzy legs and feet.

"Aki! Dude, are you okay?" Abby's voice sounded distant. "Help! Someone, help!" Then the world went black.

CHAPTER 23

I didn't leave my room for the next five days. Occasionally, I tried to get out of bed, and I thought about clean clothes, but it didn't seem to matter. Not enough to do anything about it.

By the third day, I started to smell myself, a mix of sleep and built-up sweat, but even then, I couldn't force myself to hop in the shower. Some days I managed to roll over and pick up a book, and for a moment or two I would remember exams and the life that lay outside my door. Abby and Ginika came by once or twice a day, bringing food from the dining hall. They sat on the floor, near my bed, for fifteen minutes, maybe less, often without saying a word. I hardly touched anything—the plates lined up next to each other on my desk, the food on them became crusty, then hard. I saw they wanted to help me get better, but this kind of healing wasn't in their experience.

On the sixth day, my friends convinced me to see a counsellor at LSE.

"Dude, you really need to talk to someone. Bottling things up is not healthy." The three of us sat on the floor in the residence room.

I thought I caught a glimpse of Ginika rolling her eyes. "Aki, unlike Abby here, I am not a big proponent of therapy, but you're clearly struggling."

"I'll get over it."

Abby reached for my arm. "We know, but it's okay to need help."

"Just try it? Please?" I'd never heard Ginika talk so softly to anyone.

"If I go, can we stop talking about this?"

"Yes! We can talk about anything you want, dude."

They left me on a plastic bench in the Student Services Centre. Ten minutes later, a short, stocky blond woman in her mid-forties appeared and gestured for me to follow her. She guided me to her office, past the service counter. The space was small—only big enough to fit a desk and two chairs, one on each side. There was nothing personal here—not a photo of her family, a drawing by a child, or even coloured pens. The only decoration on her desk was a small metal plate that read "Olivia Acton, counsellor."

I'd done the bare minimum to leave the house—put a hoodie over my pajama top and switched my bottoms for some black sweatpants from my almost-ready-to-wash laundry hamper. The metal chair in Olivia's office was made of aluminum and the cold penetrated my back and sent shivers up my spine. She moved some papers on the desk, in search of my file, I assumed. In the meantime, I surveyed the outside through the glass walls of her office. This really wasn't an ideal place to have a private conversation. But if I managed to get through forty-five minutes of this, that would get my friends off my back, at least for the next little while.

I'd rehearsed what I was going to say. Something about how I was still working through my parents' response to my coming out, how I'd just ended a relationship. Specific enough to satisfy the sharing threshold, but nothing too personal. But, to my surprise, when Olivia finally looked up from her desk and at me, she didn't ask how I was doing. She just plunged right in.

"Your friends have come forward," she said in what I thought was a northern accent, maybe Mancunian. "They are concerned about your well-being."

"Okay . . . ?" I was uncertain of how to respond to Olivia's statement. I couldn't imagine my friends walking up to the SSC to complain to a counsellor about me. Could she be bluffing? Then again, I'd been acting weird for the last few months. Maybe they had.

"Do you know what time of the year it is right now?"

"June?"

"And what's happening in June?"

I shrugged. I didn't appreciate Olivia's tone. I felt like I was being talked down to and reprimanded for something.

"Exams, Aki. We are in the middle of exams." I hadn't noticed the overall nasality of her pronunciation, or that she omitted the "h" at the beginning of words. She was definitely not from London.

"Okay . . .?"

"Do you think this is a game?" Olivia tapped the end of a black Bic pen on the glass top of her desk.

"No, I'm just confused. I am not sure what you're trying to get at. If anything, it's you who's quizzing me like we're playing Trivial Pursuit."

"Funny one, aren't we?" Olivia's face contorted into a fake smile.

"Okay. I'm done here. Can you just cut the crap? Just tell me what you want me to say and we can cut the session short."

"People like you are so entitled."

I felt my cheeks flush in anger. I got up and grabbed my backpack off the floor. "I don't need to listen to this bullshit."

Olivia raised her voice. I looked outside and saw a few people peer in. "It's exam time and your friends need to focus on their work. Instead, they are worrying about you."

My heart raced faster and faster and I fought the urge to break all of my basic fighting rules. I turned to face away from Olivia and reached out for the doorknob. "You're a shitty counsellor," I said before twisting it open.

I heard Olivia's chair move and assumed she got up, but I didn't look back to check. "You are making everyone's life harder! Think about that," she called after me. I rushed out of the SSC onto Houghton Street.

Outside, it was lunchtime rush hour. A group of people from my Econ B class walked out of the Old Building and nodded at me, while arguing about their answers to a mock exam. "You're over-simplifying Keynes," one of them said.

Who the fuck cares about Keynes?

I stood, immovable, the counsellor's words replaying in my head. Had my friends told Olivia I was making their lives harder? And if they felt so, why not just say it to my face? I contemplated buying a ticket to a place far away and never looking back. That might solve everyone's problems.

Students pushed past me in all directions. The crowd encircled me, and I felt the air get thinner, harder to breathe. I don't know how long I stood there but at some point I heard my name, then a gentle tap on my shoulder. Patience was an arm's length away. "Aki, I've been trying to reach you." I looked around. Where had she come from? "Do you have some time now? Can we talk?"

I thought of the night at the library and how my world had turned hazy, then black. I thought about her words. "There's nothing to talk about," I said, pushing her aside and walking into the crowd.

I retreated back into my residence room, avoiding everyone, but Olivia Acton's words kept circling through my head. At first, I was angry—angry at her, angry at Abby and Ginika for ratting me out. If they didn't want to be around, I could fucking manage on my own. I needed no one. But the more I thought about it, the more I thought Ms. Acton wasn't wrong.

Olivia was not a good counsellor. Delivery, awful, but not entirely dismissible. For the past six months I'd caused so much harm. I'd hurt people. Not just emotionally, but physically. I'd disappointed my parents, I hadn't supported Haru when he needed me, I'd betrayed and hurt Ayesha. I'd used Sana, I'd pushed away Patience, and now I'd let down my friends, burdened them with all the things I couldn't cope with myself. I couldn't think of one person who was better off for knowing me. That was it. I was toxic. Something had to change.

I was lost in thought, considering the ways I could redeem myself, when Haru called. He was sobbing, gabbling, and the crying made it hard to understand what he was saying. All I could hear was Becca's name, repeated over and over again.

I sat up on the bed and looked at the time. It was just after eleven o'clock. "Haru! Calm down. I can't understand a word of what you're saying."

He took one, two, three deep breaths. "Becca cheated on me with Lucas."

"What?"

"She thought I had a crush on this girl, and as a payback she hooked up with Lucas." I couldn't think of what to say. Haru filled in the silence. "And now Mom is saying she knew Becca was a bad seed. I don't give a fuck what kind of seed she is. Why did she cheat on me with my best friend?"

I struggled to find something to say. "Are you sure?"

"Yes, I'm sure." He started crying again. "I caught them."

"I'm sorry, Haru. You don't deserve this." My body tensed at each word I said. My response felt clinical, rehearsed.

"Am I stupid for being with her?" Haru sobbed. "I swear I did not have a crush on anyone else."

"No. If there's one thing I know, is that you're not stupid."

I stayed on the phone with my brother for an hour, until he cried himself to sleep. Only then did I disconnect the call, falling back on the bed and into self-pity.

By the next day, the smell in my room had become unbearable, so much so that even though I had refused service, the residence maid forced her way in and cleaned it all up. I lay on the bed with the covers over my head and listened to her move about. Plates clinked. Plastic bags rustled. Windows clicked open. I tried to feel embarrassed about the situation, but all I felt was numb. Once she was gone, I crawled out of bed and walked toward the bathroom.

The reflection in the mirror startled me. My eyes were red from not sleeping and I'd developed a rash on my face, probably a result of not showering. Bits of rice and other crumbs stuck to my hair, which now looked like the end of an old and worn broomstick. My once grey T-shirt and sweatpants combo was multicoloured with food stains and who knows what else. I'd never sunk so low. *Enough, Aki. Enough.*

I called my brother back, to check in on him. Haru told me that even though he'd asked my parents to let him stay home from school, at least for the first couple of days, they had refused to make any concessions. I guess, to them, heartbreak did not qualify as a sickness, though I begged to differ. So, the Monday after the cheating, Haru finally broke up with Becca before class and then unfriended his best friend, whatever that meant. He wasn't doing well, he told me—he felt alone, isolated. I told Haru it would eventually blow over, because that's what you're supposed to say in moments like that, and we both pretended it helped.

After I let Haru go, I took a long shower, washed my body twice, shampooed my hair. I squinted at my reflection in the mirror, fuzzing out the details. If I angled my head just right, I almost looked as good as new. I wrapped my wet hair in a towel and leaned in, observing my overgrown eyebrows.

I kept on thinking of my brother. Despite all the narratives I'd tried to concoct in my head, I was well past the point of ignoring the ways in which Haru's pain resembled what I'd put Ayesha through. Becca had cheated and so had I. As much as I hated Becca, I was just like her. Maybe I despised her because she reminded me of . . . me.

Patience's words whispered in my ear: "I thought you were a good person." *We were all wrong about that one.* I changed into outdoor clothes, socks, shoes and all. But when I was done, I couldn't think of where to go. The whole city felt tainted with a hue of rejection. If I was going to leave this safe haven, I had to have a plan. I had to take the city back, the only way I knew how.

I'd abandoned my original rules after the Southwark fight. Still, since the Holborn fight, I'd fought in defence of others or joined brawls already in progress. I still tried to make the distinction between a fight that served a purpose, and one just for my sake. All that separated me from a complete loss of control was random violence, but even that standard was increasingly difficult to maintain.

I was sitting at Lincoln's Inn Fields, just behind the New Academic Building, when groups of partying students began leaving the LSE pub, heading toward Holborn. A prick I recognized from one of my Econ B lectures seemed to think he was Axl Rose, that he was one in a million. He sang about immigrants and faggots, thinking he could do as he pleased. Before I could stop myself, I pulled up my hood, jumped off the bench and ran over to him. I swung around and kicked the back of his legs. Vicious. Then I ran west, disappearing into the dark.

I only pretended to study for the next three days. I drank, I took risks. My technique got sloppy. I had my ribs kicked behind a dumpster. One night I was so drunk I tripped face first, and the asshole I'd punched fought back. Bruises on top of bruises, knuckles that didn't get the chance to heal. I skipped out on commitments, stood up friends, missed more running practices.

My first exam was on June 9, barely two days away, and in the last month I hadn't done nearly enough to guarantee my predicted grades. I picked up one of my essay outlines from a month or two prior from my desk. At the top of the page was Patience's hand-writing. "What time do you want to go for our walk?" I'd written back, "15 mins?" I thought I'd cleared out all things relating to her, but I'd missed this. The room swirled around me and I found myself groping for my chair. I sat, then lay on the floor and stared up at the light on the ceiling until I began to see black dots. My hands went up in the air and I tried to reach for them, while I repeated Patience's words in my head. *I thought you were good.* I closed my eyes hard, the black dots turning bright orange. I shook my head trying to escape them, but they followed me.

My eyes opened to the harsh knock of someone at my door. I laid still for a moment and they knocked harder.

"Aki?" I heard Ginika, then Abby whisper. "Dude, are you okay?"

I got up and walked toward the door, checking myself in the mirror on the way. There was a large bruise just under my eye. I put the hood of my sweater up and tilted my head down, before stepping into the hallway. "Hey, yeah, I'm all right," I said, closing the door behind me.

"You don't look all right." Ginika took a step closer and the scent of vanilla bean and shea butter enveloped me. Her dark brown eyes focused on my wrists, and I wondered if she might be trying to calculate my BMI to decide how my weight loss might affect my performance—she always did have running in mind. "When was the last time you ate?"

"I had some lunch nearby." I waived an old receipt. I looked up and saw she had a new weave on, wavy brown hair resting just below her shoulders. As I hunched, trying to make myself even smaller, Ginika felt like a giant.

They looked at each other, then me. "We're going down for dinner now, and then we're going to the cinema. Do you want to come?"

"No, it's okay. I'm meeting someone. But thank you." I gave them a half smile. We all knew I had no plans, but they made way for me to walk through them. I rushed out, afraid my friends might follow me.

A light breeze pushed me north. I gained confidence with each step until my stride became the longest it had ever been. I zoomed past people on the sidewalk, catching snippets of their conversations. A group of students talked about the swine flu outbreak. A tourist asked for directions to the nearest tube station. A couple argued about the movie they'd just watched. A homeless man held out a paper cup, asking for change.

I walked for maybe an hour, until I couldn't recognize my surroundings anymore. Never-ending rows of mixed-use, three-storey buildings. It was hard to distinguish one block from the next. I knew I was somewhere near Camden Town station, so I decided to walk west. If I keep on going in this direction, I would reach Regent's Park. Thoughts of Ayesha rushed in. I wondered how she was doing. Abby and Ginika occasionally mentioned her name—I assumed they all still saw each other, though how often I wasn't sure.

I looked up at the tips of the tallest trees in the park. Maybe I could find the place near the boating lake where Ayesha and I went the night we met. No, that felt pathetic and overly sentimental. Surely, the better plan was to drink my problems into oblivion. I walked into a convenience store. There were only three narrow aisles, but I went up and down, accumulating chocolate, candy and gum in my hands. When I was done, I dumped it all at the cash register and pointed at the cheapest bottle of vodka. £10.29. I rummaged through my pocket. Loose change fell on the floor. I stepped on the coins to stop them from getting away. Three pounds short.

"There's a cash machine outside." The clerk pointed to the door. He had a thick accent and a haircut similar to my dad's. I walked over to the ATM. The screen was cracked, the buttons covered in sticky goo. I used my coat sleeves to punch in my PIN and grabbed the £20 bill from the machine before walking back into the store.

"Did it work?" the cashier asked.

I nodded, sliding the twenty toward him. He put everything in a bag. I walked along the Outer Circle, tracing the edges of the park without venturing in. It was getting colder, so I buttoned up my coat. Except for cars, the streets were quiet. Every few hundred meters a dog and its owner emerged from the park. I tried to make the walk into a game—a gulp of vodka for every person I encountered.

I was a third of the way through the bottle when my phone buzzed. A text message from Patience. "Can we talk?" What could she possibly want? I downed another third of the bottle, twisted the cap on and walked into the park. Lamp posts illuminated the trails. The world looked so different in the night.

One of the things Mom made me promise when I moved to London was not to walk in parks in the dark—something about it being too quiet, too far from the roads. A place where no one could hear you scream. But I didn't plan on being the one who screamed tonight. Fists closed, I walked, south toward the Open Air Theatre. Scattered strangers. A man sleeping on a park bench. Two lovers rolling around on the grass. Three French bulldogs and their owner. A group of teenagers smoking pot.

From a bench, I surveyed the park for my next opponent. There was hardly anyone around. But just as I was about to give out, I saw two men in matching Adidas tracksuits walk in my direction. They were about the same height. The one on the right was wearing a cap. The one on the left had a faux hawk. I felt my body tingle with anger—from my gut to my chest, to the tips of my fingers gripping the bench. They were perfect.

The two men stopped a few feet away. Everything about them bothered me. The track trousers tucked inside their white socks. The shaved eyebrows. The blades of grass stuck to their muddied sneakers. Their air of entitlement. My eyes rested on their arms. They crossed them and stared at me.

"Mind if we sit?" the taller one asked. I clenched my jaw.

They walked over and sat, one on each side. Their breath smelled of beer and cigarettes. The one on the left stretched his arm on the bench, resting his hand on my right shoulder. Shivers went up and down my spine. I shifted forward. The man on the right leaned in for a kiss, but I turned my face away and gripped the bench tighter. At another time, I might have waited for another transgression, something bigger. I might have even given them the opportunity to back down. But tonight, I was done with foreplay. I lifted my hand and punched his groin. He curled over and cried out.

"Ooo, a fighter," his friend said, grabbing my leg. I turned and elbowed him in the nose. His head jerked back. He held both hands to his face, blood gushing through his fingers.

"Ima bang you out," the man to my right said. I got up and took a few steps back. He kicked the side of my leg. My body thrust sideways and I fell. A kick to my left side. My ribs screamed. I rolled over. The two men look down at me. I dug my hands into the ground, pulling out weeds. I don't remember what happened next. Maybe it was the alcohol, but when my senses returned, I was towering above the two men, my hands covered in blood. They grunted on the damp grass, unable to move. The park bench was at least fifteen feet away from us. I looked down at my trembling hands. I'd gone too far this time. The light above us flickered and in the distance I saw two figures running toward us.

Fuck. I grabbed the plastic bag with the vodka and took off. It'd been ages since I had trained with the team, but figured I could still outrun them. My thighs ached. So did my ribs. I looked behind me and saw rounded hats, dark uniforms. I needed somewhere to hide.

"Police. Stop!"

I ran across the Inner Circle and jumped over the fence, the police officers a few paces behind me. A car whisked by as I made my way through the shrubs into thicker foliage. A large structure. I was at the Open Air Theatre. I walked around, keeping an ear out for signs of them. The theatre was dark. Rows of seats like bleachers at a high school football field, only much smaller. I ran up to the highest row and lay on the concrete. Deep belly breaths.

I rolled on my back, trying to find a more comfortable position. My left side touched the cold, damp ground and I flinched. Footsteps in the distance, then silence. I looked up at the starless London sky and drank the rest of the vodka. A rogue tear travelled down my cheek. I stayed there, silent, for a little over half an hour. There was no sound, except cars driving by in the distance. Around midnight I got up and made my way across the park, around the boating lake, through York Gate. I got on the tube at Baker Street station and took it to Euston Square.

There was a "Closed" sign outside the station bathroom, but it was unlocked and I went in anyway. I washed my hands and my face and patted the dirty hoodie with damp paper to remove the more noticeable stains. When I was satisfied, I headed toward my residence. Ginika was sitting outside the door to my room. I sat next to her in the hall, back against my door. She rested her head on my shoulder. I took a deep breath and held her hand in mine.

"I'm sorry," I said softly.

"I know."

I was sitting in an exam room for the GV100 final. Thea sat two seats ahead of me; every other face in my row familiar enough for me to know I'd been in lectures with them, but not to the point where I would know their names. Abby and Ginika were taking their exam in a different room. The administration mixed students from various courses, making sure we never sat next to someone we could cheat from. My mind oscillated between the sixteen essay topics printed on a sheet of A4 paper, of which I had to pick four to write about in three hours. My knuckles ached from all the punches I'd thrown in the last couple of weeks, and the pain slowed my writing down. It didn't even matter. None of it did.

CHAPTER 24

I flew back to Vancouver at the end of June, having postponed the inevitable as long as possible. I felt numb, the previous days a bizarre dream that I was finally awakening from. I struggled to remember what I'd written in my exams, my answers fragmented and disjointed. Looking out the airplane window, London became smaller and smaller until it disappeared. I contemplated the months ahead and the time I would spend with my family over the summer break, beginning with our biannual two-week family trip to the Sunshine Coast.

We made this trip every other summer. The extended family rented out a large cabin, and we would all come up. Ojiichan and Obaachan were already there, with my aunt Emiko and her family. Dad's older brother, Ichiro, would be arriving later in the week with my aunt and two cousins. My aunt Chiyo had moved to Japan with her husband, and my oldest cousin, so we hadn't seen them for several years.

By early July, the house was in full-blown preparation. Mom and Luz were cleaning everything. "I will be tired when I come home. I don't want to clean then." Haru was oddly silent about the whole thing, still moping about the house, still upset about Becca. Dad, as always, was fretting about the work he wouldn't be able to do while on vacation. He came home later than usual, woke up earlier to squeeze in an extra hour of work—anything to assuage his anxiety about being unreachable by his important clients, even though we all knew he would bring his laptop and work phone with him. This was good, as no one seemed to notice me.

I took Terry for long walks, escaped for bike rides to Lighthouse Park, where I read my favourite book, George Orwell's *Down and Out in Paris and London* over and over again. I tried to be outside as much as I could. I tried not to wallow in self-pity, but I felt stretched thin and worn out, without any outlet for my frustration and anger now that I was back in Canada.

On the morning of our departure, I was awakened by a soft knock on my bedroom door. Five minutes later, there was a harder one. I opened my eyes to darkness and lifted my wrist close to my face. 4:49 a.m. Our ferry wouldn't leave for another three hours, but Dad liked to be at the terminal at least a couple of hours before boarding time. My hand searched for my glasses on the bedside table.

I could hear Haru grunt loudly in his room. Another knock. "Get up! We will be late," Mom said through the door. She probably would have stayed in bed for another hour were it not for Dad's anxiety-driven schedule. I sat up in bed, stretching my arms above my head. Hurried footsteps in the corridor and the sound of heavy suitcases being dragged down the stairs.

"Haru, you can sleep on the ferry. Now get up!" Mom said from the hallway. "We are leaving in fifteen minutes. Don't forget your toothbrushes." I stepped out of bed and picked up the clothes I'd laid out the night before under yesterday's newspaper, folded to a page on the riots in Ürümqi that I had been reading. The family uniform: beige chinos, turquoise polo. This was our first trip together since the coming out, the falling out, and I was committed to doing what I could to make it run as smoothly as it possibly could.

We arrived at Horseshoe Bay two hours before the first ferry to Langdale. The car lanes were empty. We waited for the café by the ferry terminal to open. There was a small self-service bar displaying a meek offering of yogurt, granola, and some fruit. Haru refused any food, while Dad picked a banana and I took a cereal bar out of my backpack. We sat at a table while my mom negotiated with the only staff person behind the counter, a small Indonesian man around her age, until he agreed to make her some eggs and toast, even though the kitchen wouldn't be open for another hour or two. "I have to have something warm in the morning," she said to my dad, whose eyes were glued on his phone, a last-minute email he needed to write, the last one, he promised her.

The ferry was busy, but not packed. We parked on the lower deck, then made our way to the passenger seating on the upper floors. Haru and I sat side by side, and my parents sat on the seats facing ours, talking through the recipes they were in charge of preparing.

I knew the dynamics of these holidays well. Though my grand-parents had always been courteous and pleasant toward my mother, I knew they would have much preferred Dad to have married some-one of a similar ethnic background, someone who could steer him in a more honourable direction. Both my aunts and my uncle had married people that looked like them, all with an inclination for academia. Why couldn't my dad have done the same?

It wasn't my mother *per se* that they had a problem with, but everything she represented: too brown, too poor, too uneducated. The fact she was a first-generation immigrant certainly didn't help. To them, it must have seemed she was pulling my dad back instead of pushing him forward, and this made them feel like their efforts to give him a better life were invalidated. Why bother to make all the sacrifices when your children can do whatever they want, without any regard for your plans for them? Maybe that's how my own par-ents felt about me.

Since I'd returned from London, they hadn't brought up the subject of my sexual orientation, to my relief as much as theirs, I was sure. We had all continued to pretend like nothing was the matter, but I wondered what would happen now that we had to spend two weeks with the whole family. I wondered what finding out about might do to my relationship with my traditional Shinto–Buddhist grandparents. Thoughts of Dad calling my grandparents rushed through my head. In my imagination, they responded with confusion. "Gay? What do you mean?" they asked. At the Christmas party, Ojiichan had told me I was like him. Maybe he wouldn't feel the same once he found out who I really was.

The ferry began moving. The four of us sat in silence, with my brother eventually offering me one of his earphones. I leaned forward for a while, trying to discern whether I'd ever heard the song that was playing before, while my parents whispered something I couldn't quite make out.

Halfway through the song I handed the earphone back to Haru and turned to the window once again. I was lost in thought, halfway to dreamland, when my mom tapped me on the shoulder.

"How are you doing?" She cocked her head, her eyes filled with concern.

"I'm okay," I responded, dragging out my words, as if to say I didn't quite understand the meaning of her question.

"Aki . . ." she paused. "I feel like things between us are better, right?"

"Sure?" I wouldn't have called it good, but I guess they were better. I'd take not talking over being lectured any time. She shifted in her seat, readjusting her navy-blue polo shirt.

"Your dad and I . . ." she stopped again and looked at her hands, glanced at my father, who was reading emails on this phone. "We are trying to understand."

"Yes?"

"Yes. We are trying to understand, but we're not sure how others might feel." Mom looked up at me, waiting for the penny to drop, but I didn't follow her train of thought. "We haven't figured out, as a family, how to communicate the news of, you know. So, we, your dad and I, think it's best if we don't bring it up with people—for now. Until we sort it all out."

Not bring it up? For now? Until we sort it all out? My relief of not having to announce my sexual orientation to my extended family was overcome by the hurt I felt—my parents were embarrassed, ashamed of me. Were they still planning on "fixing" this? A part of me had guessed that, but to hear them say it was painful. I nodded and turned back to the window, tears collecting at the corners of my eyes. My brother kicked my leg and mouthed "Are you okay?" to which I shrugged. The once blue skies were now cloudy and grey, growing darker and darker as we moved through the water. I gently closed my eyes, careful not to shed a tear, and hoped for a storm, something to keep us from reaching Langdale Terminal. But the ferry kept on moving, and it was still early morning when we arrived.

CHAPTER 25

The problem with only seeing family for two weeks every other year is that you're never able to build on relationships. I never quite felt I knew my aunts, uncles and cousins in a meaningful way. I knew their names and how old they were, and Dad made us call them every year on their birthday, but I didn't know anything that held weight in their lives, like their favourite TV show, or how they spent their free time. We were acquaintances feigning familiarity, linked only by blood.

When we drove up, my grandparents were waiting for us at the front door of the cabin. Haru and I grabbed our luggage from the trunk and made our way toward Ojiichan and Obaachan, our parents right behind us.

"*Tadaima*," the four of us said in unison, as we entered the cabin. We bowed, bringing one hand on top of the other, over our knees.

"*Okaerinasai*," my grandparents replied, Obaachan's voice barely audible. They bowed with some difficulty.

"Good trip?" Ojiichan gestured at the duffel I was carrying, offering to bring it in. His hands resembled my dad's, only they had more sunspots.

We took our shoes off at the entrance and placed them in

whatever space we could find, leaving the foyer peppered with pairs of shoes in different sizes and styles. The living area was open concept, which my grandparents didn't like, but it made it easier to accommodate all the family, even when we couldn't all be sitting at the table. The cabin had floor-to-ceiling windows around its perimeter and the living room opened up to a large deck with a barbecue and a view of the water. The cabin was surrounded by trees on the other three sides. No neighbours in sight.

My aunt Emiko came into the room and hugged my mother, then my father. She lived in Edmonton with my uncle Tom, a professor of Japanese Literature at the University of Alberta. They had two boys, a year apart, roughly our age. She was Dad's favourite sibling, and the second oldest of four—my dad being the youngest. She was warm and friendly, and unlike my dad's other siblings, always tried to bridge the cultural gap between the rest of the family and Mom, doing her best to make us all feel like we belonged. She kept in touch, and knew the small things, like which grade we were in and what sports we played.

The table was set for four, blue and white plates and bowls arranged in patterns in front of each seat. My dad apologized for the time of our arrival, just after everyone had eaten breakfast. My grandparents and aunt sat at the table, while the four of us efficiently ate a bowl of rice each, with some miso soup and tamagoyaki.

Ojiichan was wearing black shorts and had a small white towel wrapped around his neck for dabbing the inevitable sweat drops. I looked at my grandmother. She seemed even more distracted than when I'd seen her at Christmas. Her back arched forward so she could only stare at the table while we all chatted. She wore an oversized dress with a gaudy light blue and white print on it, and her hands trembled. In the past couple of years, she'd aged so quickly. She barely spoke now. I suspected it was dementia, but no one talked about it. Obaachan had been a huge reason Haru and I took

Japanese lessons on the weekend. She and Ojiichan wanted to make sure we never took our heritage for granted.

Dad sat next to her, and throughout breakfast he looked at her with concern, offering her some cold tea, trying to engage her in conversation. I watched his careful movements around her and considered, for what felt like the first time, that he was a son before he became my dad.

The following day, I awoke to some commotion in the cabin. As I emerged from my room, Haru and our two cousins—Hiroshi and Kaito—rushed back and forth from their room, all three dressed for fishing.

"Aren't you going to wait for Aki?" Aunt Emiko's voice travelled down the corridor.

"Aki doesn't like fishing." While Haru was right, I didn't appreciate him speaking for me. "Plus, she's not up. We need to go before the weather turns."

Then, my mother's voice. "Be careful!" I could hear Haru's eyes rolling.

I spent the morning reading out on the deck, occasionally raising my head to watch the clouds pass by. By 11:30, Aunt Emiko joined me outside. "Mind if I sit?" She gestured to the wooden lawn chair next to me.

"Go ahead."

"It's so beautiful here. Whenever we come, it makes me miss BC." We looked out to the water in silence, then she turned to me and asked the only question everyone seemed to have for me since I'd left for college. "How's London?"

I smiled. "It's big, much bigger than Vancouver."

"You know, I left BC when I was around your age."

"Yeah?"

"I think Ojiichan and Obaachan had expected me to live with

them until I got married, but it felt like the only way I could figure out who I was." She paused. "It didn't help that your Aunt Chiyo followed every one of their rules."

My aunt had never shared so much with me. "You know, Aki, they expect us to be meek, quiet, submissive. That's how my mom had to be, Chiyo and even me to some extent."

"Yeah . . ." I said, trying to fill the silence, unsure where the conversation might be headed.

"I know your mom's had a tough time being a part of this family, but I admire her for having an opinion. I wasn't allowed to have one growing up, you know."

"Oh."

"You're the only granddaughter in this family, Aki. Don't let them crush you." Her eyes overflowed with tears. She tried to wipe them quickly so I wouldn't notice.

I sat up and faced her. "I won't."

"Good!" She laugh-cried. "Don't let them dampen your voice, okay? You are more than what they see."

"I won't," I said, trying to make myself believe my own words.

On Thursday, Uncle Ichiro and his family arrived. My cousin, Masashi, a year older than me, was socially awkward at best and downright spoiled. As an only child, he'd never heard a no and lacked the basic skills to co-exist with other people his age. He avoided eye contact and only opened his mouth to brag about studying STEM at U of T. I worried Masashi had no friends, no life outside of his narrow interests.

The balance of this family vacation shifted, as it always did. The two brothers had spent their lives competing for my grandparents' approval, with my uncle emerging victorious every time. As the firstborn, Ichiro stipulated the schedule and rhythm for the day. The whole family would wake up at 6:00 a.m. even though we were on vacation, because my grandparents ate breakfast early and we had to eat meals together. Sometimes my brother, Hiroshi, Kaito and I would go back to bed and nap for an hour or two. Other times, I sat next to my grandfather and watched the news, while my grandmother sat in the background obsessively combing her thinning hair with a small pink brush and a matching hand mirror. For the most part Haru spent his time with Emiko's sons, but sometimes my parents, my brother and I went for silent mid-morning walks, a sought-after reprieve for my parents.

Lunches were served promptly at 11:30 a.m. and over the days we were there, my mom slowly took over the kitchen, each day preparing foods my grandparents weren't used to eating, like arepas, arroz con pollo, and sancocho, dishes too exotic for their palates. In the afternoons, Ojiichan and Obaachan would nap. I would read outside and the boys would go out fishing or kayaking. Masashi always stayed behind, following his mother around. Everyone, no matter where they went in the afternoon, made sure to return home for dinner at 6:00 p.m.

On the third night after Uncle Ichiro arrived, Aunt Emiko and Aunt Yuki prepared yakisoba in three large electrical skillets placed at equal intervals along the dinner table. One of them was pork-based, another was chicken-based and the last one was vegetarian. There weren't enough seats for everyone at the dining table, so my cousins, brother and I sat in the living room.

I heard my grandfather's voice. "Yuto, did you know Ichiro has been continuing some research I started when I used to teach ethics?"

"Yes, I think you mentioned it," my father responded tersely. I looked up, noticing a shift in the mood.

"You know," Ojiichan said, turning to my mom. "Yuto was very smart. He would have been a great academic."

"Yuto *is* smart." My mom reached out for my father's hand. Dad pulled his hand away and wiped his mouth with a napkin.

"Smart is not enough. It's what you use it for."

In an attempt to relieve the tension, Aunt Emiko chimed in. "This pork is so flavourful. It—"

"I just hope your children don't follow in your footsteps." Ojiichan stared straight at his younger son. The adults fell silent. "*Tomi wa chie no jamaninaru.*"

My mom turned to my dad, as if to ask for a translation. She was the only person at that table who didn't understand Japanese. My father, however, sat frozen, jaws clenched and breathing deeply.

"Wealth gets in the way of wisdom," Uncle Ichiro said finally.

"How much does a professor make? Because last I heard it wasn't little." Dad struggled to contain his anger.

"There's a difference between seeking money and making money, Yuto." Ojiichan shook his head, as if to say he was once again missing the point.

My father got up slowly. He put his palms together in prayer position and bowed. "*Gochisousamadeshita.*" He headed straight to his bedroom without looking back. Mom followed.

The evening was over. Ojiichan and Obaachan went off to sleep, and the others retreated to their rooms. Haru and Emiko's boys retired to their bunk beds, though I could hear them laughing for hours after. And Masashi read in the living room, avoiding the other boys altogether. I needed some space away from all the tension in the cabin, so I went outside and sat on one of the chairs on the deck. I was watching the stars, contemplating what I might do for the rest of the summer when Uncle Ichiro joined me.

At first, he sat in the chair next to me, sipping on bourbon, but with each passing minute he became more restless. "You know, I wish your dad and I were closer. We were always so competitive with each other." I felt confused about the shift in the conversation, so I just let him fill the silence. "I've always envied him. He got to chart his own path, when I had to follow in someone else's footsteps."

"It seems like you're doing pretty well for yourself."

"I'm not happy." He threw his hands up in the air as if to say, it's out in the open now. "There. I said it."

I wanted to veer the conversation away from the emotional. "Didn't Socrates—"

"My point is, I see a lot of myself in you. Don't let someone else's vision dictate your journey. Whether that's your dad, Ojiichan or even me. You can't be happy by pleasing others alone. You just can't."

For our last night, Mom planned a three-course meal for the whole family. To start, an arugula salad with walnuts, goat's cheese and honey. For the main course, spaghetti alle vongole, because clams were my grandparents' favourites. And for dessert, flan, which she made with condensed milk, just as her grandmother had done.

Dinner went smoothly. On one end of the table my grandfather spoke loudly with his sons and son-in-law, gesturing profusely and reminiscing about a fishing trip they'd taken somewhere east when my dad was eight. At the other end, Mom and Aunt Emiko exchanged cake recipes, while Aunt Yuki quietly nodded. Haru and my cousins, in an attempt to be useful, stoked the fireplace. They even tried to include Masashi, who awkwardly tossed in logs from a distance. The only one who remained silent and mostly unengaged was my grandmother, arched over her food, next to my dad.

After dinner, Ojiichan invited my dad and uncle for a whisky on the deck while my mom and aunts washed dishes in the kitchen. All in our own way, we pretended for one last time that the past two weeks had been sublime. It was a way of reassuring each other we'd show up at this same cabin two years from now.

My grandmother was still seated at the now empty table. She seemed to be chewing on something, her eyes half open, staring at the empty table in front of her. Would she be with us two years from now? The conversation on the ferry rushed back into my head. "Don't bring it up with people—for now." Now was all I might have with Obaachan.

I walked over to the table and sat next to her. Then, I took a big breath and leaned in. "I'm gay," I whispered softly in her ear. She continued to chew, eyes staring blankly ahead. I tried it again, this time a little louder, "I like women." Obaachan slowly tilted her head and turned toward me, her whole body shaking slightly. For a second or two I believed she might have understood what I said, but she said nothing, her expression still, immutable. I smiled softly and bowed instinctively, not quite knowing what my gestures were communicating. Obaachan closed her eyes slowly and smiled back. Then she returned to her initial posture, shoulders arched forward, neck bent down staring at the edge of the table.

CHAPTER 26

Once we got back to West Vancouver, my parents took turns pencilling me into their schedules. First was a father-daughter trip to the Jericho Tennis Club. Even though there were other tennis clubs much closer to our home, Jericho conveyed status in a way that no other place could, somewhere Dad could meet potential clients and entertain old ones. The courts were pristine and the pool wasn't bad either, but I hated the all-white clothing policy. It was hard not to read between the lines and feel like we—Mom and me in particular—stuck out like the nail Dad was so fond of.

"I can't remember the last time we went to the club together." Dad turned his head toward me momentarily before returning his gaze to the road.

"Before I left for London. That's for sure." We got on Lions Gate Bridge. "You know, I always feel out of place whenever we go there."

"What do you mean?"

"You know. That whole white clothing policy feels heavy-handed."

"I am not sure I follow."

"Dad, come on. Don't you remember the time they mistook Mom for a cleaner? Maybe Haru passes for Japanese, but I certainly don't."

He mumbled something to himself. We drove through Stanley Park in silence. Then, instead of driving to Burrard, my dad turned right on Bidwell and pulled over. He turned off the car and looked at me.

"Aki, you belong anywhere you are."

"That's not what I mean, Dad."

"But it is."

I struggled to find the right words. "It's more complicated than that."

"No. No, it's not." He put his right hand on my shoulder. "You've got to believe it."

"How about the nail sticking out?" I turned to look at him, but he was staring down.

"That's different, Aki."

"It doesn't feel different to me. If I have to change who I am to make someone else feel comfortable, then I don't belong."

Dad opened his mouth but no words came out. He started the car, but instead of continuing to the club, turned right on Comox. We parked near the Stanley Park Tennis Courts. It was ten o'clock on a Saturday and the courts were packed, people dressed in every colour in the rainbow, in shoes that would e have been considered improper for the courts at Jericho. We made our way to a group of players who were waiting outside the courts.

"Is this the line?" A man in his mid-fifties nodded. Dad turned to me. "You know, I never liked Jericho anyway."

When we got home, Mom was waiting for us in the kitchen. We'd barely come in when she began, "I was on the phone with *tía abuela* Carmen." She looked down at her hands.

"Yes?" I waited for her to continue, but she hesitated. "Is she all right?"

"Yes, yes. She's okay." My mom took a deep breath. "I wanted to talk to her about our predicament, about you being . . ." She looked up to the ceiling, like she was remembering something. "Gay."

A sinking feeling in my stomach. Dad and I had had such a lovely morning. I didn't want to fight them now. Up until this moment, she and my dad had tried to hide this piece of information from everyone. Why bring it up with her youngest sister? I panicked. I tried to think of what to say, but nothing came out.

"When I told her, her response was, 'So what?' Can you believe that?" I watched Mom fidget with a piece of paper in her hands.

"No, not really." Dad smiled softly and made his way to the kitchen counter where Mom was seated to give her a kiss.

"She said who you like is none of my business or your dad's business." Their eyes met, but they didn't say anything to each other.

Relief, confusion—my emotions felt undefined. I searched my mother's face for a clue to how I should react, but I couldn't read her expression.

"Anyway, I thought you should know," she said abruptly, before getting up and returning to the breakfast nook to read the newspaper. Later, she headed out for afternoon tea with her friends. I don't imagine the word "gay" came up in their conversation.

When my mother returned that evening, she and Dad spoke for hours in their room, while Haru and I rewatched some episodes of *Friends* for the third time. We started with an episode in Season 1 where Ross sees his son Ben, who has two gay moms, playing with a Barbie doll. For the ensuing twenty minutes, Ross loses his shit, blaming his ex-wife and her partner for his son's choice of toy and trying to convince the one-year-old to play with an action figure. I watched it in disbelief. For the first time, it dawned on me that the show I loved growing up played into the worst aspects of heteronormativity and homophobia—like the time Joey was made fun of for wearing a shoulder bag, or when Ross couldn't handle having a male nanny, or Chandler's never-ending fear of seeming gay.

Haru paused the DVD. "Do you know what they're talking about?" He propped himself on one of the arms of my couch. My parents' door was open, but their room was two floors up, so we couldn't make out their words.

"Yeah," I answered, unenthusiastically, still unsure about the earlier exchange with my mother. "*Tía abuela* Carmen said, 'So what' when Mom called her and told her I was gay."

"What! Did she really say that?" Haru raised his voice.

"Shush!" I whispered. "Yeah, something along those lines. Not sure what it all means, though."

"Well, she didn't have to call *tía abuela* Carmen to get *that* opinion." Haru rolled his eyes and pressed play again. "Why don't people just listen to me?"

Haru and I looked at each other and laughed.

CHAPTER 27

When August came, the Pascals came to stay. They were family friends, who used to live in West Vancouver but had moved back to Montreal three years ago. I'd met Madeleine, their daughter, when we were both in Grade 8. We quickly became inseparable—playing tennis after school, going on trips together, driving around the Gleneagles Golf Course in golf carts. When they moved, Madeleine and I tried to keep in touch, sending letters to each other, but the distance had diluted our friendship. I certainly hadn't come out to her yet.

Alain, Madeleine's father, was in a similar line of work to my dad's—investment banking—and Colette, like my mom, was a stay-at-home parent. Guillaume, Madeleine's brother, was Haru's age and height, only his hair was curly like his mom's. Guillaume was quieter than Haru, but still popular. He was a good student, and like his father played tennis instead of a contact sport like rugby or lacrosse. Madeleine was slightly taller than me. She was artistic and aspired to become an architect—a way of blending her creative side with the need for a "real" job, as her parents had insisted. The four of them had light brown hair, fair skin and piercing blue eyes. Unlike our mixed family, there was no doubt that they were related.

When they arrived at our door, late in the evening, Madeleine lunged forward and gave me a hug. She had always been overtly affectionate. I remember when we were in middle school, and she kept on asking me why I didn't like being hugged or kissed. I guess in the end it didn't matter because she never stopped doing it.

Haru took Guillaume straight up to his room, while the parents made their way to the garden outside. I stood awkwardly at the door, somewhat unsure about how to proceed.

"So . . . how was the flight?"

"I could have done with better entertainment. Domestic flights have such limited options!"

"Yeah, I know what you mean." We looked at each other. As much as she was still a close friend, I wondered how Madeleine might react to the news that I liked women. "Want to drop your stuff off in my room?" I followed behind her as she made her way up the stairs.

Madeleine was conservative in a peculiar way. It wasn't that her family was religious, or her parents overtly strict, but the time we'd grown up together, I'd always gotten a sense that she felt uncomfortable with anything that strayed from the norm, or the rules—like the girls in school who folded their skirts so they'd be shorter, or the boy a year older than us who liked to wear lipstick. She would never confront anyone, or even comment on it. Instead, she would grow quiet, look at her hands and plot a quiet escape.

"How have you been?" I stood at the doorway while she put her suitcase on one side of the queen-sized bed and opened it.

"Do you mind if I shower first? Then we can catch up. I just feel so dirty."

"Yeah, no worries. I'll get ready for bed."

"I won't be long."

I lay under my pink and white flowered duvet and waited for Madeleine, going over a speech in my head, trying to iron out my lines. I figured if I planned what to say, the reveal would go better than it did with my parents. She was an important person in my life, and I wanted to be truthful about who I liked. That was the gist of it. I wouldn't say anything about the fighting and the sleeping around. Manageable doses. I stared at the wall of bookcases opposite my bed, going through my favourite titles in my head to distract myself.

Madeleine came back into the room wearing nothing but a light green towel. With her back to me, she changed in front of my closet's mirror. "Can we catch up tomorrow morning?" she said, looking over her shoulder. "We'll be here all week, so we'll have a lot of time to talk." Madeleine towel-dried her hair and turned off the lights. The scent of green apples filled the bedroom. Her bodywash, not mine.

Another night. Twenty-four hours. I could wait that long. But then I blurted out, "I'm gay." I closed my eyes, like somehow not seeing the darkness meant it wasn't there. The room remained silent, the palpable discomfort growing with each second.

"Madeleine?" I whispered, half wondering if she'd fallen asleep.

"I heard."

I waited for something more, my heart beating so loudly I was certain she could hear it. But she didn't say another word. Madeleine turned away from me, creating more distance between us in the bed. My instincts were right—she would not be okay with this. I recalled the three months in Grade 9 when she refused to speak to me because I kissed a girl on a dare. Back then, I thought the issue had been that I kissed anyone at all. Madeleine was a puritan when it came to anything remotely sexual. Now I wondered if her silent treatment had more to do with it being a girl. My mind raced through moments in our friendship, as I searched for clues of what this new silence meant, but it was futile. Without her confirmation, it was only a guessing game. Eventually, I willed myself to sleep.

When I woke up the next morning, Madeleine was already gone. Downstairs, I saw her in the dining room, eating breakfast with our parents. They seemed to be talking about something serious, by their expressions, and I wondered if they were discussing me. But the atmosphere didn't change when I walked into the room. Nobody seemed uncomfortable with my presence, so I discarded that possibility.

In the days that followed, things between Madeleine and me were lukewarm at best. We hung out, but mostly in the company of our brothers or parents. When we were alone, we rarely mentioned anything personal, avoiding the subject of romantic relationships altogether. I sensed a fear in her that perhaps I would be interested, that I would make a move. It hurt to know that our friendship was so fragile. Yet another disappointment. To avoid any more friction, I created distance as best as I could, sitting across from her at the table, dividing my attention, leaving the room when she came in to change. We managed for the week, our awkwardness only noticeable to each other. By Saturday, I could only think of how close they were to leaving.

On his last night in West Vancouver, Guillaume was set on going out clubbing somewhere downtown with Haru, but our parents wouldn't let them go unless Madeleine and I went too, "to supervise."

"Come on, Aki, please?" Haru supplicated.

"I don't know. I'm kind of tired."

"Don't be a wet blanket," Guillaume continued.

With our mothers only a few feet away, I half-looked at Madeleine, sitting on the couch adjacent to me. "What do you think?" I anticipated the answer would be no, but I had to play this part. We both did.

Her eyes moved from Haru to Guillaume, who had both kneeled. "I don't know," she said. "It might be fun." I fought to hide the surprise on my face.

"Okay, fine. But two is my limit. And somewhere with more than a handful of women. I don't want to be surrounded by thirsty creeps all night." Haru and Guillaume sprang up and darted toward their room to change. Madeleine looked at me, "I'm not sure I have anything to wear."

In my room, Madeleine and I rummaged through her suitcase looking for anything that might work. Shirts, polos, cardigans. Among the full J Crew catalogue, we found a pair of black skinny jeans and a black and white striped vest.

"How about this," Madeleine said, holding up the vest. "But maybe I won't put a shirt underneath—from a country club look to a clubbing look."

I smiled a forced smile. "Yeah, I think that will work. I'm sor—"

"Please don't say anything. I am just trying to survive this week."

"Yeah." I took a deep breath. "Okay, that's fair."

After I finished putting on my clothes, Madeleine took over, insisting that I needed to put make-up on. My ineptitude in the art of face painting was such that after my initial attempt, she wiped it off, and started all over again. In her enthusiasm, with our mothers in agreement, she decided straight hair would be a better clubbing look for both of us. Despite my protests, the three of them proceeded to iron out chunks of my hair over and over again, until burnt was all I could smell. By the time they were done, I looked like no one I could recognize. But everyone else seemed to disagree with me, especially my mother. "This is the best you've looked in months, Aki."

At 11 p.m., Haru called a cab to take us to The Clinic, a medical-themed bar in Gastown. As the eldest, I sat in front, next to the driver, even though I had no idea where we were going.

The cab came to a stop about a block away from the bar. Apparently, we would have to walk the rest of the way. A steady flow of people lined the streets between bars and restaurants.

The Clinic was darkly lit, with wheelchairs and hospital beds for seats, a bright glow shining from operating lights, and servers dressed in medical whites. I'd never much liked hospitals. But it didn't feel fair to ruin everyone else's fun, so I pushed down the sinking feeling in my stomach and tried to focus on the alcohol instead. *The faster you drink, the less it will matter.*

I started with the green-coloured liquid served in a test tube that everyone seemed to be having, then graduated to a purplish drink in an IV drip bag. Everything on the menu was overpriced, with bizarre drug-sounding names, and a sweet aftertaste that left me slightly nauseated. Even so, I continued to drink into the night, my mother's credit card in hand. Eventually, I managed to find a place to sit, but Haru and Guillaume really wanted to dance, so we all headed to a room in the back, about half the size of the front room and with twice as many people.

The DJ played all of the summer hits, from Ciara's "Love Sex Magic" to Lady Gaga's "Poker Face." He even added a few slow songs. Madeleine seemed into it, dancing with our brothers, throwing back test tube after test tube. She maintained her distance from me, and I pretended to be more concerned about other things, like the time and the cute, tall blond sitting alone at the corner of the club, when I was hit with the overwhelming smell of Axe body spray.

It made me uncomfortable, like when someone stands too close, like warm breath on your neck. I turned around to find the source and saw three men in their mid-twenties approaching us. White, tall, brown-haired, brown-eyed, slightly pointed noses. They looked like they might be related. One of them yelled something, and I heard the hint of an Australian accent, but the music was so loud I couldn't make sense of what he was saying.

He leaned in and whispered something in Madeleine's ear. His two friends—brothers?—stood at least a step back, sipping from IV drip bags. Madeleine's expression changed to disgust and she moved back. He put both his hands on her shoulders and tried again. Haru and Guillaume looked at Madeleine, then at me.

"Leave her alone! She's not interested," I yelled in his direction, hoping a direct approach would scare him off. But instead, he smiled, turned and arched forward so I would hear him better.

"She doesn't look like she's not interested." He'd put his arm around Madeleine, but I pulled her toward me.

"Why don't you go bother someone else."

The man looked back at his friends, or maybe his siblings or cousins, and they shared the sinister laugh only creeps know, the one that makes the hair on any woman's arms rise. "But this is so much fun."

Madeleine's nails dug into my arm.

I felt the familiar rush of blood from the pit of my stomach to my head.

"Oh, sorry. Is this your girlfriend?" the man said. My jaw tightened and from the corner of my eyes, I saw Madeleine shift in discomfort and step back. That was it. My hands tingled in anticipation, and all I could think about was how I would get rid of Madeleine and our brothers.

"Haru, take Madeleine and Guillaume. Get out of here."

"What? Are you crazy? I'm not going to leave you."

"I'll be right behind you. Just go."

Focused on me, the men didn't notice my brother and our friends back away. When they had blended in with the crowd, I lunged forward, punching the one who'd made a pass at Madeleine in the stomach. He went down fast, coiling over, then retching. Not enough. I elbowed his back and hooked his left leg. I wanted him on the ground. He landed awkwardly, groaning. One of his mates dropped the IV bag he was holding and rushed toward me, but before he could do anything the palm of my hand met his nose in an upward motion. He stumbled back, holding his bloodied face. Two out of three. One more to go. But the third man had disappeared into the crowd around us.

It all went down so quickly, I doubted anyone knew what was going on. A couple nearby looked at the man on the floor, but the club was too packed for anyone to make a big deal of what had happened. I wiped my hands on my trousers and took a big breath before turning toward the exit.

Haru, alone. Just a few feet away. His mouth agape, staring at the man at my feet. How much had he seen? Would he tell anyone? Why hadn't he just left the club like he was told?

I walked toward my brother slowly, my arm outstretched, but he backed away, confusion fighting with anger on his face. "What the fuck, Aki!" He put his hands to his head. "What did you do?"

"Haru, it's not what it looks like. I was just defending myself. I was just defending us." I reached for his arm but he pushed me away.

"What is wrong with you?" Haru looked at me in disgust. "I get you're going through a lot, but I don't even know who you are anymore." He stepped back.

"I'm sor—"

"Don't. You know, I used to be proud of you. But this . . . " He gestured up and down. "This is not my sister. You are not my sister."

"Haru, please."

"You are not someone I know." He turned and I stood in the middle of the dance floor surrounded by strangers, watching one of the last people that truly cared about me walk away.

On the ride back home, Guillaume and Madeleine talked non-stop about the three men, going over what had been said, asking me what had happened to them. Haru remained silent, staring out the window, looking into the distance—anything to avoid meeting my eyes.

CHAPTER 28

The Pascals left the next morning, and Haru began to avoid me. It was the same the next day and the next. He stopped having breakfast with us in the morning, and when he came home at night, he ate his dinner quickly and then went up to his room. To my parents, it looked like he was just busy with summer and rugby camp, but they didn't know what Haru had seen, *who* he'd seen.

I couldn't talk to him at home, so after four days, I decided to drive to the Capilano Rugby Club in Klahanie Park, where I knew he was practising. I walked alongside the river, waiting for the session to end, and when I saw a group of tall boys begin to pack up, I headed in their direction.

"Haru!" I raised my arm, waved.

He'd been smiling but stopped as soon as he saw me. He left his friends and walked over. "What are you doing here, Aki?"

"I feel like you're avoiding me."

"Yeah. So what?" He looked away. I saw his jaw clench.

"I want to explain what happened."

"Aki, I'm not an idiot. I saw what happened."

"But you don't have the context. Let me—"

"I don't need the fucking context, Aki. You hurt people—physically hurt people. I just can't be okay with that."

"Haru, please!"

"You should sort out your shit, Aki." Then he left and caught up with his friends.

My whole life I'd taken my brother for granted, assumed he was too rebellious, too immature to understand the pressure I was under and what I was going through, but I'd been wrong. Now he was seeing me for who I really was, and he wanted nothing to do with me. Without Haru, who would I have truly on my side?

I couldn't spend another month at home, living with my parents' disappointment and Haru's disgust. It was only a matter of time until my parents and I started arguing again. Only now, my brother wouldn't have my back anymore.

When I got home, I emailed Abby. She'd been talking about a three-week summer program she was going to attend at UCL, trying to convince Ginika and me to join her. "You can get a taste of classes at another college, Aki." I knew my parents wouldn't say no to more studying.

On my last night at home, before I flew to London, we went to Le Crocodile for dinner. It was something of a tradition for our good-byes—healthy servings of dishes cooked in butter helped distract us from the impending separation. Halfway through our meal, I excused myself to go to the bathroom. Haru followed. But instead of heading in the right direction, he pulled me past the hostess out onto the brick-paved valet parking area outside the restaurant.

"What is it? Are you all right?" I quickened my pace, trying not to trip.

"I am still mad at you. But now you're leaving, so this might be the only time I get to say anything before you're back in London doing God knows what." I held my breath. He stopped walking and turned to face me. "Why did you do it?" Haru shivered in the warm evening breeze.

"I was just defen—"

"Aki, I don't want the bullshit reason. I need to know the truth!"

"Those men deserved it."

"Deserved it?" Haru scoffed and looked away from me. He took a step back. "Who are you to decide that?"

"You don't know what it feels like to be a woman in a situation like that." I stared at the ground. We weren't going to agree on this.

I felt Haru move closer. "I love you, you know that, right? You're not alone." He paused. "But whatever you were doing, it's not right, Aki. I don't know if that was a one-off thing, but I'm going to pretend it was."

"Haru—"

"Don't. Please. I just need to finish saying this. I don't care if you did this before." He looked into my eyes. "I just need you to promise you won't do it again." I extended my arm toward my brother, but he didn't move closer. "Please. Just promise."

I moved and hugged him. Instead of reciprocating, Haru's body tensed. He still wasn't okay with me, with who I'd become. "I promise," I said, more hopeful than honest.

On the ride home, Haru asked to turn on the radio. It played pop song after pop song until Katy Perry's "I Kissed a Girl" came on. I tensed, expecting one of my parents to change the station again, but nothing happened. Instead, it continued to play as I looked out the window. When we finally parked in our driveway, Mom turned the engine off and the music stopped. I opened the door and stepped out, and as I turned back to grab my phone I heard Dad, still sitting in the passenger seat, saying the words to the song under his breath.

It was mid-August when I got back in London, a month before the LSE Michaelmas term was due to start. The residence wasn't available, so Abby's father had rented her a one-bedroom flat near Russell

Square. I was going to sleep on the sofa—not ideal, but better than being at home.

I got off the Gatwick Express and walked to the front of Victoria Station, where Abby was waiting for me.

"Dude! I've missed you so much. How have you been? You look good, healthy." She threw her arms around me.

"I'm all right. You know. Surviving. Glad to be back in London."

"I'm starving. Let's grab something to eat."

We went back into the station and found an Itsu with some metal tables and chairs. I was jetlagged, not in the mood for a full meal, so I ordered a couple of onigiri, while Abby had a curry bowl.

"Dude, you won't believe who's here in London."

I waited, gesturing for her to continue.

"Aren't you going to guess?"

"I don't know. Your boyfriend?"

"No, I wish. Ayesha. Ayesha is here."

I shuffled uncomfortably in the metal chair. No place was safe. Drama followed me everywhere. Or maybe I incited it. "What do you mean? I thought she was in Bradford."

"Nope, her whole family is here in London."

"Wait. Why?"

"Her dad's taken a turn for the worse. He's getting treatment at the Royal Marsden. There's a specialist there, with some new treatment."

I felt my cheeks flush. Ayesha was back in London. I put the onigiri down. My stomach tensed and I felt whatever I'd just eaten rise. I inhaled slowly, thinking I might be sick.

"Aki, are you okay?"

"Yeah. I'm all right." I tried to process what Abby had just said. "Can we head to the flat? I'm really tired." The whole way to the flat, I felt on the verge of a panic attack. It was like my body was infested with microscopic insects crawling all over my skin and scalp. No matter how much I tried to focus on Abby's stories about her time back home, all I wanted was to punch the idiot with the dopey smile and wandering eyes sitting across from us in the tube.

The apartment was small, with a kitchenette that opened up into a living room, a small bathroom, and a bedroom with a standard-sized closet and a double bed. I unpacked, making the most of my half of the closet, while Abby fell asleep almost instantly.

After a quick shower, I opened my suitcase and fished out four hotel-sized bottles of vodka I'd stolen from my parents before leaving. One by one, I opened them and downed the contents in one gulp, then lay on the sofa bed and contemplated the odds of bumping into Ayesha. I grabbed my phone and read the long thread of messages I'd sent to her over the past months. They all started and ended with "I'm sorry." There were no replies.

With too much to drink on a nearly empty stomach and not much hope, I composed a new text. "Hi Ayesha, I know you might not want to see or hear about me, but I'm in London and Abby said you're here with your family. I'm sorry to hear about your dad. I hope his treatment is successful. Anyway, I miss you." I hit send before I had the chance to sober up and come to my senses, and waited for a reply that might never come.

The next morning, Abby and I took the tube to Spitalfields Market to one of our favourite brunch places. Abby went on and on about Lyam, and what the second year of our program would be like. I pretended to be engaged but my legs bounced uncontrollably under the table, and I obsessed about my phone, whether it had enough battery and whether I had good cell reception.

I finally received the message I'd been hoping for while Abby was shopping for new shoes on Oxford Street. I quickly opened it, half expectant, half anticipating an angry reply, but all it said was, "I miss you too." These were the first words I'd heard from Ayesha in half a year, and they inspired so much hope, like somehow it was still possible for us to be on the same page. I looked out the shop window, tears blurring the view of a family of four—what looked like an older man, two young boys, and a pregnant woman. Another buzz on my phone, then Abby's. She cocked her head to one side, reading the text, and then looked up at me. Ayesha had texted us both, inviting us for dinner that evening at the apartment where she was staying. In her message, she said it'd be just us, her and her parents. Asad was back in Bradford.

Abby said something to me, but all I could focus on was the feeling in the pit of my stomach: excitement sinking into dread. I touched my right hand to my forehead. Could this be a delayed hangover?

A gentle tap on my arm. "Dude, are you okay? We don't have to go."

I nodded instinctively, staring blankly ahead, while possible iterations of the night played in my head, and I tried to decide whether to accept Ayesha's invitation. *This might be your only chance.* I'd spent the last six months waiting for this moment, and if I chickened out now, I knew I wouldn't forgive myself. Hangover or not, I was going to set myself straight and attend that dinner.

Knowing I would meet her family, I tried to dress as modestly as possible, in beige chinos and a navy-blue polo that Mom had picked out for me. I tied my hair in a half ponytail, curls dangling on each side of my face. I even considered wearing glasses instead of contacts in an attempt to look more serious, but, in the end, decided that was a silly idea.

Ayesha's grandmother's flat in Bayswater wasn't large enough to accommodate the whole family, so the Hussainis had rented an apartment in Finsbury Park. It was an older brick building, the outside tinged in grey dust, with visible cracks where the walls met. Abby and I walked up to the entrance and pressed the intercom. Before we could say who we were, the front door opened. Apartment 107 was at the very end of the corridor.

We were greeted by Ayesha's mother, who resembled Sana more than her own daughter. She was small, with dark, long hair with a few strands of white. Like Ayesha, she didn't wear a headscarf. Mrs. Hussaini smiled a lot and gestured for us to come in. The flat was small, with a low ceiling. Two faded armchairs and a sofa with an intricate gold and red print hugged the walls and faced the centre of the room, where four bowls with brightly coloured snacks were laid out on a table. I examined the bare walls, before sitting down beside Abby on the sofa, across from Mrs. Hussaini. Ayesha emerged from a room in the back almost as soon as we'd all made ourselves comfortable.

She looked exactly as I remembered, maybe a little more tanned from the summer. Her hair bounced with each step as she made her way across the room. She was still just as beautiful. Abby and I got up and she hugged Ayesha, but I stayed back, unsure of what I could or could not do. That half second where I stood still felt like an eternity, until Ayesha walked up and embraced me. The familiar smell of argan oil and cigarette smoke enveloped me, and I felt unbalanced.

The next half hour was an exchange of pleasantries. Mrs. Hussaini asked Abby and me about our International Relations degrees, and how we knew her daughter, while Ayesha served us a lemon-mint drink made with orange blossom water, no vodka in sight. I wished they'd serve us alcohol; it was a struggle to remain calm and act natural without having my senses dulled.

Right before dinner, her dad joined us with much difficulty. Frail-looking and greying, he appeared older than his wife, though that was probably the cancer. He slowly made his way to the head of a small four-person table around which we'd all squeezed. We ate lentil soup, followed by baingan bartha, and for dessert a bread pudding, soaked in milk, cardamom and saffron. I sat across from Ayesha and stared at my food for most of the meal, afraid her family might be able to read my feelings for her in my face.

After dinner, Ayesha invited Abby and me back to her room. With our backs to a small twin bed on a wooden frame, the three of us sat on the floor, our bodies just inches apart. This could be the closest I'd ever get to her again. After some time of playing pretend, Abby excused herself to the bathroom and left us alone, unchaperoned.

"Are you okay?" I said tentatively, rubbing my hands together with too much force, trying to stay present without being too intense.

"I don't know." Ayesha stared ahead at a small closet in the corner.

I looked around at the small room, paint peeling from the walls. "Why are you staying here?"

"We don't know how long it will be before my dad feels better." She shook her head. "If he feels better." Ayesha picked at a hangnail. I watched a lone tear travel down her cheek. We sat in silence, staring in the same direction.

It didn't feel like the right time to ask, but I didn't know if I would ever get another chance. "Do you think you could ever forgive me?" My whole body tensed expecting her response.

"Has it crossed your mind that maybe, just maybe, that's not top of my mind right now?" She turned to me. "My father is sick. Money is tight, Aki, and there's no one in my family making it. We're just spending and spending."

"I'm so—"

"You haven't changed one bit, you know. I don't know what I was thinking. You are selfish, spoiled." Her brows furrowed. "There's pain outside your own, Aki."

My chest tightened, and I worried I might pass out, just as I'd done that day at the library after speaking with Patience. I pinched my leg hard trying to stay conscious. Abby walked back into the room. "Dude, it's getting late. Maybe we should leave. I don't want to stress out your parents, Ayesha."

"Yeah, yeah. Of course." I got up, unsteadied. My surroundings blurred. Abby left us alone again and I turned to Ayesha, or the smudge I assumed to be her, still sitting on the floor. "Will I see you again? Can we grab coffee next week?"

"I don't know, Aki." She paused. "I'm clearly not ready to have you in my life. Not now, at least."

Not now? When then? Her words cut through me, and I felt my chest tighten even more. I reached for the wall, to support my weight. "Okay, I will give you space." Words betrayed my heart, and I tried to suppress all the ways I'd longed for her over the last few months. My breathing quickened, water overflowing from my eyes. "And when you're ready you'll tell me?" I said, voice trembling.

"If I am ready, I will," Ayesha replied standing up to meet my eyes. "Promise."

CHAPTER 29

Abby and I started the three-week course at UCL the following Monday. Being back at a university, albeit not mine, helped me focus on something other than our visit to the Hussainis, at least during the day. Falling back into a routine with Abby felt natural, though sharing a flat with her did not. She was messy, and I found myself stepping on clothing in the middle of the night on my way to the bathroom.

Despite my best efforts to drink myself to insensitivity at night, while Abby snored in the room next door, Ayesha's words would come back, full force and without fail, almost like clockwork. *You haven't changed one bit.* I sipped directly from a full-size bottle. *You are selfish, spoiled.* I closed my eyes, imagined her brows furrowing just like they had that day. There was resentment in her expression. *There's pain outside your own, Aki.* Empathy is only possible with the acceptance of one's ignorance.

The three weeks went by in a blur, each day uninspiring, each night painfully contemplative. By the time classes resumed at the end of September, London had me on edge. I oscillated between finding life completely unfair and random moments of clarity, where I saw the hole I'd dug for myself.

Ginika, Abby—all of my friends had moved out of the residence, living in flats around the city. I was in the same room as last year. My parents had insisted I stay. Perhaps they thought my opportunities for romantic encounters would be limited there, that it'd be easier to focus on what I was in London for in the first place—my studies. "We're not going to be funding another year of partying, Aki. If you're not living in residence, you will have to pay for things on your own. No more allowances. No credit cards."

Pushed by nothing other than a need to make London work, I went to class every day, trained regularly with the running team and went out often.

"Dude, I can't believe you're still living in residence." Abby had a mocha Frappuccino in hand. "It's nice to have a kitchen."

"At least she's still within walking distance of LSE." Ginika chimed in. She'd moved to a flat in Soho, while Abby was now living in Canary Wharf with two Venezuelan friends.

I looked down at my ham and cheese panini without saying anything.

"Aki, are you all right? You know, I was just making a comment. I'm sure residence is great."

"Yeah, of course." I mustered a weak smile. "I'm all good."

Ginika reached for my arm. "How about we have a sleepover at my place? I'm still not used to being in that flat by myself. This weekend maybe?"

Abby looked out the window from the Starbucks on Kingsway and waved at some people walking by. "Sorry, guys but I'm meeting Lyam in five. Can we pick this up later?

I got up. "I should probably get going too. Don't want to be late for my seminar."

"Aki, your sandwich." Ginika held it out to me.

"I'm not hungry." I picked up my backpack from the floor. "See you later."

As I was leaving, I heard Ginika scold Abby. "Couldn't you have waited another minute before saying you were leaving? You're so oblivious sometimes."

I'd promised to give Ayesha space and time, so that's what I did, though I struggled to resist half-drunken urges to call her at 2:00 a.m. When I wasn't thinking about her, Haru was on my mind. We hadn't spoken properly since I'd left Vancouver and, despite my best efforts to set up a time we could talk over Skype, my brother was full of excuses. "My schedule is packed this weekend. Maybe next Saturday?" "I'm busy with a group assignment." "We have a rugby match, and then a bunch of us are going out for pizza."

No matter what I suggested, there was always an excuse. He didn't want to talk to me, and it was hard to remember the first months of the year, when he'd called me so often, when he'd wanted to support me. I tried to pretend that this was payback for all the times I'd blown him off, but I knew better. Haru's distance wasn't out of spite—it was because of what he'd seen. It was because of me and who he thought I was. It scared me to think this is what we would be to each other from now on—estranged siblings, tolerating each other.

I'd kept my promise to Haru, but by the second week of October, I couldn't resist the urge anymore. I needed a fight. I needed the physical pain that grounded me, forced me to focus on the now. After dinner at Ginika's flat I'd excused myself from a night of clubbing by feigning a headache. I walked home through the Soho district, up and down lanes and back alleyways. I remained watchful, looking for an opportunity. When I turned the corner on Goslett Yard, I saw a woman stumbling toward Charing Cross Rd, high heels in hand. A man followed right behind her, though it was hard to tell if they knew each other. I quickened my pace down the dark, narrow road.

"Hey!"

They continued walking.

"Hello!"

The woman turned, confused, then realizing there was a man behind her, picked up her pace. So they didn't know each other. The man lunged toward her and grabbed her arm. I ran toward them.

"Let her go!"

"Mind your own business." He tripped me and I broke the fall with my hands.

"Help!" The woman held her high heels as weapons.

A uniformed man, a security guard maybe, stopped under a streetlight on Charing Cross Road. "Is everything all right?" he said, then walked toward us, his hand on his baton holder.

The man, startled, let go of the woman's arm and ran in the opposite direction.

I pushed myself off the ground and wiped my hands on my pants. My phone buzzed.

The guard extended his arms toward the woman. "Are you okay? I work a few doors down. Should I call the police?" She shook her head.

"How about you?" The guard turned to me.

"All good." I tried to hide my disappointment. I had really wanted to beat the shit out of that creep. My phone buzzed again. I took it out of my pocket. Ayesha. My hands shook in surprise, and I hesitated for a second, maybe two, before accepting the call.

"Hello?" I expected silence on the other end. Maybe she didn't mean to call. It was possible this was a butt dial.

"Hi." Her voice was soft but warm. There was a pause. I could hear Ayesha's breathing, the pace quickening. "Can I see you?" she said as if she were ripping off a band-aid.

"Oh, hm." I couldn't think of what to say.

"You know what. That was stupid. I'm stu—"

"No! Not stupid. Sorry. I'm just a little shocked. Yes. Of course, yes."

Ayesha agreed to meet me at Victoria Station. As I got off the tube, I looked up high at the arches and remembered the night I'd stumbled off the Victoria line and onto a train to Oxted. Another fight I'd picked. Victoria Station hadn't changed since then. I want to believe I had, but I was struggling not to fall back on old coping mechanisms. Maybe with Ayesha, I could break the pattern for good.

As I stood under the big live departure board, I imagined I'd be waiting for her for a while. After all, she was usually late. How would I greet her? Should I hug her, or would that be too presumptuous? Should I extend my hand, or would that be too formal? Before I could decide, Ayesha came up from behind and surprised me with a full-body hug. She still smelled the same, and I nestled my head in her hair, while she gripped tighter and tighter. Her warmth confused me, but I didn't contest it. I'd waited for months to hold her again. I wasn't going to let my mind ruin it for me.

Ayesha and I stood there, holding each other, for a minute, two, maybe five, until we noticed people staring. Then, she let go and looked at me with a familiar expression. "I've been thinking about doing this since I saw you in August."

It was nearly 10:00 p.m., so we opted for a pub just outside the station. As it was a weekday, it was much emptier than the last time we'd been there together, before I broke her heart. The pub was small, darkly lit, with one TV on the first floor and another on the second and that familiar scent of piss and beer. Large windows illuminated a narrow set of wooden stairs that led up. Ayesha and I had once spent the whole night standing in that corner of the pub, our bodies turned to each other, ignoring the waves of drunken people who wanted to reach the bathroom on the second floor.

Tonight, though, we sat at a small table in a nook by the door. Ayesha ordered a gin and tonic and I asked for tap water. I wanted to be sober, so I could remember this moment, all its nuances.

"How have you been?" I asked. I wanted to move beyond small talk but didn't know how. "How's art school?"

"I'm getting by." There was sadness in her eyes. "I don't really connect with anyone in my classes, so it can get a bit lonely."

I paused, unsure of what to say. Instead, I extended my hand, and she placed hers on mine, before forcing a smile. I cocked my head to the side, trying to decipher the things hidden in the distance between us.

"It's okay, really."

"How's your dad?"

"He's feeling better. Parents are back in Bradford."

"How about money?"

"It's tight. My grandma is helping out, in addition to the free rent."

"How are things at home?" I asked. What I really wanted to say was, how are things with your cousin, knowing they probably still lived together, but saying Sana's name was harder than I had anticipated.

"They're all right," she said, reading between the lines. "We don't talk about it. It's like you never happened."

My heart sank. Like I never happened. Did that mean before or after Sana? Did I never happen for one or both of them? Ayesha sipped on her gin and tonic, and I stared out the window, watching another rainy night in London.

"Do you want to get out of here?" she said finally, getting up from her seat.

Back at my residence, we stopped at the corner of Malet Street and Torrington Place.

"Can I come up?" Ayesha asked.

I didn't know. Could she? I wanted to ask if she was sure, but that felt patronizing, like somehow I assumed I knew what was best for her. Instead I nodded.

When we got to my room Ayesha walked to the bed and lay down. I did the same, right beside her, our bodies softly touching, until we both dozed off. I woke up around 3:00 a.m. to a sliver of light and the sound of the door closing. I reached out to find emptiness. I raced to the door, looking for my shoes, but they were all mismatched. I searched for the light, to find the right pair, when it occurred to me she might not want to be chased down the street. Maybe the reason she'd left in the middle of the night was indeed because she wanted to leave.

I moved toward the window and opened the curtains. Ayesha stood at the bottom of the steps of my residence for a few moments, a streetlamp flickering above her. Then, she turned right toward the British Museum. I watched her for as long as I could, until she disappeared into the darkness.

I wanted to be around Ayesha, but not like this. I needed to give her the space she needed, and I needed to work on myself. I needed to dial back on the drinking and partying. I needed to stop looking for fights. That night, I typed up a list of resolutions on my Blackberry.

I cut back on the vodka. When I went out to a pub or club, I left my card at home and only took cash to limit my alcohol intake. I also limited my partying to friends I knew weren't the type to stay out late. And I studied. It felt like turning a corner. I didn't know for sure where it would lead, but somewhere better nonetheless.

CHAPTER 30

Ayesha started texting me again, and that was all that mattered. The first time she messaged me was to ask for my help with a class project. The next day, she asked for a restaurant recommendation. A week later, she sent me the trailer of a movie she was interested in seeing. We never talked about her leaving in the middle of the night.

In a way, it felt like a reset. After a couple of weeks of random messages, we upgraded to short phone calls, then longer ones, and finally to coffees, lunches and dinners. There was no handholding, no cuddling, no kissing. We didn't talk about the past, about Sana, Asad or how I'd hurt her. We didn't acknowledge the months we'd spent apart. Instead, we acted like we were meeting for the first time.

Then, one day, after lunch on Edgware Road, she asked me to help move a piece she'd been working on at home to her studio at Chelsea College of Arts.

"What?" I said in disbelief.

"It's too big for one person to carry. I promise it won't take more than an hour."

I looked at Ayesha, hoping this might be a joke, but she wasn't laughing. Did she not remember what had happened the last time we were there together? Did she not remember I slept with her cousin and she caught us in bed?

"Ayesha . . ." I was going to have to break the illusion we were operating under, this illusion that we didn't have a history. "I would love to help, but I'm not sure this is a good idea, all things considered."

We both stopped walking. "Don't worry. Sana is away." She started moving again, but I stood still.

"Still, are we ready for this? Things have been going so well. I just don't want to mess anything up."

"It's just a painting, Aki."

As we made our way to her apartment, Ayesha talked about an upcoming show for second-year students and how unprepared she felt. But my mind was only half-listening, the other half too pre-occupied with being back in her space again. How would things look? Would I see Sana's room? What should I talk about while we were there?

When we arrived at her floor, I stood back while she opened the door, and for a while even after she'd walked in. "Are you coming?"

"Waiting here is not an option, eh?" I said, laughing halfheartedly.

An orange-tinged afternoon light shone in through the large windows in the living room. At first glance the place still looked the same. To the left was Sana's room, the door half-opened, clothes on the floor. Ayesha rushed to close it, but I recognized the baby pink overcoat on the bed as the one Sana had worn the night she came to my residence, the last time I'd seen her. I was glad she was away, whatever that meant.

A new photo of their extended family on the wall—Sana and Ayesha only three people apart. A pile of unopened correspondence next to a vase. The vase. The broken vase was still there. My hands extended toward it, my fingers tracing the cracks. She'd kept the vase. Even after all this time. I smiled to myself.

"Are you going to join me here?"

"Coming!" I rushed to her room, to find Ayesha behind a large canvas that was taller than it was wide.

"What do you think?" She looked at me in anticipation.

A woman with a similar build and features as hers stood in the middle, looking down and away. Her black hair was braided, and she wore dark clothes with a long overcoat. In the backdrop, the London skyline from Regent's Park, the exact view from the spot we'd gone the night we met. I recognized it from the many times I'd visited it in the months we hadn't spoken to each other. I moved closer to the canvas. Behind the woman, head bent over her left hand was a second person, with long curly hair. This was a take on Arthur Hughes's "April Love."

"I started painting it after you came out. Then, when everything happened, I didn't know if I should throw it away." She paused for a moment. "Anyway, I couldn't do it, so I kept it under my bed until I came back from the summer break."

Tears collected at the corners of my eyes, and the painting became blurry. "Is it us?"

"A version of us, at a certain time and place."

"I really like it," I said, my voice breaking.

Ayesha smiled, then tilted the painting on its side. "Shall we go?" She lifted one end, and I the other, and we slowly maneuvered the canvas out of the apartment, down the stairs, out of the building, and into a cab.

In the days leading up to Ayesha's art exhibition, we spent most of our free time together talking, studying, procrastinating. We would meet after morning lectures, have lunch, go back to our classes or seminars, and convene later for dinner, drinks or sometimes a movie. It wasn't until I walked into the large studio space I'd helped her move her artwork into that I realized things might not be going as well for her as I'd thought. I was Ayesha's only guest. None of our friends were there. At first, I tried not to read too much into it. It was possible she invited them at the last minute and they had other plans. She could be a forgetful person. And yet, I couldn't recall a conversation about asking them, nor could I remember one with Abby or Ginika. I wondered if the two of them were sick of the drama and just wanted out of whatever was going on between Ayesha and me. But that felt weird too, because just two days ago Ginika asked me how things were going.

While Ayesha talked to one of her instructors, I stepped away and texted Abby, "Are you coming?"

"Coming where?"

"To Ayesha's exhibition."

"Pretty sure she didn't invite me, dude. In fact, I haven't heard from Ayesha since the beginning of term. I don't think any of us have."

CHAPTER 31

I stood outside Queensway station and waited for Ayesha. We were going out for a quick dinner before I met Ginika and a few of the girls from the team for a movie. Maybe it was best to cancel. I looked at my watch—just past 6:00 p.m. People came out of the station in rhythmic bursts. Where was she? I checked my watch again—6:07. I took out a book on Chikuro Hiroike, the father of Moralogy, out of my backpack and began flipping through the first few pages. I was a few sentences in when I heard a shout.

"You!" I raised my head and saw a man pointing at me. A group of girls looked back and forth between me and him. He looked familiar. I squinted, trying to make out his features. No, he wasn't from one of my classes. Dark curly hair, full eyebrows, big nose. Trailing behind him was Ayesha, her nose red, her eyes swollen. She'd been crying. Why was she crying? Then I recognized him. It was Asad.

Ayesha clung to her brother's arm, trying to hold him back, and stared at me, begging. She said something, to him or maybe to me. I couldn't make out the words. Asad pulled his arms away from her. "You!" he repeated. Ayesha held her cheek with both hands.

Asad quickened his pace, crossing the street in my direction. I picked my bag off the ground and stuffed the book inside. Ayesha mouthed one word: run. Then she shook her head and turned away.

I took off, dodging the crowd coming out of the tube station, and headed across Bayswater Road to Hyde Park. I knew the paths there well—the running team trained here once a week. I told myself I didn't need to fight him, I just needed to outrun him.

Foot traffic in the park was beginning to die down. Few people liked being around when the light began to fade. I slipped and almost fell, catching my balance inches off the ground. If I could see better, I might be able to stick to the paths, but the sun was setting over the London skyline. The grass was still wet from the October rain, so I shortened my stride and tightened the straps of my backpack to prevent it from hitting my back.

I periodically looked over my shoulder to see how much of a lead I'd built. Asad was a few paces behind me, already out of breath. He looked as athletic as his sister had on that first day in the park, his form equally appalling. I was confident I could outrun him. If I made it to Knightsbridge Station, I could get on the tube home. I quickened my pace, cutting through Kensington Gardens.

But running would just make it worse for Ayesha. Ever since I met her, I'd done so much to hurt her. I'd outed her to her cousin. I'd cheated on her. And now I'd put her in danger. It was all leading to this. How could I not see it? I slowed down, then, stopped. Puffs of steam swirled around me as I tried to catch my breath. I had to let him have this.

I stopped and turned around, watching Asad run toward me. His breathing was laboured. He put his hands on his knees, like he might vomit, then wiped his forehead with his sleeve and straightened his back. He was almost two feet taller than me. I raised my head and closed my eyes, bracing for the expected blow. His knuckles met my left cheek. My head moved sideways, and my body followed. I fell on my hands and knees. There was no fight left in me. He pushed me down and kicked me on the side twice. *Spoiled. Selfish.* Ayesha's words. I deserved this. I lay flat on my stomach, then curled to one side. A constricting pain, like someone was gripping my lungs tighter and tighter.

"You had the guts to show up to my parent's flat, to eat their food."

"How do you—"

"How do I know it?" He scoffed. "They told me what Ayesha's 'kind' friends looked like." He gestured air quotes.

"I'm sor—"

"You're a sick homo," he said. "Leave Ayesha alone." Asad spit at me and walked away.

I hugged my knees to my chest. Then I crawled to a bench and pulled myself up. I coughed, red speckles landing on the grass below. Placing my backpack at one end of the bench, I rested my head on it. Overflowing tears.

I replayed the last year in my head. *This is not natural. You are making everyone's life harder. I don't even know who you are anymore.* I'd lost everything: my family, myself, now Ayesha. I had messed things up with everyone. Would Ayesha be okay? Would Asad hurt her too? Could I call Sana and ask for help? No. That would only make things worse.

I counted the seconds between my breaths, trying to slow down the rhythm of my heart. Every inhale brought a sharp pain below my ribs. I felt beaten, like nothing I could do would ever make a difference, like I could not be better for Ayesha, like I could not keep my promise to Haru. This was rock bottom. It had to be.

CHAPTER 32

For three days I didn't get out of bed. Didn't answer my phone or respond to texts. I ordered the little food I ate and had it delivered just outside my door. On the fourth day, I dragged myself out, the pain in my side fading but not the bruises. In the moment, I had thought taking the beating would absolve me of some guilt. Damn, I'd thought it might even be noble. I knew taking the beating was probably all I could do to prevent Asad doing something worse to Ayesha. In reality, it was the last part of me giving up on everything and everyone. Still, part of me couldn't help but feel Asad shouldn't have been the one dishing out punishment. I was confused and also fucking angry.

I didn't realize I was back in Hyde Park, near Bayswater tube station, until I found myself sitting on the same park bench, a half-empty vodka bottle in hand. It was dark. The air was crisp. Branches swayed above me, the wind picking up as I situated myself. Besides the few homeless people that slept near the bushes or on benches away from the pond, I seemed to be the only person in the park. I gulped down half of what was left in the bottle, the vodka burning the back of my throat as I looked toward the place where Asad had pushed me to the ground, where he'd beaten me up. I thought about how things might have been different if I'd fought back, if I hadn't let him win.

I was gathering my belonging to leave when I saw him—tall, dark hair, black overcoat. Could it be Asad? Was he back to finish what he'd started? I moved closer, trying to focus, squinting to see better. My pace quickened. He was fidgeting with something, looking down. I inched closer. That's when he shook his head and turned to walk away, toward the north end of the park.

"Hey!" I waved for him to stop, but he ignored me. I needed to see his face. I jogged after him, shoes slipping on the wet grass. The man looked behind every few steps, panic in his stride.

He wasn't fast or fit, though he was tall, which helped him keep some distance from me. But just as we approached the park gate near Queensway Station, he slowed, gasping for air. I kicked the back of his right leg so he wouldn't run away again. He stumbled forward, trying to steady himself. I lifted my fists in front of my face, ready for a fight, but when he turned my heart sank. He had a large nose, like Asad's, and a similar build, but as the streetlamp shone softly on both our faces, it wasn't him.

He put up his hands—they were shaking—facing me.

"Don't, don't . . ." Fear. That's what I saw in his eyes.

"Do you want my phone? Money? You can have anything you want." He fumbled with his pocket, one hand still raised in supplication, his wide eyes not leaving mine.

My stomach churned. Who had I become? This wasn't Asad, no matter how badly I wanted it to be him.

"I'm sorry," I said softly. "I thought you were someone else."

He backed away while I stood still, my hands shaking. I wanted to go over and comfort him—he looked so vulnerable, so scared. He turned, ran to the road and hailed a cab.

I bent over and vomited.

I lay on the wet grass for a while, until my breath felt even again. It was almost five. The tube would start running again soon.

I walked. Past my residence to Camden Town, then back down. It took me an hour, maybe two. I don't remember. Faces blurred past me, the voices in my head blocking out every other sound.

You are not my sister.

You are selfish, spoiled.

I used to be proud of you.

I'm clearly not ready to have you in my life.

You are not someone I know.

There's pain outside your own.

That poor, frightened man. I was exactly like all those arrogant, entitled pricks I'd fought. I wasn't a victim. I wasn't a saviour. I was an aggressor.

Since coming out, I'd told myself I was the victim in every situation. With my parents. With Ayesha. With my friends. It was all about me, little, quiet me. I told myself I fought according to my rules and principles, but I didn't. I was fighting for me, for the pain I needed to feel and to inflict, so I could be in control.

The West Vancouver bubble. The private school. The money, the holidays. The designer clothes and trappings. The top grades and sporting success. And my parents smiling on and on at their perfect daughter.

Could I go back? Could I go back to the Aki and the world where my privilege was justified?

A sob escaped me. A vortex of loathing howled inside me.

By the time I got to the glass doors of my residence, I had convinced myself the world would be better without me in it. For the past ten months I'd caused so much harm. I'd hurt so many people I loved, physically hurt people I didn't. I couldn't think of one person who was better off for having me in their life. I was toxic.

I didn't go to my room. Instead, I headed straight to one of the shared bathrooms on my floor, the only ones with bathtubs. I closed the door behind me, felt for the taps and turned them on. With the room still dark, I crawled inside the bathtub. The water was tepid, and I felt it soak my clothes through, my pants and shirt first, my underwear and socks last. I shivered and I lay there, waiting for the water to engulf me.

Mom. Me. Tourists. Snorkelling. The warm ocean waters around an island in Panama. The edge of a coral reef. The current pulling us, sweeping us away. Saltwater burning my nose, my throat. The panic in the eyes of our guide, so clear behind his mask. Mom, struggling, her head beneath the waves. Me. Screaming in every language I knew for a life jacket. Dragging one onto my mother. Using all my energy to pull her to shore.

I closed my eyes, held my breath and let my face slide under the tepid water. My clothes inflated and I pushed my legs against the sides of the bathtub to prevent myself from floating up.

My heart pounded. Lungs ached in starvation. I knew I wouldn't last long. My hands moved toward my neck. I was running out of air, my mind slowly fading. Then one involuntary breath, water travelling up my nose and down my windpipe. An agonizing burn. Nothing.

I awoke in a room painted completely white. There was a nurse, and then a doctor. I was in University College London Hospital, just a few blocks from the residence. They were asking me how I had found myself in an overflowing bathtub and explained that I had been found by one of the residence maids, who'd noticed water spilling out from under the bathroom door.

"The paramedics revived you. You're a lucky girl," the nurse said. All I could think of was how I managed to mess up dying. I wasn't even good enough at that.

I tried to lie, to say that I was really tired from pulling all-nighters studying for my midterms, even though LSE didn't have those for International Relations. I said I'd fallen asleep in the bathtub, but they didn't believe me. The doctor kept me over night on suicide watch. The next morning, I was sent back to my residence.

CHAPTER 33

In the days that followed, I felt empty, as if all the contents of my mind had oozed out into the bathtub and travelled down the drain to somewhere I could never recover them. My family called incessantly on Skype, Mom sobbing with her hand over her mouth, Dad holding her tightly at his side. I couldn't do anything more than sit in front of the camera.

"Aki, what is going on!" Mom had unbrushed morning hair and her eyes looked tired and swollen.

"Aki-chan, why did you do that?" Dad's customary stoicism was replaced by small teardrops that formed at the corners of his eyes every time he uttered a word. He looked fragile, breakable.

I didn't have an adequate response. Suicide had felt like the only option in that moment, so it felt unreasonable not to act on it. I wanted to say that wasn't how I felt right now, though I couldn't promise I wouldn't feel that way again. I said none of that.

"Come home, Aki. Take the year off."

"No. It will be fine."

"Aki, I'm getting on the next plane to London. You need me and I have to be there."

"No, Mom."

Ginika and Abby visited daily. They wanted me to go back to the LSE counsellor, but Olivia Acton wasn't what I wanted. I didn't want to see the "I told you so" in her eyes.

"You have to see someone, Aki. You need to talk to someone." Ginika handed over a printed list of psychologists in Central London.

"Therapy isn't that bad, dude. Everyone does it now."

"I really can't see how a therapist will fix this." I fluttered my hands around me.

"Do you have a better option?" Ginika pressed her lips together and looked intently at me.

"I guess pushing my feelings down isn't an option." I smiled.

"Promise you will try." Abby touched my shoulder. "We've called around and highlighted the ones we think might be a good fit."

"Thank you." I looked at Abby, then Ginika. I wasn't sure I would call any of these people, but for perhaps the first time since, I could really see the effort they were making. Their sincerity. "I mean it."

"We're here for you, Aki."

"Yeah, dude. We're not going anywhere."

I replayed the last year obsessively in my head. I thought back to the young woman before the rupture, remembering how she wanted nothing more than to fit in, leave West Vancouver and disappear. I thought about the years of collecting grievances, forcing them to fit in a tight space, without ever letting my emotions breathe.

I wondered if the fight had always been in me, just waiting for the right moment to make an appearance. With every fight, I wore down the impotence, the numbness I'd been feeling. The hurt, the sadness, the anger. I felt it all. Every explosion was an opportunity to obliterate the whole. Every fight was a way to see the parts. Every recovery was a chance to reinvent the self. So, I did that until I could no longer remember who I was before I became a fighter. But attacking another person, no matter how awful they are, kills a part of your humanity, bit by bit.

Perhaps the break, the explosion, was unstoppable, inescapable. But inevitability eliminates responsibility. I thought of the ways in which I'd stayed the same. Then I thought about the fighter. She was also me, wounded and raw, fighting for the existence of the imperfect parts of myself I'd never let surface. Perhaps I'd finally learned the difference between fighting yourself and fighting *for* yourself.

As my future went from bleak and immutable to the possible "whatever you make of it," I decided fresh air couldn't harm me more than being stuck in a stuffy residence room by myself.

It was on a stroll a couple of days after Abby and Ginika had brought the list of psychologists that I bumped into Patience on Charing Cross Road. She was coming out of TK Maxx with two large bags. I began to turn away when she called my name.

"Aki!" I wanted to keep on walking away but my legs stopped. Patience said my name again, and I could tell she was much closer.

I turned to see her. "Hi . . ." Her hair was braided back in a ponytail and she wore a puffy green jacket.

"I thought that was you!" She touched my arm. "How have you been?"

"Uh, I've been good. How are you?" I was confused by the warmth.

"I'm happy. Enjoying my last few months of LSE."

"That's right." I took a breath and looked at the floor "It's your last year, isn't it?"

There was an awkward pause. Patience touched my arm again. "Hey, can we talk? Like, do you have time to talk now?"

I looked around, trying to shape a satisfying excuse out of thin air. "It's okay if you don't."

"No, no." The words slipped out. "Let's talk."

We crossed the road and went into Foyles, which was busy

with Christmas shoppers, and searched for the café. She ordered a mocha and I had a shot of espresso. We found a table to sit near the window. Then Patience jumped right in.

"I'm sorry for the way I ended things. I could have handled it better."

"I don't think you could have." I looked down at my hands. "Anyway, it wasn't your fault. I was going through a lot, and it shouldn't have been on you to figure out my shit."

"I know you're saying that, but I also know you probably needed more from me than what I could give you."

"Yeah, but that's my problem, isn't it?" I took a sip of the espresso, my jaws involuntarily tightening.

Patience sighed. "Aki, I know you might not want to hear this, but when you live your life in extremes, you miss all the important nuances of just being human." She reached for my hands, and her warmth sent a shiver down my back. "I've thought a lot about you these past few months. Being with you, there were so many highs and lows, but very little in between."

I looked out the window and tried to hold back the emotions. Patience continued, "The versions of yourself you've separated are not mutually exclusive. I was so shocked when I saw you in that alley, beating up that man. Surely, that couldn't be the person I was dating—the kind, quirky, thoughtful Aki."

Patience paused. Tears trickled down my face.

"But it was all of you, the parts you wanted me to see, and the parts you felt you had to keep hidden. I wish I would have had this clarity in May. You are not a bad person, Aki. I never should have made you feel like you were."

"I'm sorry I treated you like a ticket out of my misery. I wanted you to be perfect, uncomplicated, because my life felt anything but that. I never truly gave us a chance. You deserved to have the space to go through your own shit too, and I didn't give you any space."

"You know, I finally came out to my parents."

I wiped my eyes. "Really?"

"Don't sound so surprised! I just needed to do it on my own terms, you know."

"I'm happy for you." I truly meant it. I felt like I was really seeing the person sitting across from me. Really seeing her.

"Are you still getting into your back-alley shenanigans?"

"No, I've been *good*." I winked at her.

"Being mixed, we're conditioned to compartmentalize." Patience brought the mocha to her mouth, then sat it back down in front of her. "That's the way society keeps us fragmented and under control. Imagine how wonderful it would be to be everything at once? Asian *and* Latina, privileged *and* oppressed, strong *and* vulnerable."

"What is it you're studying again?" I laughed. Then I sat with that thought for a moment, imagining all the shades of grey I'd been depriving myself of.

"Aki, what I'm trying to say is don't let someone else—whoever they might be—define your story and tell you what box you can or cannot fit into. Anyway, that's what I should have told you that day in the library. The choice of who you are, who you want to be, is yours. No one can take that away from you unless you let them."

Patience and I made plans to hang out as friends, once we returned to London after the holidays. Maybe that's all we should have been in the first place. We'd both searched in each other for an answer that we could have only found through self-discovery, and neither of us wanted to repeat the mistake.

In the days that followed, I kept on coming back to her words. *The choice of who you are, who you want to be, is yours.* Patience was right. There had always been a choice, even when I had felt circumstances had forced my hand.

Keeping emotions bottled up had never served me well—not

when I managed to hide them back in West Vancouver, and certainly not when I began to explode after my move to London. I'd started fighting to try and control what was happening around me. It'd served a purpose, despite its pitfalls, and part of me would always be afraid that I might relapse. The fighter would never leave me, but she might grow and change. And maybe that was okay too.

CHAPTER 34

One Saturday morning, in early December, there was a knock on my door. I'd been reading Naomi Klein's *No Logo*. When I opened it, I was amazed to see Haru standing there. He'd grown another inch or two and put on some weight. His chest was bigger and shoulders broader, and he'd traded his shaggy haircut for a military crew cut. But he was still the brother I'd left a few months ago in Canada.

He hugged me tightly without saying a word.

"Good flight?" I said instinctively.

He laughed. "Sure, good flight, Aki. Look. I'm staying at a hotel in Kensington. Come with me to help me check in?"

He'd packed light, with only a medium-sized suitcase and what appeared to be a mostly empty backpack. The tube arrived at Russell Square station, and I let Haru go in first. The car filled in quickly, and he struggled to hold on to his suitcase while keeping it out of the way.

"Just put it between your legs and hold on with your knees."

"That's what she said," he smirked.

I laughed. "It really *is* still you. Just bigger and without any hair."

Haru felt the top of his head. "Just you wait. In a couple of months, you'll be rocking this too. It's the prime lesbian look."

There was a pause. "Sorry you had to come."

"I get to skip school for a couple of weeks. Nothing to be sorry about. Mom thought maybe you could use the company."

"So you're Mom's spy." I got serious. "I'm getting my shit together. Promise."

Haru held my hand and smiled. "I know."

The first night, we had dinner in his room. Haru was jetlagged and fell asleep early. His phone had been lighting up ever since he'd arrived, and before I left, I snuck a peak at it.

Every message was from Becca. "I miss you," and "Please talk to me," were two of her favourites. I turned his phone face down on the table—I didn't need to know Becca's desperation intimately. Then I left Haru to sleep.

Back at my residence, I worried. I wanted to ask Haru what that was all about—why, how, were they back together—but I worried about what that might push him to do. He was, after all, the king of the contrary. Whatever you told him not to do, he would, without a doubt, do it.

The next afternoon, we were walking in Kensington Gardens, when Haru's phone rang. He walked a short distance from me to take the call, but I overheard some of the conversation.

"I will. I will ask her! Let me do it my way, please. Otherwise, what's the point of sending me instead of coming yourselves?" He looked at me, and said, "Gotta go. Bye."

Haru wanted an English high tea, so we walked to a place Lyam had taken Abby near Harrods. We both knew we had to talk about the episode in the bathtub, and the earlier we got it out of the way, the quicker we could move on to talking about other things.

"Aki, can I ask you something?" Haru took a sip of his tea.

"Yeah, sure. Shoot." I tried to sound like I didn't know what this was about. It was my way of trying to relieve the tension.

"I mean, it's not really a question. Or maybe it is."

"Haru, just go for it."

Our eyes met. My brother took a big breath. "Are you going to do it again?"

"You mean, try to off myself?"

"Well, that's morbid. But yeah."

"I don't feel like I am. Not now, anyway."

"Did the fighting have anything to do with it?" The waitress brought out the three-tiered plate stand with little sandwiches, scones and cakes. "Thank you," Haru said to her.

I waited for her to leave before starting. "Maybe? I'm not sure, to be honest. I'm still trying to figure it out." I paused. "I think the fighting stopped me from trying it sooner."

Haru looked confused.

"What I mean is, I needed something to control. And fighting gave me a sense of that, for a while. But then, after, you know, The Clinic, I began to feel unhinged. and I think in the end the fighting turned against me."

"Are you still fighting?"

"Not since I've come home from the hospital."

"Are you going to fight again?"

"I don't want to."

We both smiled.

Haru and I went to Camden and explored the market. And continued to eat. We took a double-decker tour bus around the top sights. We walked along the river and watched the sunset over the city atop the London Eye. On Tuesday, we found ourselves right outside Buckingham Palace waiting in the rain for the changing of the guards.

"Isn't it fucked how the monarchy is still a thing?" Haru shook his head.

"Not as fucked as Canada being part of the Commonwealth."

He turned to face me. "Can I ask you a question?"

I continued to stare across the space between the gate and the palace, wishing the damn thing would just start. "Sure. What do you want to know?"

"How would you feel if I got back with Becca?"

"Are you? Already?" I said, without looking at him.

"Not officially."

"Do you actually want to know my opinion?" If Becca were a man, she'd be everything I'd looked for in a target—arrogant, misogynistic, argumentative, prone to violence. But taking her— or them—down wasn't my responsibility. Not for now.

"Haru, you know I don't like Becca, but after the shit year I've had, I don't want to ever make you feel like I won't take your side. If you feel like Becca is the right decision for you, then I'll learn to be okay with it."

Haru smiled. "Thank you."

"Just promise me one thing."

"Yeah . . ."

"Promise you won't force yourself to stay when you outgrow the relationship. It's okay for things to end, you know?"

"Promise." We heard drums, followed by trumpets. "Now shut up. We don't want to miss the royals," he said sarcastically.

Abby, Ginika and I sat in a pub, waiting for Haru to return from the bathroom. "Your brother is cute." Abby followed him with her eyes. "If he were a little older, I'd entertain the possibility."

"No, thank you." Ginika wagged her index finger. "He's a boy. Look at that baby face—no hair. He can't handle this." She ran her hands down her figure.

"I'd rather we didn't discuss my little brother in this context."

"Don't be a prude. You know he's cute," Abby continued.

"Did I miss anything?" Haru sat between Abby and me.

"No, just Abby forgetting she's got a boyfriend." Ginika took a sip of her drink.

"So, what is Aki like in London?" Haru looked over at Ginika and Abby. "I only know Vancouver Aki."

"Sexually liberated," they said in unison.

"What? That's not true. Can we change the subject please?"

"No, no. I want to hear this. Those are not the words anyone would have used to describe my sister in high school."

"Aki's slept with half of the lesbian population of London," Abby said between swigs of her cranberry and vodka.

"Oh, wow. Are we talking about this Aki over here?" Haru looked me up and down.

I shook my head. "Come on. Look, what are we going to do? The night is still young."

"The Zoo!" Abby shrieked.

"Definitely. This boy needs to get down at that club," Ginika agreed. What started as a modest hangout soon turned into something more. Abby invited Lyam, Ginika invited Kwaku, and I called Anaïs, who I thought might spark Haru's interest. I was planning on being on my own that night, but to my surprise, Anaïs decided to bring Ayesha too.

We went into Zoo Bar as pairs, and even though Ayesha and I were not together, we kept each other company. We started the night at the bar drinking shots, then made our way through the dance floor to a corner of the bar with a couple of velvet stools.

Eventually a woman, not much taller than me, with long brown hair and dark eyes approached us. She wore black jeans and a white T-shirt, with black Converse hi-tops. Allison introduced herself and told us she was studying to be a nurse. After some awkward chatter, she asked Ayesha to dance, extending her right hand in a funny gentleman-like manner that made me laugh inside.

I watched them and remembered the night I first kissed Ayesha, how I'd stepped in when someone else tried to flirt with her, telling him I was her girlfriend. But that wasn't my place anymore. I'd had

EMI SASAGAWA

my chance. Ayesha and I looked at each other for a while. Then, I nodded and imagined myself letting her go. She placed her hand in Allison's and they moved away from me, to the other end of the room.

Eventually, I found my way back to the group on the dance floor. Lyam and Kwaku had decided to leave and meet their basketball team at the Penthouse, so it was Haru and four women. "Are you having fun?" I yelled into his right ear.

He smiled without saying a word. The music was too loud. Zoo Bar was getting crowded very quickly. I surveyed the club looking for familiar faces. I spotted a couple of boys from LSE, and a tall blond man with shoulder-length hair walking toward us. He was no college kid, more likely someone in his thirties. As he approached, he locked eyes with Haru.

"Are any of these taken?" The man gestured toward Ginika, Abby, Anaïs and me.

Ginika and I looked at each other. "Excuse me. We can speak for ourselves." I stepped between the man and Haru.

"Patience, babe. I haven't made my choice yet."

"Whatever it is, we're not interested." I stood on the tips of my toes, making myself as big as possible.

"Okay, okay. I pick you." The man put his right hand on my waist and pulled me toward him. Haru stepped forward and shoved the man's shoulder.

"Fine! I was kidding. Can't take a fucking joke."

"Are you okay?" Haru put his arm around me.

"I can handle myself." I shrugged him off.

"I'm done. Let's leave." Ginika grabbed my hand and led the way to the door.

Once outside, the five of us stood awkwardly looking at each other, not knowing what to suggest next. Anaïs texted Ayesha to let her know we were leaving. "She's okay. She's going to stay with Allison."

"So much for a night out, huh?" Ginika tried to alleviate the tension.

"That was insane, dude. Thank God Haru was there to handle that sleazebag."

Haru looked at me but didn't say anything.

Abby, Ginika and Anaïs decided to go for a late-night Chinese.

"Do you want to go, Haru?" I asked.

"No. I'm good. I'd just like to get back to my hotel. Flight tomorrow."

The two of us walked to Leicester Square tube station. At the entrance, Haru stopped. "Can we talk about tonight?"

"I really don't think now's the time for it. We're both tired." I turned away to go into the station, but Haru grabbed my shoulder.

"Aki, I think I get it now." He sighed. "I get why you beat up those men at The Clinic."

I stopped in my tracks, my breath quickening.

"You're a badass. You will still be a badass even if you don't beat up people, you know." He smiled. "Even if some of them deserve it."

I laughed.

"Plus, there are other ways of fighting." He paused. "But I bet you already know that."

CHAPTER 35

Haru's flight wasn't until late afternoon. I met him at his hotel in the morning, and he checked out, leaving his suitcase and backpack with reception.

"Where are we going, badass?"

"I hope that's not going to be your new nickname for me," I said, punching him lightly on the shoulder. "It's a surprise. Follow me."

Takibi's salon was just behind Oxford Street. He was a tall, thin man in his mid-twenties with choppy hair that reminded me of Shane from *The L Word*. I'd done my research and decided that a Japanese stylist was the right professional for this job. I'm sure the place was usually busy, but on that Tuesday morning, I was his only client. He placed me in a chair and went to bring some *genmaicha*, roasted rice green tea.

Takibi's smiled above and behind me, his reflection in the mirror showing two overlapping front teeth. "Why do you want to cut your hair? In Japan, women want to grow their hair long, to look more feminine."

"I don't know," I said, lying. I didn't want to explain to him that the long hair was not right for me anymore. That this new person who had emerged the last year didn't match the way I looked on the outside. "I think I need a change. I've always had long hair."

I anticipated a follow-up question, but instead, Takibi gestured okay with his hands and led me to a wash station. He laid a towel on my shoulders, tucking the end into my shirt. *Well, that was easier than I expected.* He turned on the tap, lukewarm water wetting my thick hair. I closed my eyes, trying to take the moment in. Next time I showered, that heaviness, that weight, would all be gone.

When I got back to the cutting station, Haru had dragged a chair to a few feet behind me, so he could witness the transformation. "How are you feeling, Aki?" Our eyes met through the mirror and he smiled.

"First, I will tie her hair in a ponytail and cut it," Takibi explained. "Then, I will trim what's left, from the back to the front."

"I can't wait for how badass you're going to look!" Haru took a photo with his iPhone. "This one is for posterity."

Takibi tied my hair in a low ponytail, being careful to brush back as many of the curls as he could. Then, looking at me in the mirror, he said, "Are you ready?"

My eyes met Haru's. He gave me a thumbs-up.

"Yes, cut it."

Three snips of the scissors, and the large bundle of hair fell to the ground. My brother raised both fists in the air triumphantly. I turned my head so I could see what had been cut, while Tabiki removed the tie to reveal what was left of my hair—a neck-length clump that he freed with his hand, adding volume each time he ran his fingers through it. Haru took a photo of the bundle on the floor.

"This is so sick!" He patted me on the shoulder. "I'm so glad I'm here for this."

Takibi spent the better part of an hour trimming the back of my hair. Without a mirror behind me, I just sat there, unable to see the progress, half curls dangling at the sides of my face. My only indicators of how it was going were my brother's expressions, which seemed to alternate between surprise, excitement and pride. The situation made me wonder about the ways we change, and how, sometimes, when we are in the thick of it, we can't quite see the process, just the end result. It also got me thinking about the people around us, and how they are in a better position to witness the transformation, observing up close or from the sidelines.

Eventually Takibi began cutting the hair on the sides of my head, and then what was left at the crown. When he was done, he twirled me around, grabbing a large mirror propped against the back wall, near the sinks. He moved it from side, showing me a 360° view of my new haircut. I ran my hand through the top—three-inch loops curled around my fingers. I turned my head from side to side, examining what looked like sideburns. The look seemed familiar, a reminder of who I was. But there was also a newness to the contours of my face, something this new hairstyle had brought out, accentuated.

Haru clapped effusively, "Bravo, Aki!" I smiled wide, my chest spilling over with confidence. I got up and brushed little bits of hair from my face and neck. How would everyone else react to the new look?

Haru and I left Tabiki's salon just after noon. We stopped by HMV to buy our dad a couple of DVDs, then started walking toward Marble Arch, Haru intermittently exclaiming, "I love it. Do you love it?"

"I'm starving. How about you?"

Haru nodded.

"I'm thinking. . .Thai? There's this place Abby, Ginika and I go all the time."

"I could eat Thai."

We turned back. Right before we reached the pub where I'd gotten into my first fight, on the day my parents had found out I was gay, we crossed the street. Then right on Store Street. Almost at the restaurant, there was a warm touch on my shoulder, followed by a tap. I turned around to see Ayesha, standing there, hand to her mouth.

"I thought that was you!" She moved her hand toward my hair. "It's so short! Can I touch it?" I nodded, surprised.

"Hey, Ayesha, right?" Haru reached out his hand.

Ayesha hugged him. "Yes! Sorry we didn't talk much last night at the Zoo Bar."

"No worries. I could hardly hear anything in there!"

I considered inviting Ayesha to join us, but before I could say anything she looked at her watch. She was running late to meet someone, maybe the nurse from the club, Allison. I didn't ask. We watched her run awkwardly down the street. Her gait was still terrible.

"Have you and she, you know . . ." Haru asked, Ayesha still in sight.

I smiled without saying a word and started walking toward the restaurant's entrance.

"I think she still likes you." He trailed behind, still looking at Ayesha.

"I'm learning just because you *can* do something, doesn't mean you should."

EPILOGUE

"Get up!" My mom opened the blinds in my room loudly. "Come on, Aki!"

"What!" I hated being woken up this way, especially during my summer break.

"Time to get up." From the corner of my eye, I saw her catching her reflection in my full-length mirror and readjusting her hair and straightening her bright pink polo.

"Why do you do this?" I put the cover over my head.

"We're going on a mother–daughter day trip." She pulled the covers away from me and threw them over the armchair in the corner of my room.

"Get ready. We are leaving in ten minutes."

"Where are we going?"

"You'll see. We are going to try something together."

I thought trying anything together wasn't going to work in my favour, but I didn't seem to have a way out of this. Once I came downstairs, a minute shy of my ten-minute allotment, Mom rushed me to the garage.

We drove to the ferry terminal in silence. I watched Vancouver turn into Richmond, then Delta and finally Tsawwassen. We took the eighty-minute ferry journey to Long Harbour on Salt Spring

Island. I stood in the upper deck, looking back at where we'd come from. There was still time for Mom to give up and take me home.

We drove through dense forest, following signs for Musgrave Landing.

"You know, when I was your age, I had a friend who liked women."

I looked at her confused by the abruptness of this revelation. "Yes?"

My mom gestured to her purse. "There's something in the inside pocket." I pulled out a faded photo of three women standing side by side, smiling to the camera. I recognized my mom almost instantly. She was the one in the middle, her hair longer than I'd ever seen it. Next to her was a woman of similar stature, with black hair and a fringe, and on her right, a blond woman with a pixie cut who was almost a head taller than Mom. I tried using my gaydar on the photo, but the results were inconclusive. So instead, my eyes bounced from Mom to the photo, back to Mom, looking for clues. When was this photo taken? Was it after she started dating my father?

I opened my mouth to say something, then closed it again. Growing up, Mom had never exactly fit in. She was never close to her mother or siblings, and she'd never felt at home in Medellín. When she moved to Canada with her grandparents as a teenager, she had been looking for more than a better life. She had wanted a way out of her upbringing. Still, Mom? Bicurious at some point in her life?

The car came to a stop beside a small house behind a wooden fence. How had my mother heard of this place? Mom rang a copper bell stuck to the fence.

A tall, blue-eyed woman in her mid-forties stepped out of the house wearing an off-white, flowy dress, with long sleeves folded up. Her blond hair was long and her arms were covered in metal bracelets that clinked as she moved. She opened the wooden gate and gestured for us to come inside.

Mom got back in the car and we parked in front of the house.

"Where the heck are we?"

"Aki! Language." She turned to me. "This is a reiki healer."

"A what? What is going on?"

"I can't lose you." She reached for my hand. "I need to make sure you're okay."

She reached behind her seat and grabbed her purse. Then she got out of the car. I sat, immobile.

She walked around and opened the passenger door. "Aki, please. If not for you, do this for me. I feel like we're running out of options to mend our relationship." The reiki healer watched us from her doorstep.

"Fine!" I got out of the car and put my hands inside my pockets. "But this is not going to work."

Mom extended her hand for a handshake, but the woman bowed instead, then woman showed us the way inside. The living and dining rooms were covered with metal bells, dreamcatchers and candles. The sickening scent of overly sweet incense filled the main floor.

"Welcome, Aki and Aurora. My name's Andrea and I'm a reiki master." She walked a few paces ahead of us, turning occasionally to make sure we weren't falling behind.

"Really?" I whispered. "You told a stranger our real names?"

We navigated between piles of books on the hall floor to a healing room covered in Hindu symbols: a fabric hanging of Om took up an entire wall, statues of Shiva and Ganesh rested on the top shelf of a bookcase.

"Please, sit down," Andrea offered us the floor. We sat in a corner, around a low wooden table.

"So, your mom tells me this is your first time doing reiki."

I nodded reluctantly. "I guess so."

"Well, let me walk you both through the next hour. First, we will have a consultation. Aurora, you are welcome to stay for this portion. Once we begin the actual treatment, you will have to leave."

Great! Leave me here in a room alone with a total stranger, Mom.

"Once your mom has left, Aki, we will do a few exercises together, to loosen that energy inside you."

I resisted rolling my eyes.

"Then, you will lie down on the message table and the healing will begin. The last five minutes will be for debriefing." Andrea turned to my mom. "You can rejoin us then if you'd like."

The healer and my mother talked at length about the past couple of years, and how tumultuous they'd been. Occasionally she asked me, "Is this true?" to which I always nodded. They talked about how traumatic my coming out had been to the family, how we were all still learning to be with each other again. At moments, I wanted to interject, but this was about my mom, not me.

"We will start the treatment now." The healer gestured for Mom to leave the room.

"Be open," she said, clasping my hand briefly on her way out.

The healer smiled across the table. "Now let's do a few exercises." She grabbed what looked like a brass mortar and pestle and started mumbling something, while rubbing the pestle along the rim of the mortar. Her motions produced a high-pitched echoey sound that raised the hairs on my neck. "I'll ask you a few questions and you will sing out the answers, okay?"

I shook my head. "No. That won't work for me."

"Let's give it a try. How do you feel?"

I said nothing.

"Please. Describe how you feel."

"No. I refuse to take part in this."

"I will demonstrate." She cleared her throat. "I feel so sad that you won't do this exercise with me. Please try." She sang off-key.

She continued to rub the pestle along the rim of the mortar for another minute, accompanied by her tuneless humming. I stayed silent, not breaking eye contact. Then, she finally gave up.

"Take your shoes off and lie on your back on the massage table," she said once the nonsense of the first exercise was over and done with. "I won't touch you. Instead, I will be massaging your energy, helping it flow better."

She put on some instrumental music and asked me to close my eyes. I didn't feel comfortable, lying down in an unfamiliar place with an unfamiliar woman, but this beat singing out a Q&A, and the music was actually very soothing. Water sounds, followed by bird sounds, with a harp in the background.

I tried to embrace the moment as best as I could. I was more than skeptical but knew how much my mother wanted this to work. I let my mind wander, to the day of *The L Word* DVD box. I watched that Aki look at her phone and make her way out of the lecture hall. I floated above her, so I tried to wiggle my way down. I wanted to warn her, to let her know what would happen next, but my body was pinned to the ceiling and she couldn't hear me. I wiggled harder, stretching my arms forward, trying to grasp her. Still nothing. My breathing quickened; my hands tightened into fists.

I tried to think of something happier. I remembered the time Ayesha got us into a club by pretending to be royalty. She'd told me I could be her escort for the night. That was before we slept together for the first time.

The healer changed music, the new track more fast-beat, more agitated. The last year of fighting replayed in my head—the pubs, back alleys, deserted parks. Phantom aches all over my body, the ghosts of every beating I'd taken. The hurt, the sadness, the anger. I felt it all. Emotions churned inside my chest, until they formed a hot bundle that rested on my sternum. Asad, chasing me in Hyde Park. The fight. The man I'd terrorized in the same park. The ball moved up my chest to my throat. The healer hummed something. She leaned close and asked for my name again. The ball continued to move up my throat to my head. It expanded and pulsed faster and faster to the rhythm of the music. My mind filled with fragmented memories bleeding heads punctuated by screams of agony, grown men in fetal position, crying uncontrollably. I'd taken down anyone who stood in my way. The pain was like a migraine, on both sides of my head. I inhaled deeply and wondered if she had somehow slipped me something.

Then, out of nowhere, a loud, sharp bang. I opened my eyes to the healer standing over me holding a golden gong twice the size of my head. She gestured for me to close my eyes again. I heard shuffling, and assumed she was moving toward my feet. She hit the gong again and sang out my name three times, attempting to match the melody of the music. I struggled to contain my laughter. More shuffling followed by another bang and my name again. This continued for two or three minutes and, in the absurdity of it all, I lost track of the pulsating ball in my head. Maybe it fell out of my body, forced out by the high-pitch sounds of the gong and the healer's off-key singing.

Mom came back into the room with a smile on her face. I wondered what she'd been able to hear through the door and whether she too was trying hard not to laugh.

"There's dark, heavy energy inside Aki." Andrea stared at me but talked to my mother. "It's best if she comes back in two weeks, so we can continue working on this."

Mom nodded. "Yes, yes. That makes sense." She paused. "We are away for the next week, but I will call you later to make a follow-up appointment."

Away? We weren't going anywhere, as far as I knew. As we made our way out of the house, the decor appeared even more eccentric, the colours more vibrant, the bells and chimes more excessive, like it had all multiplied in the span of an hour. As Mom backed out onto the road, we both waved to Andrea, complicit in our mockery. Once we were no longer in sight of her property, we broke out in laughter.

"What was going on in there?"

"She sang out my name!"

"And there was a gong too?"

"Yes! She nearly gave me a heart attack with that thing."

I threw my head back and laughed, harder and harder until the muscles around my stomach began to spasm and ache. Tears of laughter rolled down my mother's face. Things weren't the same, but this felt right.

My whole life I'd forced myself to be the perfect daughter my parents wanted. When I moved to London, I only saw two options: Continue on the same path or break with the old. I'd never imagined I would have the permission to do both. To honour my family and the good girl they'd raised, while charting out my own path, filled with complexities and contradictions.

In the end, it was never really about whether the fighter saved or broke me. She was—she is—more than I could ever describe. Without the fighter, I might never have known myself as someone fierce and vulnerable, strong and reckless. Without her, I might never have found the strength to live outside of social narratives. Without her, I might never have learned I could fight like a girl.

ACKNOWLEDGMENTS

Growing up, writers were magical beings, capable of weaving invisible thread into narrative. Back then, publishing a book was a far-fetched dream, something an alternate version of myself would do in a parallel universe. Only having gone through the process do I understand the labour and care that goes into a project, by myself and those around me.

J.J. Lee, you were there when the idea for this book first emerged, and through its many iterations you've supported me with nothing short of unrelenting enthusiasm. Without your encouragement, I don't know that I would have continued to push through. To Aislinn Hunter, you've stayed with this project throughout the pandemic. You helped me develop and edit this work, and for that I have the deepest gratitude.

To my wife, who's been so incredibly understanding about my intermittent absence and exhaustion, I appreciate all the ways you've taken care of me over the years, so I could make this childhood dream a reality.

To my parents and my sister, thank you for being there for me, unconditionally. Your love allowed me to write from a place of freedom and compassion. *Amo vocês.*

To my TWS writing cohort: Jo Kakwinokanasum, Averill

Groenenveld-Meijer, Julie Gordon, Joanna Baxter, Ann Wilson, Marian Dodds, Vicki McLeod, Georgia Swayze, erica hiroko and Dayna Mahannah—you've seen this project at its infancy and cheered me at every step along the way. For that, I thank you.

Thank you to all my friends and extended family, from near and far. Kathryn, Hillary and Neil, Valeria and Kelli, Roquela and Manj, and Loraine and Bruce—you've been there for me over the past five years, celebrating each achievement, big or small. To Minelle Mahtani and Shirley Nakata, thank you for your care, for the generous way you give, and for always uplifting me.

For their support, encouragement and patience, I want to give special thanks to my editor, Kilmeny Jane Denny, and Lynn Duncan of Tidewater Press.

Thank you, Chelene Knight, Danny Ramadan and Kevin Chong, for volunteering your time to read and support this work.

ABOUT THE AUTHOR

Emi Sasagawa is a settler, immigrant and queer woman of colour, living and writing on the traditional, ancestral and stolen territories of the xʷməθkʷəy̓əm, Sḵwx̱wú7mesh and Selilwitulh Nations.

In her writing, she explores identity and belonging through the lenses of mixedness, queerness, oppression and privilege. Emi is a graduate of The Writer's Studio at Simon Fraser University and is currently completing an MFA in Creative Writing at the University of British Columbia.